Acclaim for the [Writing] of VICTO[R GISCHLER]

"Edgar-finalist Gischler offers tornado-paced shoot-'em-up action in this can't-put-it-down thriller."
    —*Publishers Weekly*

"Gischler is one of those authors who writes so smoothly that he makes it look easy. It isn't, of course, except for the reader who gets to jump aboard his books for the exciting ride."
    —*Rocky Mountain News*

"Teems with enough violence to fill an entire shelf of crime thrillers."
    —*St. Louis Post-Dispatch*

"Gischler keeps the humor at a high level throughout with witty asides and sharp, nasty observations…hilarious."
    —*Detroit Free Press*

"A perfect fit for the high-octane crowd."
    —*Booklist*

"As fast and funny as what we've come to expect…it's just that this time out it hurts more, the characters dig under a couple more layers of your skin."
    —*BSC Reviews*

"Funny, mordant, crazed, riveting, sardonic…Bravo for Victor Gischler."
    —*Mike Resnick*

"Gischler keeps readers on the edge of their seats...and the writing is always well done. It's a fun read and a read that once begun is difficult to put down."
        —*Examiner*

"The tension is perfection, the writing is smooth and addictive...Not to be missed. This one screams blockbuster."
        —*Blake Crouch*

"Gischler has the unique gift of being able to write intense action and brilliant comedy in the same moment. The juxtaposition of the two is simultaneously hilarious and thrilling. This book proves Gischler's skill as the master of the game."
        —*Crime Spree*

"This is a damn fine book by a damn fine writer, and I want more."
        —*Greg Rucka*

"Crazy, sexy, and action-packed."
        —*Bookgasm*

"Victor Gischler is one of my favorite crime writers."
        —*Sean Chercover*

"A marvelous addition to an already remarkable body of work from one of the most creative crime writers in the business."
        —*Michael Koryta*

I spotted Stan in a back booth, sat across from him.

Stan had looked old even when I'd first known him. Now he sat shrunken inside his pinstripe suit. But his bright blue eyes were hard and alert.

Stan produced a rolled-up paper bag, slid it across the table to me. "Look inside."

I looked.

The bag contained the metal receiver box for the hidden microphone we sometimes used, also the cordless earpiece and the tiny tape recorder. I looked at Stan.

"Beggar Johnson's in town tonight," said Stan. "I want you on the listening end."

I nodded.

"Then stick around after," he said. "I might have an errand for you."

"Sure. What am I listening for?"

"You'll know when you hear it." He stood and dropped a twenty on the table. "Wait a few minutes before you leave."

He walked out. I sat.

I thought about what Stan had said, but even more about what he didn't say. The unhappy stink of change was on the wind. A big shake-up coming our way...

**SOME OTHER HARD CASE CRIME BOOKS
YOU WILL ENJOY:**

JOYLAND *by Stephen King*
THE COCKTAIL WAITRESS *by James M. Cain*
THE TWENTY-YEAR DEATH *by Ariel S. Winter*
BRAINQUAKE *by Samuel Fuller*
EASY DEATH *by Daniel Boyd*
THIEVES FALL OUT *by Gore Vidal*
SO NUDE, SO DEAD *by Ed McBain*
THE GIRL WITH THE DEEP BLUE EYES
by Lawrence Block
QUARRY *by Max Allan Collins*
SOHO SINS *by Richard Vine*
THE KNIFE SLIPPED *by Erle Stanley Gardner*
SNATCH *by Gregory Mcdonald*
THE LAST STAND *by Mickey Spillane*
UNDERSTUDY FOR DEATH *by Charles Willeford*
CHARLESGATE CONFIDENTIAL *by Scott Von Doviak*
A BLOODY BUSINESS *by Dylan Struzan*
THE TRIUMPH OF THE SPIDER MONKEY
by Joyce Carol Oates
BLOOD SUGAR *by Daniel Kraus*
DOUBLE FEATURE *by Donald E. Westlake*
ARE SNAKES NECESSARY? *by Brian De Palma and Susan Lehman*
KILLER, COME BACK TO ME *by Ray Bradbury*
FIVE DECEMBERS *by James Kestrel*
THE NEXT TIME I DIE *by Jason Starr*

Fast
CHARLIE

by **Victor Gischler**

**ORIGINALLY PUBLISHED AS
'GUN MONKEYS'**

A HARD CASE CRIME NOVEL

A HARD CASE CRIME BOOK

(HCC-S09)

First Hard Case Crime edition: December 2023

Published by

Titan Books
A division of Titan Publishing Group Ltd
144 Southwark Street
London SE1 0UP

in collaboration with Winterfall LLC

Copyright © 2001 by Victor Gischler,
originally published as *Gun Monkeys*

Cover photo courtesy of Vertical Entertainment

"I Walk the Line" written by Johnny Cash. © 1956 ® 1984
House of Cash, Inc. (BMI)/Administered by BUG.
All Rights Reserved. Used by Permission.

All rights reserved. No part of this book may be reproduced or
transmitted in any form or by any electronic or mechanical
means, including photocopying, recording or by any information storage and retrieval system, without the written
permission of the publisher, except where permitted by law.

*This book is a work of fiction. Names, characters, places, and
incidents either are the products of the author's imagination or
are used fictitiously, and any resemblance to actual events or
persons, living or dead, is entirely coincidental.*

Print edition ISBN 978-1-80336-448-3
E-book ISBN 978-1-80336-449-0

Design direction by Max Phillips
www.signalfoundry.com

Typeset by Swordsmith Productions

The name "Hard Case Crime" and the Hard Case Crime logo
are trademarks of Winterfall LLC. Hard Case Crime books
are selected and edited by Charles Ardai.

Printed by CPI Group (UK) Ltd, Croydon CR0 4YY

Visit us on the web at www.HardCaseCrime.com

For my wife Jackie.
Thanks for softening up
a hard-boiled guy.

ONE

I turned the Chrysler onto the Florida Turnpike with Rollo Kramer's headless body in the trunk, and all the time I'm thinking I should've put some plastic down. I knew the heap was a rental, but I didn't like leaving anything behind for the inevitable forensics safari. That meant I'd have to strip all the carpeting in the trunk, douche out the blood with Clorox, and hope Avis took a long time to notice. I should've just taken a second and put some plastic down. *Shit.*

"Slow down, Charlie. You'll flag us." Blade Sanchez popped a Winston into his mouth, crumpled the pack, and tossed it into the backseat.

I grabbed the cigarette out of his mouth and jammed it into the ashtray. "You light another one of them fucking things, and you're in the trunk with Rollo."

"Christalmighty, that's my last one. Jesus, Charlie. What the fuck?" He pawed at the cigarette, but I'd smashed it up good. "I just said slow down is all. You want the state police should pull us over and find Rollo?"

It's your fault he's back there, I thought. But I slowed down. He was right, and that made me like him even less.

"You botched this good."

"So you keep telling me," said Blade.

Me and some of the other boys had been riding Blade Sanchez hard about his lack of originality. We called him "Blade" because he always whacked his marks the same way: a quick flick of his stiletto, an ear-to-ear smile. That's a sure way to tip your hand, doing it the same way every time. Not quite as bad as leaving a thumbprint, but it sure helps the profilers put together an M.O. when you fall into a pattern. Everyone knows what everyone's up to. It's just the difficulty proving it that keeps guys like Blade out of stir.

Now me, I'd never, ever developed bad habits or fallen into a routine, and as a result my name wasn't on a single piece of paper in a single precinct in any state in the union or the District of Columbia.

Anyway, we were riding Blade pretty good about his knife at O'Malley's over beers. And mostly we were kidding, but he was getting pretty sore, because he knew it was true. That's when guys get the most sore, when they know something's true. It was the night before we got this Rollo job, and Blade pulled me aside and practically begged me to let him be trigger man. He already knew I didn't want to work with him, and now everyone was on his case about his knife, so he was all eager to show he could bump this Rollo guy in some new and improved way. As if me and the rest of the boys still wouldn't think Blade was a moron. So I had a couple of drinks, and he wore me down. And before I knew what I was saying, I told him he could do Rollo, only don't screw it up or he'd have all of our balls in a vise.

Of course, it all went to shit. I should have known better.

When I picked up Blade the morning we were supposed to whack Rollo, gray clouds hung heavy in the winter sky but didn't quite threaten rain. All January the temperature hadn't dipped below fifty. Got to love the Sunshine State.

Blade had a fresh box of doughnuts all tied up in a yellow ribbon. I thought maybe they were for us.

"Hands off," said Blade. "They're for Rollo."

"Last meal?"

Blade tapped a finger against his temple. "Research, *compadre,* research. Old Rollo's a doughnut junkie."

Rollo's neighborhood looked like something God had scraped off His shoe. Dull brick buildings hunched along the wide street. Every third car was stripped and up on cinder blocks. The front lawns were yellowing postage stamps of dying grass. I pulled the Chrysler into an empty spot across from Rollo's rented house.

Blade looked up and down the street shaking his head. "Whoever said crime don't pay must've been thinking of Rollo."

I didn't answer him, but I understood. It was like any other job. You were either good at it, or you weren't. Rollo Kramer wasn't very good at his job. He'd been a middleman for Beggar Johnson, a big-time boss hood from down in Miami. Rollo thought skimming off the top of Beggar's take would be a good way to supplement his income. Beggar caught Rollo with his hand in the till, and Rollo fled north. Orlando. Our territory. Since Beggar knew Blade from the old days, he'd asked Stan personally to put Blade on the job.

But the problem was that Blade Sanchez was a grade-A screwup, and Stan had him on probation. Sanchez had stuck his knife into the wrong guy in Detroit, and a month before that he'd dropped the ball in Tampa, letting a city councilman with a bull's-eye on his chest slip out of the crosshairs. So there I was in the car next to him on babysitting duty, making sure Blade didn't eat his own gun or forget to breathe or some damn thing. I'd made it clear I wasn't happy with the job, but since I had Stan to thank for every nickel hidden in my safe deposit box, I couldn't really turn him down.

Blade slipped into a Do-nut Barn jacket and delivered the box to Rollo's front door. When he returned, I gave him the fish eye.

"What? Poison?"

Blade shook his head. "You'll see. I told him it was a gift from an admirer."

"Just what? Wait?"

"Wait."

So I waited. I pulled an old issue of *National Geographic* out of my topcoat and looked at the front for the hundredth time. On the cover, the beautiful brown face of a young Polynesian woman hovered in front of an expanse of virgin beach and deep green sea. I'd read every word of the article three times. I folded the magazine. It bulged awkwardly in the pocket of my topcoat, so I dropped it on the floor.

Waiting sucked.

"That was Rollo at the door?" I asked.

"Yeah."

"Why didn't you push him inside and whack him right then?"

Blade frowned. "Whatever."

God damn hotdog amateur.

Long seconds crept past.

"If he's such an addict, don't you think he'll already have doughnuts?"

"These are fresh."

The explosion shattered the windows in Rollo's house and shook the rental car.

"What the fuck was that?"

Blade grinned big. "That would be the Boston cream."

We tumbled out of the Chrysler and ran up the walk and into Rollo's house to the scream of car alarms set off by the blast. I kicked in the door, and we found what was left of Rollo still sitting in a ladderback chair blown back about ten feet from the kitchen table.

"Holy shit, Blade."

Rollo's neck still oozed dark liquid. It pooled around his

body on the linoleum. The walls and ceiling looked like a giant anteater had sneezed a watermelon. Thick chunks of red gunk dripped from the kitchen cabinets, and hung in gelatinous strands from the ceiling fan.

Blade looked around like he couldn't believe what he'd done. "Where's his head?"

I squinted hard at something fuzzy and bloody in the sink. "I think this is a piece here. Crap. What'd you put in that doughnut?"

"Four blasting caps."

I shook my head. "Idiot."

Blade looked hurt. "He's dead, isn't he?"

"We're supposed to bring back the body to collect our bonus," I reminded him. "How's Beggar supposed to identify the body without the head?"

"Gimme a break, Charlie. I stayed up all night thinking of this. I got up at five in the morning to suck out all the cream with a straw. Then I shoved in the caps with my thumb and squirted the cream back in."

He seemed genuinely upset that I didn't appreciate his genius. Right about then I wished he'd just stuck his knife in the guy. I went into the living room and came back with Rollo's ugly green drapes. I spread them on the kitchen floor and motioned for Blade to help me lift Rollo.

Blade made a sick face. "But he's a mess."

"You dumb shit. Everybody in the neighborhood heard that Boston cream go off. Somebody's called the cops for sure. Now shut up and help me wrap Rollo up in the drapes."

The blood was already soaking through the drapes when we stashed the corpse in the trunk of the Chrysler. I threw the doughnut box in on top of the body. Blade looked like he'd swallowed a bug the whole time. I didn't see how he made it in this business. I guess everyone has his limit. The police sirens grew in the distance as we pulled out of Rollo's neighborhood.

We zig-zagged around for about twenty minutes before I finally pulled into an Exxon station and told Blade to wait in the car while I made a phone call.

"Who're you calling?" asked Blade.

"Just wait here."

Stan was my boss. Blade's too. We worked for him, but he rented us out freelance whenever he smelled a buck. That's when we earned the real cash. I'd been with him for years and never had any reason to question his judgment until now, so I was a bit relieved when he finally picked up the phone after thirteen rings.

"Yeah?"

"It's me," I said.

"You in a jam?"

"Right."

"Tell me."

I spilled out the story, Stan snickering the whole time on the other end of the line.

"I don't see what's so damn funny."

"Just you with that bozo, Sanchez," Stan said. "How'd you guys get paired up in the first place?" Like he had nothing to do with it.

"Are you going to help or not?"

"You stay put," said Stan. "I'll call you back in ten."

I gave him the number to the phone booth, then hung up just as Blade came and knocked on the glass.

"What now?"

"We wait," I said. "If you want to be useful, go into the gas station and get us some coffee."

Blade left, then returned and handed me a Styrofoam cup about the size of a gnat's jock. "You couldn't spring for a large?"

"It's just the way you like it," said Blade. "Lots of cream and sugar."

"Why the hell would you say that? You've never gotten coffee for me before in your life."

"I thought you'd like cream and sugar."

"Next time, black." I poured it on the ground.

Blade wrinkled up his face at me like some little kid and stood pouting next to the rental. He folded his arms across his chest and kept an eye on traffic. My hands balled into fists just looking at him. Guys like Blade were why this business wasn't what it used to be.

I dropped in another thirty-five cents and dialed my mother's number in Winter Park. She answered on the third ring.

"Charlie, don't tell me you're calling to postpone again."

"Sorry, Ma. I got tangled up."

"You work too hard."

"Maybe."

"When can we expect you? You know Danny really would like to see you."

"I know. I want to see you too. And Danny."

Ma lowered her voice gravely. "I can't do a thing with him, Charlie. If your father were still alive—"

"Danny's a big boy now."

"But you'll talk to him?"

"Sure, Ma. I have to go. I'll call and let you know when I'm coming down."

I hated to put Ma off like that, but business was business. My little brother Danny would keep for a while. He was a good kid. He wouldn't push Ma too far.

I'd just about talked myself into crossing the street for

another cup of coffee when the phone rang. I picked it up.

"Yeah?"

"Rollo's ex-wife lives in Sanford." Stan's voice. "She can identify him."

"We don't need her to identify him. We need the guy who's paying us to identify him."

"Do what I say. You put the grab on her and take her to meet Beggar's boys. If she sticks up for you that should be good enough."

"If you say so."

This deal was going down the tubes quick. I was used to a certain level of professionalism. Maybe that's one of the reasons I preferred to work alone. Or maybe I just didn't like people.

I pulled the car off the turnpike and onto I-4, pointing it toward Sanford. We rode through the town in silence, Blade getting fidgety because he hadn't had a cigarette in a while. Rollo's ex-wife had an acre of land and a ranch-style house out by the regional airport. We turned down her long driveway and parked close to the house. The shrubs out front were over-grown. Big oaks kept the house in constant shade.

"I hope she don't have dogs," said Blade, scanning the yard. "I hate it when they have dogs."

"I'll go talk to her," I told him. "You stay here and keep an eye peeled for dogs."

I knocked, and she answered. Stan had told me that the former Mrs. Kramer's name was Marcie, thirty-four years young. My eyes took a quick trip up and down her body. She was casual in blue jeans, a Hilton Head T-shirt, and open-toed sandals. She wore her red hair short like a boy's, and her breasts knocked around heavy and braless under her shirt. Her skin was smooth and bright. It was only around her brown eyes you could tell she had some miles on her. Not so pretty that I felt like a troll standing next to her, but pretty.

I said, "Miss Kramer, I'm Charlie Swift. I don't know how to say this, but Rollo is dead."

"Murdered?"

"Yes."

She took me in with those eyes, looked past me to Blade waiting in the car, nodded slowly, her eyes lighting on me again. "You're not police."

"No."

"You killed him and now you want something from me." It wasn't a question.

"Yes." Her penetrating brown eyes made it pointless and silly to lie.

She nodded, raised an eyebrow. "Yeah. Knowing Rollo, I thought he'd get it sooner or later. What is it you think I can do for you?"

I was tired from the drive and tired of Blade's company. I told her I had a proposition for her, and I sent Blade into town with a twenty-dollar bill and instructions to bring back Chinese food for three. He shot me an evil look before climbing behind the wheel of the Chrysler.

Usually, I'd have slapped some duct tape over her mouth and shoved her in the backseat of the car, but there was some quality about Marcie I didn't want to spoil. She had that subtle characteristic which made her seem good without making me seem clumsy or crude. She wasn't afraid, but she was careful, and I suspected she knew the ropes from being kicked around a lot. Anyhow, I thought she was tough enough to deserve a break, or maybe I just wanted to talk to a pretty woman. Either way, I was glad when she asked me in.

She pulled the tabs on two cans of Schlitz, and I sat across from her at her drab Formica-covered table in her dim little kitchen. I told her the story, and she knew how to listen, asking the right questions in the right places.

"I really expected to hear he was dead before this," said Marcie. "The kind of people he ran around with, you know? Anyway, I wished him dead a couple times myself. I haven't seen an alimony payment in nineteen months."

"I might be able to help you with some money, if you'll help us."

She smiled. "I'd have killed the little prick myself if I'd have known he was worth anything dead."

There'd only been a trace of anger in that remark. Mostly, she was being practical, just another on a list of people who'd figured out the world was better off without Rollo Kramer. That toughness again, but I sensed deep down she had the ability to be soft if she wanted. Or maybe that was just something I wanted to think. Anyhow, I liked her.

"You didn't seem frightened when I came to the door."

She shrugged. "You were going to do what you wanted anyway. I couldn't see how freaking out would help. You should have seen some of the wild characters Rollo dragged home. At least you seem well-groomed. Clean. When I was with Rollo I used to keep a loaded gun by the door. It's in a closet someplace, I think."

"Why'd you marry a guy like that in the first place?"

"Young and stupid, the usual story." A little smile crept across her face, like she was talking about some dumb kid sister instead of herself. "Every teenage girl wants to ride off with a young rebel." She shook her head. "It's horrible and shocking to realize you're a cliché. I grew up."

"So what do you do?" I sipped my beer.

"I make my money as a taxidermist, but I consider myself an artist."

"Isn't it creepy working with dead things?"

A little smile pushed up the edges of her mouth. "I don't know. Is it?"

Blade returned, and over sweet-'n-sour pork, we agreed to cut Marcie in for ten percent if she identified Rollo's body.

"My brother's a tattoo artist," said Marcie. "For our wedding present, he gave Rollo and me matching tattoos. They say *Rollo Loves Marcie* inside of a heart."

"Where?"

"On our butts."

I raised an eyebrow. "You too?"

"I had mine removed. It looks like I sat in acid."

Too bad.

We adjourned to the back of the Chrysler. I opened the trunk and peeled Rollo out of the drapes. Most of the blood had dried, but he was still as headless as ever.

"Oh God." Marcie swallowed hard.

"You gonna be okay?"

She nodded.

I pulled down Rollo's slacks just enough to reveal the tattoo. It was bigger than I thought it would be.

Marcie's sudden intake of breath made the hair on the back of my neck stand up. I stiffened, realizing I'd leaned too far into the trunk, my back to Marcie and Blade. I got the sickening, dull ache of stupidity in the pit of my stomach. I turned slowly and found myself on the bad end of Blade Sanchez's 9mm Luger.

"That's all I needed to see," said Blade. "I guess old Rollo and I will be going now, and I'll take the whole bonus."

"Don't be a blockhead, Blade. Stan won't stand for this."

"I don't think so, Mr. Smarty-fuck hired gun. I know something you don't. Beggar Johnson was in Raiford with Rollo for two years. They were cellmates, so I'm sure he's seen that cute little tattoo in the shower. Beggar says I can go work for him anytime."

"Even so, Blade, this ain't professional. It's gonna look bad."

"To hell with you." Blade quivered and shook the pistol in my face for emphasis. "You been riding my back since we took this job. You think you're just the shit, the big-shot trigger-man on the block, huh? So you team with me like I'm some kind of charity case. Well, I'm getting the last laugh. Now give me the car keys, you smug, cigarette-hating, black-coffee-drinking son of a bitch."

I gave him the keys.

Marcie and I stood and watched as Blade tore out of the gravel driveway in the Chrysler. Thank God I always rented under a fake name.

Marcie turned to me immediately. "If I give you the keys to my Volvo so you can go after him, will you cut me in for his half?"

I blinked at her, not quite sure if I'd heard right. She'd just seen her ex-husband's decapitated body without flinching. Now she wanted me to go after Blade. I liked her a lot.

"Well?" She jingled the keys in front of me. "He's getting away."

"Deal."

"I'm coming with you."

Her baby-shit yellow Volvo was about ten years old but in good shape. It didn't take us long to catch up with Blade. I'd seen him drive once, so I wasn't surprised he was taking it easy. He didn't recognize Marcie's car, so we came up behind him slow. I made like I was passing him, but he recognized me when I pulled alongside. He tried to gun the Chrysler, but I got ahead of him a little and swerved hard into his lane. He went off the road and smacked the rental into a pine tree. I pulled the Volvo over and told Marcie to stay put.

Blade was slumped heavily over the steering wheel, a trickle of blood running from his forehead to his chin where he'd bashed his head. I reached in the driver's side and pushed Blade back in his seat. His eyes blinked open, and he pointed his pistol at me groggily.

I said, "You smell that, Blade? Smoke. You've landed in tall, dry grass and your exhaust pipe's caught it on fire. Give me the gun, and I'll pull you out." While he thought about it, I went around to the passenger side, opened the door and grabbed my *National Geographic* off the floor.

Back around on Blade's side. "What's it going to be?"

He glanced in the rearview mirror, and when he saw the smoke billowing behind the Chrysler, he handed me the Luger. I pulled him behind the Volvo and dropped him on the ground. Rollo was still in the trunk, but before I could go back for the keys, the whole car went up in flames.

I walked over to Blade, thought about him pointing his little Kraut gun at me and flushed hot around the ears and up through my cheeks. The smug expression on his moron face when he thought he'd put one over.

I squeezed the trigger and put a bullet in his chest.

Marcie got out of the Volvo and stood next to me.

"What a mess."

"Yeah. You'll have to pay your brother out of your half," I said.

"My brother?"

"To tattoo *Rollo Loves Marcie* on Blade's butt." I sized up Blade's carcass. "He's roughly the same build as Rollo."

She raised her eyebrows in appreciation. "Okay, but I'm not cutting off his head."

Right. With no head and a tattoo on Blade's ass, Beggar wouldn't notice the switch. I hoped.

"Just help me get him in the trunk before the sheriff comes."

Marcie sighed as she opened the Volvo's trunk. "I just wish we had some plastic or something to put down." She rolled up her sleeves and went to work. Good girl.

"Marcie."

"Yes?"

I felt suddenly clumsy and foolish. I didn't like feeling that way, so I hurried ahead to get it over with. "Maybe when we take care of this, I could take you to dinner? Do something that doesn't involve dead bodies?"

"Someplace nice?"

"Yeah."

"Sure." She bent, took Blade under the arms. "Get his legs, will you? This son of a bitch is heavy."

TWO

The deal went off without a hitch, and thankfully Beggar Johnson sent two of his muscle boys to meet us instead of coming himself. They'd driven up from Miami, and we met them in the desolate regions of a mall parking garage in Altamonte. The car ride had been quiet and nervous.

Beggar's goons identified themselves as Norman and Vincent. Norman was in charge, a gangly scarecrow of a man who tried to hide his lack of bulk inside a suit too big for him. Vincent knew he was just there to kill anything if Norman told him to. He was short but wide, a big, meaty guy with thinning hair and a sweaty face.

"You bring him?" asked Norman.

"In the back." I jerked a thumb at the Volvo.

Vincent was looking hard at the back of Marcie's car, maybe getting the tag. I didn't like it, but also didn't see how I could complain.

When they saw Blade's body, Norman flipped open his cell phone and described the tattoo to his boss. He nodded a lot, grunting without emotion. I started to feel a little moist under my arms. My eyes kept darting into the corners of the garage, looking for trouble. I'd sent Marcie into the mall and told her I'd join her for coffee when the exchange was completed. I needn't have worried.

Norman folded up the cell phone and looked at me. "What a fucking mess."

"Sorry."

"What did you do to the poor slob?"

"He got out of line, so I bit him."

Norman frowned. "You're a laugh riot."

They took what they thought was Rollo's carcass and stashed it in the trunk of their black Mercedes. There was a nice layer of plastic in the trunk, all ready for the body. Bastards. Norman handed me a wrinkled manila envelope. I didn't bother looking inside. I knew the money would be there. We nodded to each other, and I walked away trying not to hurry. In the mall, I found a pay phone and dialed Stan.

"I got it."

"Understood," said Stan.

We hung up.

I didn't know how to explain to Stan that one of his guns had cashed it in, so I pretended it never happened. I was counting on the fact that Blade was a flake and nobody would miss him. Or at least I'd wait, maybe think of a better way to explain how it couldn't have been helped.

I located Marcie in the food court, sipping on a frappy-crappy-amaretto coffee something. I sat down, put the envelope on the table, and slid it across to her. "Take a look."

She cracked open the envelope and peeked inside. Her breath caught, and she coughed up a nervous chuckle. "Oh, my."

"Half is yours. Five grand."

"Wow." She blinked at the cash. "It worked."

"Dinner?"

"Let's just get a room. We can order up."

We quickly found the Hilton. Wrapped in the mingled glow of champagne and leftover adrenaline, we slipped between the sheets and completed our discovery. After, I lay awake for long hours, content to feel her curled against me. I'd have to call Ma tomorrow, tell her I got tangled up again.

°

We drove back to Marcie's the next morning. She said I should hang around awhile. I called O'Malley's and got Benny on the line. Told him to cover for me.

Marcie was out running errands, said she'd be back to fix me lunch. I poked around the place. I went through the side door in her kitchen, which led to the garage. It was dark. I felt along the wall for the light switch. No luck. I felt on the other side. Nothing.

I stepped into the darkness, felt something on my face, and jumped back.

A string. The light. I gave it a yank, and two rows of fluorescents flashed to life.

An eight-foot-tall polar bear charged me, its claws outstretched, its mouth twisted into a savage snarl. I stepped back, one arm flung up to ward off the bear, the other hand flying into my jacket, drawing the revolver from my belly holster. I backpedaled toward the kitchen, legs tangling. I fell on my ass, but the pistol was out. I squeezed the trigger three times, dotting the polar bear's chest with a neat triangle of .38 caliber holes. But the bear didn't drop.

As a matter of fact, he didn't budge at all.

Marcie was a taxidermist.

I stood, moved close to the polar bear. Marcie had done a good job. The bear was incredibly lifelike, and she'd fixed the animal with an expression that was likely far more terrifying than nature had ever intended. The bear was a perfect picture of rage. It felt like he was actually mad at *me*.

I explored the rest of the garage. A large worktable. Tools. Bottles of liquid. Various animal anatomy texts side-by-side with art books, cubism, sculpture. Alien to me. A large freezer took up one corner. It creaked open, and I found an assortment of packages wrapped in butcher's paper. I picked up one about the size of a big ham, turned it over in my hands. In black Magic Marker was written *Raccoon*.

"Ew." I shivered, dropped the package back into the freezer, and closed it.

God damn ghoulish way to earn a living. Okay, I killed people, but I didn't keep any souvenirs. I looked at the bear again, shook my head, laughed.

I went back in the house, flipped on the television. I made a couple laps around the channels with the remote control but nothing was good. Bored.

I wrote Marcie a note.

Thanks for a nice evening. Sorry I couldn't wait. Work. I'll call you.

That's the thing about Orlando: it wasn't a tall city, but it had a bad dose of the sprawl, creeping out in every direction, soaking up communities like Altamonte and Longwood and places that used to be rural like Sanford and Oveido and even Bithlo. All of Central Florida from Disney to the Space Coast was a snarled clusterfuck of beltways and mini-malls and cookie-cutter housing developments and hotels, hotels, hotels.

In Longwood, I'd managed to find a nice apartment over a two-car garage. It was far enough away from 17-92 that traffic noise was almost obliterated if you turned your TV up loud enough. The lady who owned the garage and adjacent house was about seven hundred years old and hadn't raised the rent once in the eleven years I'd lived there. The house was on a pond that everyone in the neighborhood pretended was a lake so the sign at the entrance to the place could say Lake Potter.

The taxi let me out, and I paid the guy. I took the stairs up the side of the garage and let myself in. The place was just like

I'd left it. One chair. One single bed—made, sheets and blanket tucked under the corners. No dishes in the sink and a two-thirds-full bottle of Chivas on the small, round wooden table.

I showered, changed into fresh clothes. Charcoal slacks. Tweed jacket. Muted paisley tie.

I fixed myself a roast beef sandwich, horseradish, tomato, cut it in half—diagonally. A glass of water, no ice. I read the *National Geographic* while I ate, the one with the story on French Polynesia.

The phone rang.

I picked it up. "Yeah?"

"Stan's looking for you." It was Bob Tate. I could hear the crowd murmur and clink of glasses from O'Malley's behind him.

"Why?"

"I don't know. He seems irritated."

"What did you say to him?"

"I didn't say nothing. He's the boss. He can be irritated if he wants."

"I mean did you tell him where I am?"

"I didn't know where you were."

"You still don't. Understand?"

Bob cleared his throat, made unhappy noises. If he had something to say, I really should have heard him out. Benny and the new guy Morgan—and even Blade when he was alive—usually knew better than to second-guess me, but Bob was next down on the totem pole. He'd seen about as much shit as I had, and believe me, there was plenty to see. Stan's organization was into everything. Numbers, protection, fencing, bookmaking. If there was a dirty buck to be made, Stan was on top of it. And if anybody looked at Stan sideways, he gave us a ring in the back room at O'Malley's. The monkey cage, Stan called it. I'm still not sure why.

Me and Bob and the others were Stan's enforcers. The guys with the guns, the knives, the brass knuckles. The guys with the deep voices and the long shadows. The guys with the heavy footfalls on the stairs late at night. I'd read all that in a dime novel once.

In the years I'd known Bob, he'd been shot three times, stabbed, had his ribs busted with a baseball bat, and been sideswiped by a Toyota. In all honesty, he'd earned the right to speak his mind. He wouldn't bother unless it was important.

But I guess I just wasn't in the mood to listen.

"Tell him I had some personal business, Bob." I cradled the phone against my shoulder, tore the cover off the *Geographic* and folded it, put it in my pocket.

He cleared his throat again, code for Stan ain't going to like that, but he said, "Sure, Charlie, whatever you say."

"Thanks."

I hung up the phone and went downstairs to my Buick Skylark. I didn't want to go back to O'Malley's. I wasn't ready to explain to Stan about Blade, and if I stayed around the apartment he might call.

It only took me a second to think of someplace to go.

I found Marcie on her front porch. She sat on the wooden bench sipping a gin and tonic.

I stopped in front of her, just off the porch. "I shot your bear."

"You what my what?"

"The big stuffed polar bear in the garage," I said. "I shot it. With my gun."

"Why the hell'd you do that?" She stood, balled her little fist.

I shuffled my feet, shoved my hands deep in my pockets. "It sort of startled me."

"My God. A grown man." Marcie stomped into the house trailing obscenities.

I followed but paused in the kitchen. She'd left the door open, so I could hear her growling from the garage. I tossed some ice cubes into a glass and drowned them in gin. I went into the garage.

Marcie fingered the singed fur around the holes in the bear's chest. She frowned at me with every muscle in her face. "Well, that's just great."

"He's not getting any more dead. What's the big deal?"

"This is my work."

"Don't you have some stuff to shove in the holes? Just use some white shoe polish on the burn marks. When the people come to pick it up they'll never notice."

"It's not a job for a client," said Marcie. "It's one of my art pieces."

"Oh."

"And you shot it."

She huffed back into the kitchen, built herself another gin and tonic.

I stayed in the garage, looking up at the bear's snarling mug. "How's this art?" I shouted over my shoulder.

"I wouldn't expect you to understand," she shouted back from the kitchen. "You're an uncouth Neanderthal crap-head."

That seemed a little harsh.

"I have a master's in art from SUNY Buffalo for fuck's sake." She loudly slurped the gin and tonic, sucked ice.

And the bear, the way he looked, seemed angry. Not merely savage like an animal hunting food or defending its territory, but actually angered by some wrong. Like somebody had insulted the bear's shoes. Or kicked his granny down the stairs.

I told this to Marcie, voice raised so she could hear me in the kitchen.

She came back into the garage quietly, her drink leading the way. "He looks angry? Really?"

"Is that wrong?"

"No." She was surprised. "That's what I meant. I was going for angry."

"Yeah?"

"When people bring in an animal for me to mount, I try to give each piece an expression that matches the owner's. It's hard to give animals human emotions. Most people don't think they can love or hate or be angry like people. But the bear's mine. I wanted him to look angry."

"So this is your art, huh?"

She laughed, put her hand on my arm. "I can't exactly claim my work is wildly popular." She kissed me on the cheek. "But thanks for getting it."

I wasn't sure I was getting it, but I was glad she wasn't yelling at me anymore.

On a whim, I fished out the folded-up picture of paradise, the cover of the *National Geographic,* and showed it to her. "Let's go here sometime."

"Here?"

"Why not? Doesn't everyone want to go someplace like that? The beach. Palm trees."

"Who gives a shit about palm trees?"

"Who gives a—are you kidding? Look at the picture. It's paradise."

"I want to see pyramids."

"Egypt?"

"Or Mexico," said Marcie. "We could go to Acapulco. They have beaches and pyramids both."

I slipped an arm around her waist. "Well, that's one idea, I guess. I'll take it under advisement."

"Are you staying here tonight?" she asked.

"Yeah."

We drank our drinks and stood for a while looking at her angry polar bear.

In the morning, Marcie got a call for a taxidermy job and took the Volvo to pick up a dead pelican.

I put last night's plates in the dishwasher and cleaned up the kitchen. That took fourteen minutes. I made the bed. Three minutes. I showered, shaved and dressed. Twenty-one minutes. I had a cup of coffee.

I had some guns in the trunk of my car, fetched them out. I took the Belgian .308 apart and cleaned it and the Browning automatics too, even though I hadn't fired them, and they were spotless. I did a quick inventory of my ammunition. I had a hundred .308 shells and two hundred .45 rounds including what was in the spare clips. I had eighteen bullets for the .38 revolver. I drank another cup of coffee.

Time to call Ma.

I dialed her number, and she answered after four rings. She was happy to hear from me, then immediately bawled me out for not calling sooner. She filled my ear with news of aunts and distant cousins.

"Ma, you didn't want me to call just to tell me Aunt Nora was having her gall bladder out, did you?"

"It's Danny," said Ma. "Your brother's making me crazy."

"He's a Swift. Comes with the territory."

"I know, and I'm probably worrying over nothing. You know, if your father were still alive—"

"I know, Ma."

"Sometimes, he needs a man to talk to. I do my best."

"I know."

"Come over. I'll cook for you."

"Soon." I cleared my throat. "I've met somebody."

There was a pause. "Oh?"

"She's nice. Smart. Has a master's degree from college."

"Well, be careful, Charlie."

I fought down my irritation. "Why would I need to be careful?"

"I know you're an adult, of course." She lightened her tone and put a chuckle into her voice. "It's just that no one's good enough for my baby."

"She's good enough. Maybe too good."

"Let me know when you're coming."

We made our goodbyes, and I hung up the phone.

I poured a third cup of coffee. It was 8:41 A.M.

I picked up the phone. No more stalling. Marcie had her work, and I had mine. Vacations were nice, but I was a professional. Stan picked up after seven rings.

"Hello?"

"Hi, Boss," I said. "You've been looking for me?"

THREE

Back in the day.

I'd been out of the army for two months, and I'd already killed five men, but I could barely pay the bills. The army hadn't really paved the way for legitimate employment on the outside.

I had a string of medals for marksmanship.

After the first seven weeks of Ranger training, a guy with bars on his shoulders ordered my transfer to a special outfit. No patches. No insignia. No name. It wasn't anything I could put on a resume.

But there was always work for someone with skills. Fists, knives, guns.

Stan had gotten word I was handy with my pistols. That's how things worked back in the day. No matter how careful you thought you were in keeping a lid on things, The Word always got around. So Stan had sent Thumbs Hogan to invite me for pie.

In the years I'd known Stan, we'd had pie four times.

The first time was when he made me New Guy in the monkey cage. I was young and hungry and smart, and I'd known a good opportunity when I was handed one.

We shook hands. I started making good money.

I didn't have set hours. I didn't punch a clock. I just did whatever Stan said. Or, more often, whatever Thumbs Hogan said. Sometimes people wouldn't come across with money they owed Stan. A laundry service or a gin mill or one time even a Lutheran preschool. Sometimes a deadbeat gambler needed a knuckle job. Sometimes people got too curious about Stan's business, and I was sent to convince certain parties to take up other hobbies. Variations on a theme solved any problem. Me and a gun. Me and a set of brass knuckles. Me and a baseball bat. Me.

Then there were those times that somebody called Stan for help and was willing to pay big money to have a problem go away. And Stan would put me on a plane to Denver or Little Rock or Portland, and I'd disappear the problem into the night. Sweep it away in a clap of cordite, a .45 caliber stab of light into the darkness.

It had been after one of these trips that Stan and I had pie for the second time.

I'd been sent to pull the plug on an assistant D.A. in St. Louis, but I'd been handed a bad scouting report. I walked into a room full of guns and had some trouble getting out in one piece. The bullet I'd taken in the belly had me out of action for three months. Before Stan would pass me okay for work we'd met for pie. He'd wanted to look me in the eye. To see if I could still handle it.

"We got to stick together," Stan had said.

"I know."

"If we can't stand by each other," Stan had told me, "the rest don't mean shit. You remember that."

"I'll remember."

The third time we'd had pie was after Thumbs Hogan took it in the back.

He'd been giving a delinquent gambler a knuckle job. The gambler was having a bad football season and was into Stan for ten grand. So Hogan had the gambler down on the gambler's carpet in the gambler's living room, breaking the gambler's ribs when the gambler's fourteen-year-old daughter screamed into the room, tears smearing down her face, yelling for Hogan to get off her daddy as she unloaded a .22 caliber pistol into Hogan's back.

So two bites into my pie, Stan had told me I was in charge of the monkey cage. The new chain of command went from God to Stan to me to the boys. I wasn't quite an executive, but I was more of a somebody than I'd been before. Congratulations.

The fourth time for pie had been six years later, just after Dad had died.

Now Stan had called and said it was time for pie again. Something was up. I said pie sounded like a good idea, but my gut twisted into a little knot.

I walked into Troy's Diner just after three in the afternoon. I had my explanation all rehearsed and ready for when Stan asked about Sanchez. Self-defense all the way. Still, you didn't retire one of Stan's boys without Stan's permission. It was a matter of etiquette.

The diner was full of unwashed college kids with too many tattoos and too much time on their hands. Stan wanted to meet someplace where nobody would see us. I spotted Stan in a back booth, sat across from him. The coffee and pie arrived a few seconds later, brought by a pale twenty-something waitress with black hair and black lipstick. Hot apple pie with a scoop of vanilla ice cream on top.

"Stan."

He nodded to me. "Charlie."

Stan had been in the South since before I was born, but he still retained his deep Bronx accent. He came south in 1955 with a pistol and an attitude. His voice sounded like a bag of rocks in a tumble dryer.

Stan had looked old even when I'd first known him. Now he

sat shrunken inside his blue, pinstripe suit. His head was bald as a melon, dotted with dull brown liver spots. His face was a wad of sagging red flesh, but his bright blue eyes were hard and alert.

"Beggar Johnson's in town tonight," said Stan.

Beggar Johnson and Blade Sanchez had been tight. Sanchez had even gone as far as saying he was going to work for Beggar. I looked at my pie like it was the priority of my life. Inwardly, I braced myself.

Stan produced a rolled-up paper bag, slid it across the table to me. "Look inside."

I looked.

The bag contained the metal receiver box for the hidden microphone we sometimes used, also the cordless earpiece and the tiny tape recorder. I looked in the bag again. I looked at Stan.

"Beggar and a couple of his men are coming up to meet me and mine," said Stan. "I want you on the listening end."

I blinked at him. "Why?"

He frowned. "Why? Because I say why is why."

I nodded. "Sure, Stan."

"Then stick around after," he said. "I might have an errand for you. And keep this under your hat."

"Sure. What am I listening for?"

"You'll know when you hear it." He stood and dropped a twenty on the table. "Wait a few minutes before you leave. See you tonight."

He walked out. I sat. Drank coffee. The ice cream on my pie melted.

I thought about what Stan had said, but even more about what he didn't say. The unhappy stink of change was on the wind. A big shake-up coming our way. I'd seen shake-ups before but never from inside the eye of the shitstorm itself. We didn't help decide policy down in the monkey cage, so if Stan wanted me on my toes, then on my toes I'd be.

I signaled the waitress for more coffee, and while I was considering my soggy slice of pie, I realized Stan hadn't even asked about Sanchez. No mention. Not a word.

Back in the day, a hot game for high stakes in the back room at O'Malley's would have meant a dense layer of gray-blue smoke. Hard men keeping cigars alive with short, nervous puffs, ties pulled loose, pistols checked at the door, a line of hookers snapping gum at the bar waiting to reward winners, console losers.

But this ain't back in the day.

The stakes aren't so high, and smoke hurts my eyes. I wasn't in charge of much, but I was sure as hell in charge of the monkey cage. You want to light a Lucky, take it out to the alley.

"That's forty bucks," said Bob Tate. He looked at Lou Morgan, and Lou looked back like Bob had just asked for a kidney.

"That's steep."

Bob shrugged. "In or out?"

Lou looked at me. "What do you think, Charlie?"

I sighed at him. Didn't answer.

"I ain't got forty, man," said Lou.

"For Christ sake," said Bob. "We just got paid yesterday. What the hell do you do with your money?"

"What about a loan?" That was Benny. Always trying to be helpful.

I said, "I'm getting bored here."

And that settled it.

"Never mind then," said Lou. "I'll pass."

I scooped the dice off the center of the board, rattled them in my fist, and rolled. Eleven. I scooted the race car around the big third turn, passed the cartoon policeman with the whistle in his mouth, left Park Place and Luxury Tax in the dust, and parked my car right next to Lou's little tin dog.

"Son of a bitch," said Lou.

I counted out forty bucks and passed it to Benny, who'd drawn duty as banker. A tenth of the normal price. That's how we'd adapted the rules to use real money. Everything divided by ten. He gave me the white square of cardboard with the blue across the top. The deed for Boardwalk.

"We might as well cash it in," said Bob. "He's got the yellow ones and the green ones and now the blue ones."

As far as Bob was concerned, nothing had a proper name. Everything was the blue one or the green one or the lumpy one or the wet one or the one that smelled like cheese. He'd been married nine years before his wife had caught him with her sister. When I asked which sister, he'd said, "The easy one."

The door leading into O'Malley's front room opened. Amber scooted through amid the crowd chatter. They had a basketball game on, and judging from the crowd's surly tone, the Magic were taking another beating.

Amber had a paper sack in her hand. It bulged with money, which meant one of Stan's mules had dropped off his weekly take. Amber scooted over to the floor safe behind the bar and dropped it in. On her way back out, she diverted toward the table, bent and gave me a quick peck on the cheek.

"Tell Danny I'll call him tomorrow, would you, Charlie?"

"No problem, honey." I beamed at her.

She turned on her high heels and swished back into O'Malley's. Everyone at the table watched her go.

Amber and my kid brother Danny had a pretty steady thing going. They'd been dating about a year, and I was pretty sure

Danny was ready to pop the question any second now. But you could see in Amber's eyes she had a lot of living yet to do. She was just twenty years old and working on her degree in theater arts at UCF. A pretty kid with her head in the clouds.

But I couldn't blame Danny. Amber was a knockout. Thick hair the brown of highly polished antique wood. Deep, dark eyes. She always had this knowing expression on her face, like she knew something you didn't. A little impish half-smile. And you desperately wanted in on the joke.

So I'd gotten her the bullshit O'Malley's job. Officially she was a "hostess." She called taxis for the drunks. Ran errands. Brought paper sacks full of money to the back room. Mostly she winked at me and the boys, made us feel like we were all twenty years old again. That alone was worth what we paid her.

But don't get the idea that any of the boys had inappropriate thoughts about her. We all sat there, a table full of doting uncles. Let someone even look at Amber sideways and wait for the bloodshed. Once a few sailors who had no business being in O'Malley's in the first place thought a little grab-ass would get them on Amber's good side. Suddenly, five ugly uncles had them by the ice cream suits. They'd woken up in the alley.

"It's late," said Benny. "Who's closing?"

"Me and the new guy." I jerked a thumb at Lou. He'd only been with us a month and was as dumb as a sack of doorknobs. But Stan said take him on. Stan said it, we did it. That's how it worked until God or Stan said different.

"How long you guys going to call me the new guy?"

"Until we get a newer guy," said Bob.

The most tedious part of the job was closing. Stan's book-keeper counted up the take for the night, balanced accounts, and locked everything in the safe. The bar out front did a good business. O'Malley's had a regular crowd, mostly middle-class stiffs who pushed a pencil from nine to five and needed a few hours to unwind before going home to the wife and two-point-three kids. But what O'Malley's pulled down in a week wouldn't even pay for the men who sat around the Monopoly table every night.

When I was the new guy, I'd always wondered why Stan wanted a bunch of goons sitting around.

I remember it had been maybe a year since Stan had sent Thumbs Hogan to offer me a job. I'd been the little tin dog then, just a kid with a steady hand, a good eye and a quick trigger. I remember the night like it was yesterday, like it was slow-motion action footage, replayed over and again. Thumbs wasn't there that night, so Tony Dale was the race car, Eddie Mex the top hat. Porky Mullins had definitely been the shoe. Strangely, that was my clearest memory the night of the holdup.

Porky held the shoe delicately between his thumb and fore-finger, his meaty pinky finger stuck out like he was drinking tea with the queen. Each time he moved the shoe a space he'd say "Walk." I thought he was about the corniest guy I'd ever met. A guy as big as a hippo in a plaid sports jacket.

Porky rolled a four. "Walk, walk, walk, walk." His little pinky sticking out. "Hey, that's Marvin Gardens. I wanna buy that."

"I already own it," said Eddie Mex. "Welcome to *Casa de Marvin.*" He camped up his Spanish accent even though he was fourth generation and born in Oregon. "No extra charge for breakfast in bed, *huevos rancheros,* and Bloody Marys."

"I don't care if you own it or not. I need it for the monopoly," said Porky. "I got the other two."

"Don't give it to him," I said. "He'll load it up with hotels."

"Hey, fucking New Guy, put a sock in it." His eyes stabbed at me from behind big, fatty folds of flesh. "I'm down two hundred bucks, and I still don't own dick here. I got Water Works and Baltic Avenue and one fucking railroad. Now I want Marvin Gardens, and I want it right fucking now."

I shrugged, tipped my chair back, watched the show.

"Okay," said Eddie. "You want it? A hundred bucks."

"What the fuck? At least pull a gun on me. Ya damn spic. A hundred fucking bucks."

Eddie smiled big. *"Lo siento mucho, seeenyooor,* but if you want the land, you better fork over a Franklin."

Tony Dale sat quietly like a big Irish lump.

Buzzzzzzzzzzzz.

We all checked our watches. The midnight drop. About five minutes early but no big deal.

Tony hit the button on the wall near his chair. The buzz stopped and the lock on the back door clicked. Eddie opened his mouth to spit another remark at Porky.

The back door flew open, and two black men dressed in dark jogging suits exploded into the room. Each held two revolvers in tight fists. They began firing immediately, spraying the room with lead.

If I hadn't been leaning way back in my chair, I'd be dead. After the first shot, I fell flat on my back, the bullets shedding drywall over me. Eddie took it in the side of the head just above his ear, slumped to the floor like he'd had the air let out of him. Porky and Tony flipped the Monopoly table, cash and dice and hotels scattering. Tony had his pistol out but never got off a shot. The first black guy drilled him square in the heart. But Porky was quick, moved well for a big man. His silver-plated .45 flashed into his hand, and he unloaded the clip into the attackers. They twitched, dropped their weapons, sprawled on the floor.

It was all over by the time I got to my feet. I stood next to

Porky, and he pointed his empty automatic at one of the dead black guys.

"Holy shit, that's Leon."

I looked at the corpse. "Who?"

"He washes dishes here," said Porky. "Son of a bitch must've been casing us for a month. He knew we got cash drops back here."

I looked at Porky. A dark stain crept out of his jacket, spread across his white shirt.

"Porky." I pointed at his chest. "You okay?"

He looked down at himself. "Aw hell." He opened his jacket. A mess.

"Aw, shit, New Guy, I'm fucked." He collapsed to the floor.

"Christ! Hang on, Porky. I'll get somebody."

I ran to the front of O'Malley's. Deserted. Everyone had hot-footed it at the sound of gunplay.

I called the paramedics, but by the time they got there all they found was Porky lying on his side, eyes open, a pool of blood around him like cherry syrup, little green Monopoly houses dotting the blood like gumdrops.

Now cash drops came through the front. We only used the back door if we needed to cut out in a hurry.

"Charlie, hey, man, you listening?"

I blinked. Looked at Lou. "What is it, New Guy?"

"I asked if you'd seen Blade."

"Yeah," said Benny. "Where's our knife boy?"

"He's not here," I said. "Are we playing or what?"

Benny and Bob took the hint immediately.

"What do you mean not here?" said Lou. "I can see that, man. Is he working or something?"

"Hey, New Guy, you don't like the way I answer your questions?"

"It's not that. I just—"

"Am I the information booth, is that it? I'm supposed to keep you informed about every little thing that goes on?"

"Sorry, Charlie. Never mind, man. I withdraw the question."

Stan came through the door from O'Malley's front room and into the monkey cage. He had the whole parade behind him. Stan's right-hand man Larry Cartwright was in tow along with a fat guy called Jimmy the Fix who made sure all the hot stuff that came through got shipped to the right place to be fenced. Jimmy and Larry were movers and shakers in Stan's organization. I didn't know Larry Cartwright too well, but Jimmy was a stand-up guy.

Beggar Johnson came next. Young compared to Stan, maybe mid-forties. Blue blazer, pink shirt open at the neck, no tie. Black hair slicked back like Pat Riley's. He stood straight and tall like he owned the world. Guys like him ran things from an ivory tower and only came down when it was doom time.

I sized up the two guys with him. Both trouble, but for different reasons. I didn't know them, but I could tell the type.

The first guy was short and twitchy. Bland, clammy face under a dishwater haircut. His eyes pinballed around the room, not really taking anything in, hand clenching and unclenching the whole time he stood swaying next to Beggar. His hand jerked up to his nose every few seconds, tweaking it between thumb and forefinger. Coke-head. You could spot one a mile away, and dangerous. Either Beggar didn't know, or he didn't care that he had a man under him who could go squirrelly at a moment's notice.

Unlike the coke-head, the other guy was dangerous by design. He was tall and Aryan, blond and stiff. Young. Wore an expensive black suit, purple shirt and tie. He was hard and cold, and his jacket bulged in the right places.

Stan broke off from his guests and motioned to me.

I told the boys to pack up the game for the night and met Stan in the center of the room.

"Tell Amber to come up to the office and see what everyone wants to drink," said Stan. He tapped his chest and gave me a wink.

He had the wire on. I nodded.

Stan led his guests upstairs where he had a boardroom with a table and enough chairs to accommodate everyone comfortably. I sent for Amber, told her to hustle it up and see what everyone wanted to drink.

I told Bob and Benny to get home.

"What's the deal?" Bob Tate had a big worried look on his mug.

"Ask me again tomorrow."

Bob nodded, gave Benny an elbow nudge. "Let's go." I told Lou to keep an eye on things out front.

I waited until he was gone then slipped on the earpiece.

"—young lady can get us some drinks," Stan was saying.

I imagined them up there. Stan and Larry and Jimmy at one end of the table, Beggar and his boys at the other, everyone wearing big phony smiles. I didn't like the idea of the guy in the purple tie being up there. He was strictly enforcement. If he was up there I felt like I should've been too. Too bad. I didn't make those decisions.

"No drinks." Beggar. "If I wanted drinks, I'd go get drinks. I'm here to talk business. I'm going to talk quick so I think you better listen."

Stan sent Amber out. I adjusted the volume.

"Okay, Beggar. What brings you all the way up from Miami? What couldn't be handled with a phone call? You wanted us to run down Rollo for you. We done it. What else?"

"How old are you, Stan?"

A pause.

"What the hell is this?"

"Don't get me wrong," said Beggar. "I have nothing but respect for what you've accomplished here. You've done a hell of a job. Nobody could have run Orlando like you. Especially in the old days. But this ain't the old days anymore. Things change. It gets tougher and tougher to keep business at the level it used to be at."

"The hell you say." Stan. "I run a tight ship. You got complaints? Let's hear them."

"This isn't just me saying this, Stan. It's come straight down the chain. You're sitting on a big fat apple here in Orlando. Hotels, bars, Disney sitting over there like a big, ripe plum. Every hotel should be using the laundry service you tell them to. Every bar should be on to your beverage service. You've maintained well here, Stan, but the town's expanded these last ten years. You haven't. It's a juicy territory, and you're not squeezing hard enough."

Stan made a disgusted noise in his throat. "And who can squeeze harder? You, I suppose."

"I suppose I could."

"So I'm out with the bathwater, am I?"

"It's not like that. Nobody wants to put you out to pasture. Just let me move some of my people up here, show you how to shake a few more leaves off the money tree."

"Bullshit. You think I don't know the slow squeeze when I see it."

"I told you," said Beggar. "Nobody wants to squeeze you out." He lowered his voice. "But it can get tough if you want to play it tough."

Stan muttered something I couldn't catch. "Okay. What am I supposed to do?"

"Good," said Beggar. "You're doing the right thing. First we need a favor."

"What?"

"There's a guy up here. In your town. Took some stuff that ain't his. I need you to go over and make him unhappy."

"Seems like all your problems run up here to Orlando."

"Can I count on you or not?" asked Beggar.

"Why me?"

"He's meeting one of your boys. Donovan."

"Small time. Owns a titty bar. A nobody. So what?"

"We know he's nobody," said Beggar. "That's why we figured you wouldn't mind giving him up."

Stan sighed heavy and ragged, the sound of his soul being pulled up through his throat, the sound of our world changing forever.

FOUR

Stan had watched everyone go, watched Beggar glide out like the angel of doom back to his ivory tower. I told Lou to lock up then take a hike. Stan's driver–bodyguard waited in Stan's Fleetwood, so it was just me and him sitting around the Monopoly table in the monkey cage.

"Get a bottle," he said.

"Of what?"

"Whatever. Bring two glasses."

I fetched a bottle of Chivas, straddled my chair backwards. I leaned forward, filled each glass a third full.

He sipped. I sipped. We sat.

Finally he said, "You heard all that?"

"Yeah."

"How do you size it up? The situation."

"They're handing you a big shit sandwich," I said.

Stan nodded. Smiled. Not a happy smile. A might-as-well-get-used-to-taking-it-up-the-ass smile. "You have a good way with words, Charlie. Charlie the Hook. Anybody still call you that?"

"Hardly anybody."

He scratched his head. "How'd you get that nickname? Been so long, I forgot."

"I killed a man with a boat hook once."

He chuckled. "Oh yeah." He'd been forgetting a lot lately.

He finished the Chivas, coughed a little. "I don't really drink anymore. Eighty-one years old. Believe that shit? All I've lived through, and it's drinking and smoking and cholesterol and shit I have to worry about. Fuck."

Yeah.

"But tonight—" He tapped his glass. I poured it a third full again. "—tonight I need a drink."

"Sure, Stan."

He drank. I drank. We still sat.

I cleared my throat some, kind of looked at him.

"Go ahead and ask," he said.

"What do we do?"

"Right now we do nothing. We toe the line. You know Kyle Donovan?"

Not personally, but I'd been listening on the wire. "Owns a titty bar called Toppers on Orange Blossom Trail. He answers to you?"

"He's pretty far down the food chain," said Stan. "He answers to people who pay me for the honor of doing business in my neighborhood."

"Who do you want me to take along?"

"Who do you need?"

I only thought a second. "Bob and Benny to cover the doors. I'll go in myself after hours. I'll leave New Guy to watch out for things here."

"New Guy? Who the fuck's that?"

"Lou Morgan. The huge guy. Muscles."

"Don't worry about that. I want you to call Benny and Bob. I want you taking care of this tonight before Beggar heads back for Miami."

"Tonight?"

"What's that? Some kind of problem?"

"No problem, Stan."

"Good. Nobody gets out. Got it? If it moves, it's dead."

"I got it."

"Now listen, Charlie. This is the important part. There's a

black, eel-skin briefcase with the initials A.A. Combination locked. Grab it. Turn the place inside out if you have to but put the snatch on it top priority, *capiche*? Beggar wants the case taken to Alan Jeffers."

Stan explained Jeffers was the twitchy coke-head that worked for Beggar. Beggar's blond gunman was a cat named Lloyd Mercury.

I said, "I understand. What's in the case?"

"What the fuck you care what's in the case? Just get it."

"Okay, Stan."

"Shit, what a fucking night. Look, forget I snapped. I'm a cranky old man, right?"

"No problem, Stan."

"I got to go. I'm trusting you to take care of this."

We said our goodbyes. From the window I watched him bend his old-man body into the Fleetwood.

As I was dialing Benny's number, I thought that Stan still hadn't asked where Blade Sanchez had vanished to. Maybe he had a reason for not asking. When you asked questions, you risked getting answers.

Benny answered after four rings. "Yeah?" He didn't sound sleepy. Night owl.

"Put your fun hat on," I told him. "We got work."

At a quarter to five, me and Benny and Bob waited in a black minivan in the Toppers parking lot. The girls had left in a steady stream, not quite as appealing out of their g-strings and in their street clothes. When the lot was empty, I told my team to check the loads on their shotguns. The plan: I go in and sweep the place clean. They wait by the exits and plug anyone who tries to bolt.

"You sure about this, Charlie?" Benny chewed his fingernails.

All of his jittery habits surfaced when it was go time. But he had his head on straight. No problem.

"Our best guess is there's about nine guys in there," he said. "We'll know better when you talk to the girl."

"Yeah, but the breakdown's okay. We got one bookworm counting the night's take, two bartenders, and two bouncers who may or may not be packing. That leaves four probably carrying heat, and I take them first."

"Look, I got plenty of faith in you," said Benny. "But maybe I should come with, huh?"

"I got it. You cover the rear."

"Okay." Benny handed me an envelope. "Her name's Candy."

"Sure it is."

I leaned against the back wall between the rear entrance and the Dumpster. Two minutes later, a ragged blond with big fake tits emerged and held the back door open for me.

"How many?" I asked.

"Nine," she said and snapped her gum. "The four suits all have guns. I sat in Myron's lap earlier, so I know he ain't packing."

"Myron?"

"Donovan's cousin from down south."

My ears perked up. "How far down south?"

"Miami, I think. What do I know? He had busy hands and wasn't much interested in talking."

"Okay. Who else?"

"Sal and Ron—the bartenders—don't carry anything on them, but there's a small silver revolver underneath the register. The bouncers got nothing but muscles."

I handed Candy the envelope. "I don't know what your plans are, but I wouldn't come back here."

She opened the envelope, thumbed through the bills briefly, then stuffed the cash into her jeans. "Don't worry. I ain't ever coming back to this shithole." And she was gone.

I entered the dim hall and closed the door behind me. A few quick steps brought me to the girls' dressing room. A curtain on the left led to the stage, and the door on the right opened into a long hall that led to the kitchen. So far, it had been just like Benny told me it would be. I took a few seconds to check my guns. The twin .45s hung snug in their shoulder holsters, and the .38 with the three-inch barrel was clipped tight to my belt just below my belly. I used to wear a little .380 on my ankle, but I'd never needed it and it made movement awkward.

My last touch was a pair of latex gloves. You can get a whole box of them for free when you see your doctor for a routine checkup. A little compensation for having to read two-year-old magazines in the waiting room. Anyway, I wasn't eager to leave fingerprints.

I drew the .45 automatics and slipped down the hall toward the kitchen.

The kitchen was completely dark except for the dusty light that spilled in from the lounge beyond. I could hear men's voices and the clink of glasses floating in from the next room. I crept up to the edge of the doorway, staying in the shadow, and peeked in. One of the big bouncers still sat on his perch near the front door. He looked bored and tired and leaned heavily against the red velvet wallpaper, his eyes drooping. Both bartenders washed and dried glasses behind the bar, and the guy who had to be Myron sat at one of the big tables in the center of the room with two of the suits. Both suits looked clean-cut and serious.

I watched from the shadows for two more minutes, and my patience paid off. The other two suits returned and pulled chairs up to Myron's table. Myron was bent over some papers, reading hard and fast. The other bouncer was still unaccounted for, but I felt good enough about the situation to go in. I made a mental note of the order I wanted to start shooting people.

From where I stood, I couldn't get a clear shot at everyone, so I needed to be on the move.

I started pulling triggers as soon as I stepped into the light.

The shouting and confusion erupted like it always did. Men pushed chairs away from the table, went for pistols inside jackets. Another thing about strip clubs: most are wall-to-wall mirrors, and the effect was that blazing death had descended on them from all directions. The thick-necked bouncer awoke on his stool, his eyes widening with panic.

I swung the automatics in a deliberate arc, squeezing lead into the four suits. They spun around in a shower of blood, guns halfway out of their holsters. Myron dove under the table, and I left him for the moment, turned my attention to the bar. From the corner of my eye, I caught sight of the bouncer's back as he disappeared through the front door. I was vaguely aware of a shotgun blast outside.

Behind the long, wooden bar, both bartenders were in motion. The first bolted for the kitchen door. The other went for the pistol beneath the register, and I followed him with a rain of lead. Booze bottles danced and shattered behind him, but I had to abandon him and attend to the second bouncer who emerged from the dancers' dressing room with a sawed-off shotgun. He stood center stage and blew a chunk of wood out of the table I'd overturned for cover. I stood and emptied both clips into him, and he fell into a lifeless heap on the stage.

I dropped the empty automatics, deciding it would be quicker to pull the .38 from the belly holster than it would be to shove another clip into one of the .45s. I thumbed back the hammer and rolled along the tile floor until I was up against the bar.

The bartender might still be crouched near the register, but if he was smart he'd have crawled two-thirds of the way to the other end, so he could pop up and squeeze off a few shots at me. But I didn't know if he was smart or not, so I watched the bar in the mirror on the other side of the room.

I guess he wasn't too smart, because he popped up about ten seconds later, still near the register, holding the little silver revolver in front of him like he was trying to choke it. After the rage of gunfire, the club was now strangely quiet.

"Dave?" he called. "You okay? You get him?"

I double-checked his position in the mirror, then stood and fired. I caught him solid right behind the ear. Blood surged fleshy and wet. He slumped forward over the bar. The pistol fell out of his hand and clattered across the tile.

I thumbed back the hammer again and slowly approached the table in the center of the club. I crouched, the .38 leading the way, and found Myron flat on his stomach with his hands over his head. I was about to turn his lights out when he said something interesting.

"Who are you? You want it? Just take it. Okay? Leave me alone." He thrust a finger over his head. "In the briefcase." Myron was a portly, sweaty man with fat arms and fat legs and stubby fingers and a nose that looked like a little fist. A cowering blob in a nice suit. I'd seen a hundred like him, but I was suddenly curious.

"You stay put." I kept the revolver on him. I couldn't afford to be *too* curious. The shots would bring the sirens soon enough, but I had this gut feeling that there was more going on here than the after-hours strip club routine. I tried the briefcase, but it was combination locked with a three-digit code. The initials A.A. in gold.

I waved Myron out from under the table. "Open it."

"Sure, pal. You got it. I'm cooperating, see?" Myron worked the combination, flipped the latch and reached into the case.

I saw his shoulders tense and twisted away from him just as his fat hand came out of the case with a snub-nose revolver. He fired once where my midsection had been. I felt the hot kiss of the slug glance along a rib as it passed through my shirt and jacket. My side grew warm and wet with my own blood.

The .38 jerked in my hand three times. The bullets sprouted red across Myron's chest. He twitched once and fell across the table, slamming the briefcase closed. Locks clicking shut again.

I checked myself. The wound stung like hell, but it wasn't too bad. I kicked Myron away from the table and grabbed the briefcase. On my way out, I passed over one of the dead suits. A brassy hint of metal sticking out of his jacket caught my eye. By all the rules, I should have hauled my ass out the back door a long time ago. But some strange little tickle in the back of my brain made me stop and poke my nose into things that were none of my business. My job was done. I should be gone. But that little tickle.

I bent and shoved back the suit's lapel, revealing the shiny hunk of metal pinned to his vest.

It was a badge.

My heart shifted into passing gear, and I swallowed hard. A quick check revealed three more badges on the others. I'd just pulled the plug on four cops. This wasn't in the game plan. Not by a long shot. I pocketed one of the badges, picked up my automatics. And left Toppers through the same door I'd come in. Benny and Bob looked impatient.

"Christ," said Bob. "We almost left you. Get in the van, and let's get out of here."

"Listen, guys, something's fucked up," I said.

"Something's always fucked up," said Bob. "Let's talk about it in the van."

I flashed him the badge, and his eyes got big as hubcaps. "I took it off one of the marks in there. There's three more just like it. Somebody's not telling us everything. The shit's going to hit the fan. I just thought we should get ready to duck."

He looked unhappy. "Goddamnmotherfuckshit."

"I think we'd better go someplace. Figure this out."

"The monkey cage." Benny's suggestion.

"No," I said. "I know where. And we can get some breakfast."

I held a handkerchief to my bleeding side as I climbed into the van. The angry song of sirens chased us into the fading night.

FIVE

The sun was just percolating through the trees when Benny parked the van in front of the two-story house in Winter Park. I made the boys wipe their feet on the way in.

"That you, Charlie?"

"It's me, Ma. I got Bob and Benny with me."

"Hi, boys. I'll have food for you in a minute."

"Good morning, Mrs. Swift." Bob.

"Hope we're not disturbing you too early." Benny.

Ma made a noise in the kitchen like that was the most ridiculous thing she'd ever heard.

Two things: Ma never slept, and there was always something working in the kitchen.

I stuck my nose in the air. A quick sniff was all I needed: eggs, coffee, Canadian bacon. Ma had probably been up an hour, getting grub together for me and Danny. Ma was small and frumpy and motherly with flecks of gray in her auburn hair.

"Let me get a shower, Ma, and I'll come down for a bite. I'll get Danny up too."

"He's up," said Ma. "Punching that bag again behind the garage."

Danny had retreated home after quitting college again. He was supposed to be at Clemson University getting himself educated, but he thought punching the heavy bag and trying to talk Amber out of her clothes every night was a better use of his time. Ma was crazy with the whole situation, and I was supposed to sit down for a brother-to-brother ass-chewing session. I hadn't had a chance to get around to it.

"It's too early for boxing," I said.

"You let him alone. Let him punch. He's a good boy." Ma said that because Benny and Bob were listening. When it was just family, Danny was making her "nutso."

"I'll get cleaned up."

"Good. You look like a mess. I'll feed these boys." She led Benny and Bob to the kitchen table.

I dragged myself into the upstairs bathroom and slumped heavily onto the toilet. I made a point of taking the briefcase with me. The night's work had finally seeped into my muscles during the van ride, and I ached all over. I peeled myself out of the bloodstained shirt and went to work on the wound. It was shallow and ugly. I fished the first aid kit out from under the sink. I wiped the wound clean with water first then gave it a second going over with the hydrogen peroxide.

I turned the shower on as hot as I could stand it, bathed, dried, and bandaged the wound. I probably could have used a stitch or two. I made up for it with a few extra strands of medical tape. I slipped into jeans and an Orlando Magic T-shirt and packed last night's clothes into the hamper. I shuffled back to my room and found Danny waiting for me.

He sat in the window seat, which overlooked the street, his shorts and tank top soaked through with sweat. He'd given the bag a good work-over, and he still wore the gloves. He was a good-looking kid, taller than me, square shoulders and a flat belly. He was a sit-up junky from way back. At twenty-four years old, he was sixteen years my junior, and he'd been a surprise for my folks. Whereas I had a big square mug and a lump of granite for a chin, Danny's features were sharp, angular jawline. He got that from Ma. I took more after Dad.

Danny pulled off the gloves and pulled the bottom of his tank top up to wipe the sweat off his forehead. It didn't help much. "Hey, Charlie."

"Danny."

"Ma's got breakfast ready."

"Yeah. I smelled it. I hope there's something left when Benny and Bob are through."

"Ma tell you to tell me to go back to school yet?"

"About twenty times a day."

He shrugged. "I don't think school's for me."

I tried another strategy. "Ain't there like ten tons of gorgeous girls running around campus? You don't want to give that up, do you?"

"None of them are as good as Amber."

I couldn't disagree.

"Actually, I thought I might go to work."

"Oh yeah?"

"Yeah. I thought maybe you could take me on down at the monkey cage."

I made myself chuckle at him even though it wasn't very damn funny. "What the hell do you know about that?"

"Come on, Charlie. I hear you talking with those other guys. I know what goes on. I'm not a bookworm, okay? I've been in and out of college three times. I'm not cut out for it."

"So what then?"

He flipped back the spare blanket at the foot of my bed. Underneath was my little Mac-10 machine pistol, the spare clips and the flash suppressor. The firing pin was busted, and I hadn't gotten around to fixing it yet. Also, a 9mm Browning automatic, three Marine combat knives, and a stun gun.

"We'll talk later," I said. "I've got the boys downstairs."

Around the kitchen table three men frowned around mouthfuls of eggs and bacon. I was one of them. Coffee. Biscuits. More frowning. Ma had gone about her business. Let the boys talk.

We were all thinking the same thing. I didn't need to be a mind-reader. Dead cops. Now what?

I had the briefcase down by my ankles. We hadn't opened it. We didn't know if we were supposed to. I hadn't told them what I'd heard on the wire during Stan's meeting with Beggar Johnson. But we knew our instructions. Take the briefcase to Beggar's man Jeffers. The monkey cage wasn't supposed to ask questions.

Benny had reached that conclusion ahead of me. "Look. Just give me the case, and I'll run it over to this Jeffers character. We did what we were told. Period. We can't get in trouble for that, can we?"

Bob watched for my reaction.

I thought. Scratched my head. Drank coffee. Rubbed the stubble along my chin. Thought some more.

"Okay," I said. "What's our job is the question, right?" I looked at them.

They looked back.

Yeah, we were supposed to do what we were told. Sure. But we were also supposed to look out for the boss. If he went under, we were all sunk. "I'm going to call Stan."

I told them to wait and went upstairs to use the phone in the bedroom. None of the other boys had Stan's personal home number, so I dialed with reverence. He answered after five rings. Stan always answered his own phone.

"I got news."

"Tell me."

I told him.

"I see." He didn't really sound too surprised, went quiet for long seconds.

"Stan?"

"I'm deciding."

I waited, ear glued to the phone. When he finally came back on the line, my heart jerked up in my throat. Anxious.

"Open the case," said Stan.

"It's locked."

"Pry it open."

I didn't hesitate. I grabbed the bowie knife and pried open the latches in ten seconds flat. The briefcase contained two leather-bound ledgers, accounting books. I flipped through the pages. Rows of numbers. All Greek to me.

I told Stan.

"Bring it to my place. One hour."

"You don't want me to take it to Jeffers?"

"Who's running the show here?" His talk was tough, but his voice strained.

I swallowed hard. "Right."

"Charlie."

"Yeah?"

"You done good." His old, old sack-of-rocks voice sounded fatherly for just a second.

We hung up.

I went downstairs.

"I'm going to Stan's."

Benny shook his head, but Bob said, "Good."

"Listen," I said. "We got to keep a lid on this. Take the minivan and ditch it." It was stolen anyway. "Dump the shotguns." I handed over the .45s and the .38. "These too." I had replacements.

"What about you?" asked Benny.

"I'll get Danny to drop me by my place. I want to change before I see Stan."

They got up, and I showed them out. They had their marching orders, and I had mine.

I yelled for Danny.

From upstairs: "What?"

"Pull your hot rod around," I yelled back. "I need a ride."

✿

The first time Danny tried college, he'd surprised the hell out of everyone by getting a baseball scholarship. So we gave him the eight thousand dollars we had in a savings account that we'd been saving for tuition. He dropped three grand on a 1965 Chevy Impala, big V-8 engine, fire-engine red. Convertible. He spent a month covered in grease, rebuilt the transmission, fixed it up nice.

So we were heading up 17-92 to my apartment, Danny driving. We had the top down. Wind blew. Normally, I'd be noticing how cool we looked, but my brain kept spinning me around in circles thinking what I was supposed to do with the briefcase in my lap. Take it to Stan I guess. Keep my mouth shut. Why didn't that seem good enough?

"Have you thought about what I asked?"

I blinked, stopped thinking about who I could shoot to make things better for Stan. "Huh?"

"About working down in the monkey cage," said Danny.

I waved him away. "You don't even know what it takes."

"Oh yeah?" He wore a denim jacket. He steered with one hand and pulled back his jacket with the other. Tucked in the belt of his jeans was an enormous, nickel-plated automatic pistol. There was a scope on it.

"What the hell is that?"

He took it out, slid it across the seat. "Take a look."

I picked it up, turned it over in my hands. Danny had added a barrel extension, extra-capacity clip. What I'd thought was a scope was actually a laser sight. "I'm serious," I said. "What the hell is this?"

"That's one bad-ass chunk of serious heat. That's what that is."

"What are you, Buck fucking Rogers?"

"What's wrong with it?"

"Nothing, I guess. If you're trying to blow up the Death Star."

"Listen, man, I'm good with that thing. I've been to the range twice a week."

"Let me ask you something," I said. "Where'd you get this thing?"

"Shoot Straight Gun Emporium."

"How'd you pay?"

"Visa."

"Okay," I said. "So you shoot somebody. The cops get the ballistics and have no trouble tracing the piece right back to you. A nice, legal trail. Puts you in the slammer, twenty-five to life. Am I making my point?"

"Fine. I get it. I don't know everything. You probably didn't either at first. You had to learn."

"That's right. *I had to*. You don't."

"But—"

"Danny, it's an ugly, hard, shitty way to earn a living." I couldn't help I was good at it. "And frankly this is not a good time. Things are crazy right now, and I've got to think about what I'm going to do."

"Maybe I can help."

I exhaled, the breath huffing out of me like it had given up. "I'll let you know."

Danny let me out in front of my garage apartment, rumbled away in the Impala with his giant gun and a sour look on his face. I went upstairs.

I shed my jeans and T-shirt, slipped into a black double-breasted suit, cuffs, red tie with a subtle pattern. Wingtips.

I went into the bathroom and opened the medicine cabinet. I took out the aspirin, milk of magnesia, various antiseptics and bandages. Set them all on the back of the toilet. I pried away the false back with a penknife, revealing the hidey hole where my spare pistols hung on pegs. I left the two Colt .45s and took down the .38 police special with the four-inch barrel. I checked to make sure it had a full load, then snugged it into the belly holster. When I buttoned the jacket, the piece was almost invisible, and I could draw three times faster from across my belly than I could from the shoulder.

I put the medicine cabinet back together and checked myself in the mirror. Good. I looked professional again.

At my kitchen table, I fussed with the eel-skin briefcase. After my makeshift locksmithing with the bowie knife, I could only get one of the latches to snap back into position. I didn't want the books to spill out into the street, so I found a dark green gym bag under my bed and put the books inside. Zipped it up.

I started out the door with the gym bag, stopped, looked at the briefcase still on the table. Stan said bring it. Of course, he wanted what was inside, but why risk having to drive back? Details. That's what separates the professionals from the average jerkoff. Details.

I grabbed the briefcase and my car keys and went downstairs.

Behind my Buick, I dropped the gym bag at my feet, still had the briefcase under my arm. I slipped the key into the trunk but never had a chance to turn it.

The blow slapped sharply across the base of my skull. My eyes were swallowed by darkness; the big fireworks display went off in my head. I stumbled forward, sprawled on the trunk. The blackness drawing me down into a spiraling funnel of white noise.

SIX

My suit was dirty.

So was the left side of my head.

That's what happens when you lie facedown in a sandy drive-way, I guess. I felt the back of my head before trying to get up. No sticky layer of blood. Thank God for small favors. I got up on one knee, a little wobbly. I put my hands against the trunk of the Buick for support, climbed to my feet.

I brushed myself off.

I looked up at the sun, down at my watch. I'd been lying in the dirt all morning.

I was very very late to meet Stan.

Stan. I stood straight, head jerking around, scanning the yard. The briefcase—the eel-skin briefcase with the initials A.A., the briefcase I'd pried open with a knife, the briefcase I'd shot everybody dead in a titty bar for—was gone.

Shit.

I bent, looked under the Buick. The gym bag. I opened it. The books.

Nervous, relieved giggling elbowed its way out of my throat, skipped away on the mild winter breeze. I rezipped the gym bag, took the stairs two at a time back up to my apartment.

I called Stan's home phone. Twenty-one rings. No answer.

I dialed Bob Tate. Three rings and an answering machine. "Hey, this is Bob. I'm not here right now but—"

I hung up.

I dialed Benny. Fifteen rings. No answer.

Where the hell was everybody?

I called O'Malley's. Twelve rings and no answer. I let it ring five more times. Still nobody.

That was just wrong.

I looked out my window. Scanned the yard. No trouble. At least none that I could see.

Okay, Charlie old boy, now what?

I called Ma. She answered after three rings.

"Ma, let me speak to Danny."

"He's out back punching the bag."

"Get him."

"Is something wrong?"

"I just want to talk to Danny."

She went for him. He came on the phone panting. "Charlie?"

"Look out the front window. I'll wait."

"What?"

"Just do it."

"What am I looking for?"

"A strange car parked across the street. Maybe somebody sitting inside. Take a good look. Maybe parked down a block."

"What's going on?"

"Just do it."

"Hold on."

I waited, looked out my own window.

Danny came back. "It's clear."

"Okay. Still want to help?"

"Does this mean I'm hired?"

"Call it an audition. Still got your Buck Rogers gun?"

"Yeah."

"Keep it handy. Don't let Ma see. No sense sending her off the deep end. Stay inside and try to talk her out of going anywhere."

"She's Ma. Where would she go?"

"Keep an eye on the window. Don't let anyone near that you don't know. I'll be in touch later."

"Charlie, what's going on?"

"Probably nothing. Just being careful."

"That's what you need me to do? Guard Ma?"

"That just shows you don't know anything," I said. "First thing you learn in the monkey cage is watch after your own."

"Okay, okay. Take it easy."

"I'll be in touch."

I hung up and took the medicine cabinet apart again. I withdrew the Colts and put them in the shoulder holsters but didn't wear them. I shoved them in the gym bag with the books.

I left the apartment, locked the door. I was halfway down the stairs when the phone started ringing behind me. I ran back up, fumbled the keys out. I unlocked the door and answered the phone on the eighth ring.

"Yeah?"

"Charlie?"

Lou Morgan. New Guy. "Where in the shit are you?"

"O'Malley's," he said. "Where's everybody else? Place is locked up tighter than Bob Tate's colon after a chunk of cheese."

"Can the comedy, New Guy. This is fucking serious. How long you been there?"

"An hour maybe."

"I tried calling."

"I was across the street," said Lou. "I thought maybe it was a holiday or something, so I wanted to see if Jan's was open." The deli across from O'Malley's. "I mean it's dead here, man. Nobody out front in the bar. Nobody back in the cage. Nothing."

The wheels in my head cranked, began to turn. "Have you talked to Bob or Benny?"

"No. I tried calling Bob first."

"Lou," I said, my slow thoughts stumbling over one another, "I think maybe you ought to get out of there."

"Hold on," said Lou. "Somebody's at the door."

"Don't answer it, Lou."

"It might be Bob. It'll just take a second." I heard Lou lay the receiver on the bar.

"Bob has a key," I yelled into the phone. "Lou!"

The scene beyond the phone unfolded like a radio play. The door opening. The rush of bodies into the room. Shouts. Lou's voice: *Fuckers!* Shots. Yelling. More shots. Glass shattering. Movement. Pushing? Another voice: *Around there. Hurry.*

"Lou!" My voice urgent.

It went silent quickly. Steps. The click and buzz on the other end of the phone. Disconnect.

I drove as fast as I could without risking a ticket, knowing the party would be over by the time I got there from my apartment. What else could I do? I fingered the .38 in the belly holster. The gym bag perched on the passenger seat.

This wasn't the slow squeeze anymore. It was bad.

But when I got to O'Malley's I found out it was worse.

I got within a block. A uniformed cop held back a crowd. Squad cars.

Beyond, fire engines.

Angry black smoke poured from the windows of O'Malley's. A team of earnest firemen directed hoses, drenched the burning building.

I didn't watch long, put the Buick into gear and drove on. Behind me, a world ended, my small, fixed place in it swept clean by fire, escaping and dispersing into the wide sky with smoke.

*

Bob Tate's house was ten minutes away. I screeched to a halt in his driveway, jumped out of the Buick, left the driver's side door open. I knocked on Bob's front door. Waited. No answer.

I knocked again. Louder. Insistent.

When I tried the knob, the door was unlocked. I pushed it open, walked inside.

"Bob?"

Nothing.

I tilted my head, listened. The house was dead still except at the open windows. The cool breeze tickled the thin curtains. Where next? In the living room or up the stairs?

"Bob?" This time louder.

I decided on the living room. I found his answering machine. It blinked its story at me. Two phone calls. I played the messages. First Lou, then me. Variations on a theme. *Where the hell are you?*

Into the dining room—nothing—through to the kitchen.

A jagged scattering of glass glittered on the floor. My eyes traveled up the back door where a square of glass had been punched out just above the door handle. A break-in.

"Bob!"

Through the rest of the ground floor. I ran up the stairs two at a time and pushed open the first door I came to. A bedroom. Bob's bedroom.

Bob was there.

He lay faceup on his bed in his boxers and undershirt. The clothes he wore the night before at Toppers trailed from the bathroom to the foot of the bed. Bob wore a neat bullet-hole in the exact center of his forehead. A trickle of blood ran down past his open eyes, alongside his nose and over his lips.

Bob had been a cold-blooded, hard-as-nails killer. A brute with a sap or an axe handle or a set of brass knuckles. His wife had left him and took the twins back to Jersey. He chewed with his mouth open. He farted for comedy. No one on the planet would miss Bob Tate.

Except me.

I pulled up a chair, sat looking at Bob's cold body. After a few minutes of his vacant eyes, I got up and threw a blanket over him. I sat down again in the chair, put my head in my hands.

Would I find the same scene at Benny's place? At Stan's? I'd already heard what had happened to Lou. What now, Charlie? What now, you dumb, thick monkey? I'd spent a lot of years doing what I was told. Now I had to think for myself.

I suddenly felt tired, ragged. How long without sleep? From Toppers to Ma's to my apartment. I'd spent some time face-down in my driveway. Did that count as sleep? I didn't feel rested.

And why wasn't I dead? Somebody had clocked me good but left me alive. They'd only wanted the books.

I got to my feet, down the stairs, back out to my car.

I drove.

Where? Not back to my apartment. Fuck that. Too dangerous. I didn't want to end like Bob. Back to Ma's. Hell, no. They'd think to look there. I'd only get Ma killed with me and Danny. Better for them if I stayed away. I pulled into a convenience store, found a pay phone, dialed a number.

She picked up after four rings. "Hello?"

"Marcie?"

"Yep."

"It's Charlie."

"I know."

"I need a place to stay."

No hesitation. "Come on then."

❖

Marcie let me in, took my coat. "Are you okay?"

"I don't know yet." I handed her the gym bag. "Put that someplace out of the way. Please."

"Okay." She disappeared into the garage then came back.

I still stood in her dim foyer. "Where'd you put it?"

"In the freezer under the raccoon."

"Okay."

"Come on. You look terrible."

She took my hand and led me into the living room. I stood there like I didn't know what to do. I felt numb, listless, indifferent. She lowered me into the big leather recliner in front of the TV, put the remote on the arm of the chair but didn't switch it on. I leaned back, raised the chair's footrest. My muscles cried in relief.

I hadn't noticed Marcie had left the room until she returned. She handed me a drink. Chivas. My brand. She'd been shopping. I nodded my thanks at her.

"What happened?"

"It's a long story," I said.

"Maybe I can help."

"You can't help."

"You don't know. Try me."

I thought about it, closed my eyes. "My boss is being squeezed out by a big shot from Miami. All my buddies are dead, and the place where I work just burned to the ground. I was hit on the head and slept in the dirt. And all I got is a gym bag full of questions. Still think you can help?" I gulped back the Chivas, emptied the glass.

She took the glass from me. "Well, anyway, I can get you another drink." The rustle of her clothing followed her out.

I didn't hear her return, didn't get my next drink. I sank into the comfort of the chair, down into vivid Technicolor dreams.

The first dream was a rerun. I was looking down the barrel of Blade Sanchez's Luger again. He was talking and talking but only one thing he said really came through clear. *Beggar says I can go to work for him anytime.*

Why would Beggar want to hire your sorry, dumb ass?

In the next dream, I walked through O'Malley's. Flames licked the walls, skipped across the carpet. I kept thinking we needed to get everybody out. But Lou Morgan was there, waving a big muscle arm. "Get out, man. It's empty."

Yeah. Empty. Where were the people? The place should have been full of drunks. The bartenders. Amber. Why weren't they there? I was alone in a burning house with nobody to save.

Somebody had tipped them off. That was the only answer, and I realized I wasn't dreaming anymore. I was thinking, figuring it out. But I didn't want to think too hard about thinking. It was like asking the centipede which foot he started walking with. Think about it, and you're fucked. So I let the thoughts drift. Somebody had tipped the bartenders. They didn't come open. Patrons couldn't get in. Don't show today. Fire. Everyone gets the tip-off.

Except the monkey cage. We didn't get the word. Somebody'd set us up.

Sold us out.

I opened my eyes to darkness.

SEVEN

I sat up, shifted the recliner into its upright position.

The base of my skull ached distantly. Dim light leaked in from the kitchen, and I got up, followed it back to its source. Marcie sat at the little kitchen table, hunched over the books, reading them by the light of a low-watt bulb in the small lamp she dragged in from her bedroom nightstand. She wore a pair of grandmotherly half-glasses.

I smelled coffee.

She saw me, read my mind.

"I just made it," she said. "Want me to pour you a cup?"

"I'll get it." I took a plain white cup down from the cupboard, filled it. Drank. I took the pot to the table, refilled Marcie's cup.

"Thanks."

She'd arranged the books on the table side by side, had her finger on a column of numbers. Her lips moved quietly as she read, the finger sliding down the page.

"I thought you'd stashed those," I said.

She shrugged. "You needed to sleep, and nothing good was on TV."

"A fun read?"

"I was an accounting major for two semesters."

"Why would you want to be an accounting major?"

"That's what I asked myself," she said. "Why would I want to be an accounting major? Why would anyone? So I chucked it in for art."

"So what's with the ledgers?"

She put her hand palm down on one of the books. "These are the accounts of several businesses in South Florida, mostly in Miami. It's all here. Let's take Geno's as an example."

"Geno's?"

"A restaurant."

"Gotcha."

"So according to *this* book," she patted the ledger again, "Geno's made a profit of sixty-seven thousand dollars." She looked at me over her granny glasses, made sure she had my attention. "But according to this book," she slapped her hand over the other ledger, "Geno's made two point four million dollars in the same year."

"What? Let me see that." I grabbed the book. My eyes danced along the rows of numbers. I had no idea what I was looking at, but I didn't need the book. I knew the rest of the story.

I held in my hands Beggar Johnson's whole operation. Two ledgers. Two accounts of all the businesses under Beggar's thumb in South Florida. One for public consumption, the one he showed the I.R.S. The other book contained the real numbers. The money laundering. It completely outlined the flow of cash for his whole organization. These books should have been under lock and key. No wonder Beggar wanted everyone in Toppers rubbed clean. If these books got into the wrong hands, it could be Beggar's end.

But they were in my hands, and as far as I was concerned, they were hot potatoes.

"I got to go see somebody about this."

Marcie took off her half-glasses, set them on the table. "How bad is it, Charlie?"

"Bad."

"Charlie—"

"Bad, Marcie. As bad as it gets. I have to go."

"It's the middle of the night!"

"There's no time. I can't stay here." I gulped the coffee. There was a bag of rolls on her kitchen counter. I opened it, grabbed two rolls, shoved them in my jacket pocket.

"You can stay as long as you like. You know that."

I shook my head. "No good. If they find me, they find you. Then we're both dead."

I took the books, headed for the front door. Marcie followed.

"Charlie."

I stopped, looked at her.

"Anytime, day or night," she said.

I nodded, thought about her, the ledgers, us. I hadn't known her long, but you got to have somebody to trust, lean on. Might as well be somebody pretty.

I kissed her. "I'll be in touch."

I tried to think of what I needed more, friends or answers.

My friends were all dead, at least the ones who could help. I knew I could count on Marcie and Danny and Ma to all go to the mat for me, but I didn't see how they could help and I'd only be getting them in hot water.

I decided to settle for answers, and I figured Beggar's toady, Alan Jeffers, might have them.

I drove to a convenience store, found a pay phone.

Information had a listing for Alan Jeffers in Heathrow. I got the number and dialed it. Nine rings. It was about four A.M., so I wasn't surprised when Jeffers's machine answered. "You've reached the home of Alan Jeffers. I can't come to the phone right—" I hung up, put in another thirty-five cents, dialed again. "You've reached—" I hung up, a quarter and two nickels, dialed the digits.

"Do you know what damn time it is?" Jeffers sounded groggy and annoyed.

"Mr. Jeffers, this is Charlie Swift."

"Swift." He was putting the name through his brain, and I heard him suck in a big gulp of breath when he figured it out. "Holy shit, pal. Where've you been?"

"I got held up. When can I bring over the stuff you wanted?"

"Now. Bring them now."

"Can't. How about noon?"

"For crying out loud, Swift. Beggar's having a shit fit."

"Sorry. Noon?"

"Noon. Yeah. Okay, noon. You know where I live?"

"I know." I hung up before he could figure out a way to give me trouble.

I drove to Heathrow and parked about half a block down from Jeffers's place, close enough to watch. Nobody came or went. Good. Jeffers wasn't expecting me until noon, so I was pretty sure I could catch him with his panties down at the breakfast table. I didn't want to give him time to arrange a reception for me.

I had a dim, feeble notion of the bare bones of a plan knocking around in my head. I'd get ahold of Jeffers and make him tell me about those ledgers, about Beggar, about Stan and Jimmy Hoffa and Bigfoot and anything else I could get out of him. I didn't have the time or the temperament to be subtle.

I explored my side with my fingers. It was tender, but I didn't think it was infected. I'd need to change the bandage the next time I had a chance. I checked my .38, then slipped it back in the belly holster. And I still had the listening equipment Stan had wanted me to use to eavesdrop on his meeting with Beggar.

Now I just had to wait for the sun.

❖

I snapped awake. The glow of morning spread orange over Heathrow, reflected brightly in the windows of the houses up and down the street. My stomach was coffee sour, so I fished one of Marcie's rolls out of my pocket and ate it.

I got out of my car, rubbed my eyes, and headed for Jeffers's front door. It occurred to me as I knocked that I wasn't nervous. Maybe I was too tired, too sore from sleeping in the car, too God damn wrung out to be nervous.

A woman answered. She was lean, black hair bobbed at the ears, thick dark lips, nose pointed and predatory. She held a white cotton robe together with one hand and looked at me like I had a lot of nerve knocking her awake at the crack of dawn.

"Yes?"

"I'm here to see Jeffers." I pushed past her into the house.

"Wait, you can't just—" She padded after me, bare feet slapping against tile. "Alan!"

She shouted toward the kitchen, so that's where I went.

Jeffers was at the kitchen table, a half-eaten slice of toast in his fingers. "Tina, it's too early to be screaming all over the house for—oh, hell."

He saw me and froze.

"I'm Charlie Swift."

"You've got a lot of nerve busting in here like this. I have a good mind to—"

"Shut up. We need to talk."

He huffed and puffed a little. Tina stood in the doorway behind me, waiting to see what happened.

"You weren't supposed to be here until noon," said Jeffers. "I'm not ready for you yet."

"That's the idea."

"Do you have the ledgers?"

"No."

Jeffers frowned, then just looked confused. "What the hell's the point then?"

"Is there someplace we can talk?" I jerked a thumb over my shoulder at the woman. "Without your wife listening?"

"That's not my wife. My wife lives in Boca." He looked past me to her. "Tina, go get dressed why don't you?" He stood, motioned for me to follow. "We can talk in my office, Swift."

His office was a big, modern glass and mirrors room with electronic everything and a view of his pool in the backyard. It glittered crystal blue in the cool morning air. He sat behind the metallic bunker he called a desk, steepled his hands like he was considering my loan application, and waited for me to speak.

"I need some answers, Jeffers. And I need them without a lot of smart-guy double talk."

Jeffers raised an eyebrow. "I think you have it backwards, pal. It's you who'd better start explaining."

I started feeling all hot up through my face.

"Beggar's not happy," continued Jeffers. "He wants to know where his ledgers are and why they weren't delivered on time. He's not a patient man."

"I'm not so patient myself these days."

"Now, really, Swift, I don't think you understand who you're dealing with here."

I was across the desk quick and grabbed a fistful of his shirt, hauled him out of his seat. His eyes bulged. A little yelp of terror got stuck in his throat. I yanked him about halfway across. Pens and pencils scattered. A calculating machine flew to the floor. My teeth and jaw were set. I tried to make sure I looked like I felt. Mad.

"Are you crazy?" said Jeffers. He pried feebly at my hands, trying to pull away, trying to get back behind the safety of his desk.

"Maybe."

"You're digging your own grave, you fool. I work for Beggar Johnson."

"I'm getting a little sick of everybody saying that name like he's Jehovah. I want to know where my boss is right now. What happened to him?"

"Who?"

"Stan, you fucking pencil-neck. Where is he?"

"How the hell should I know?" Jeffers was too scared to lie. "I'm not involved with that end of Beggar's operation."

"You are now. You're down in the dirt with the rest of us."

"Please," Jeffers whined. "Let me go, will you? Let me go, and I'll explain."

I held him with a hard stare for a moment, nailed him to the desk with my eyes. I let him go, but I remained standing and close to the desk.

He was shaking a little. He opened a cabinet behind the desk, and my hand drifted into my coat and hovered over the revolver in case he was reaching for something dangerous. He came out with a bottle of Ballantine's and a tumbler. He held up the glass and cocked an eyebrow.

I shook my head.

He filled the glass three fingers' full, shot it back, and filled the glass again. He exhaled raggedly, calmed down some. He contemplated the bottom of his glass like he might find some answers there.

"You said you'd explain," I reminded him. "Start talking."

"Okay. Right." He nodded. "Sure." He looked back at the bottle of booze, thought about it a second, then shook his head.

"Like I told you, I don't see the nasty end of the business. I handle the money. I happen to be president of the Exchange

Bank in Longwood. I make sure nobody looks too closely at Beggar's deposits, and I supervise the smooth flow of monies to various offshore accounts. I take it you've figured out Beggar's taking over Stan's territory."

"You take it just right."

Jeffers shrugged. "Then you must understand. Beggar needs somebody like me who looks like an upright citizen, who has legitimate contacts in the business community. Stan's still running things like it's 1955. He couldn't modernize, so he's out."

"None of that answers my question," I said.

"You're not listening. I don't know where Stan is. That's not my job. I don't rub anyone out or give them cement overshoes or any of those other wonderful things you film-noir types do. Beggar's got a guy named Lloyd Mercury for all that."

"Then where do I find him?"

Jeffers snorted and looked at me like I was trying to push a truck uphill with a wet noodle. "I hope you don't think you can bust in on Lloyd Mercury like you did here with me. He'd kill you. It's that simple. I've never seen the man operate, but I've heard enough to know I don't want to hear any more. He's a cold-blooded professional right down to the bone."

"I'll be leaving now, Jeffers."

"But what about the ledgers?"

I leaned forward, slapped an open palm down on his desk. "You don't get dick until I hear about Stan. Get on your phone, call who you have to call, but when I get back in touch with you, you'd better tell me something useful."

"You're not being smart about this, Swift." The tone in his voice kept shifting. He couldn't decide if he was pleading or telling me off. "Stan's a sinking ship. Why are you still shoveling coal into the furnace?"

"I'll tell you why." The words came out harsh, and Jeffers

flinched. "Because when you throw in with a guy, you stick with him. Otherwise, you're just some kind of animal."

As I spoke, I pounded the desk again for emphasis, but my other hand slipped under the edge of the desk. The microphone was the size of a button and had some gummy stuff on the back so it would stay. I pressed hard, made sure it stuck.

Jeffers shook his head. He couldn't believe how dumb I was being. "Only dogs are that loyal, Swift." He opened the top desk drawer, and reached in lazily. When he came out with the little automatic, I was surprised. I didn't think he had it in him.

"If you don't put that away," I told him, "I'll take it away from you and shove it straight up your ass."

He lifted his chin, put on a brave face. "I can't have you running around causing trouble. We're going to sit here nice and quiet while I call Beggar and find out what he wants done with you."

My hand snaked out fast, and I plucked the little pistol from his grip. His eyes grew, and he looked down at his empty hand like he was trying to figure out a magic trick. When he looked back at me, my fist caught him on the chin. The *No Sale* signs popped up in his eyes, and he wilted into a little heap behind his desk.

I left his office and made for the front door.

Tina stood in my way. Her robe had fallen open, and she was naked beneath. Her robe had fallen open, because she wasn't holding it closed anymore. She wasn't holding it closed anymore, because she needed both hands to point the enormous revolver at me. It looked like a .44 magnum. It looked like it could make me one hundred percent dead if she pulled the trigger.

"Hi."

I cleared my throat. "Hello."

She was steady with the gun, held it well like she'd been trained how. She looked over my shoulder, trying to see into the office. "What did you do to Alan?"

"He's just napping. I had to put him out."

"Why?"

"He pulled a gun on me."

We exchanged long, probing looks, sized each other up, and I think we were both surprised at what we saw. It was obvious to her I'd had a gun pointed at me before. It was obvious to me she was ready to pull the trigger if necessary. Your average person doesn't know dick about aiming a gun or how to hold it or squeeze the trigger. Your average person would shit his pants when looking down the barrel of a cocked handgun. We were not two average people.

And then she did something so smart, it made me realize how dangerous she might be.

She stepped back and motioned with her chin that I should leave.

"Just like that?"

"I have to speak to Alan," she said, "before I can do anything with you."

I gave her a half-hearted salute. "Until next time."

She smiled, cold and tight. "I'll be keeping an eye on you, Mr. Swift."

I got out to my car and fumbled with the headphones, put them on, adjusted the volume. I could hear Tina helping Jeffers to his feet, getting him back in his chair. He groaned, and she said she'd get him some ice for his chin.

"What do we do?" asked Jeffers. "This is bad."

I looked in the rearview mirror. A car approached, parked behind me. It was so blatantly unmarked that it screamed "cop." I quickly plugged the receiver into the little tape recorder and stashed the whole setup under the car seat. I tugged off the belly holster, and the pistol joined the tape recorder.

A tall man climbed out of the unmarked car. I knew him. He was bent and his hair was thick and white. He wore a shiny brown suit and cheap cop shoes. He walked up to my car on the driver's side and knocked on the window.

I rolled it down. "Morning, Burt."

"Hi, Charlie." He bit his thumbnail, looked almost like he was embarrassed to be troubling me. "I think you'd better take a ride with me, okay? I got somebody back here that wants to have a word with you."

EIGHT

We didn't seem to be driving in any particular direction.

I'd known Detective Sergeant Burt Remington about five years, and he knew me. I was the guy that brought him the fat envelopes full of cash whenever Stan needed a favor from the police department. So it was with reluctance that Burt held open the car door and motioned me into the backseat with the FBI agent.

I knew he was an agent just by looking at him, the three-piece gray suit, the haircut, the standard-issue sunglasses all gave him away. He reeked of Harvard or Yale or wherever glossy G-men came from. But if that wasn't enough, he flipped open his little badge wallet and said, "I'm Federal Agent Dunn, Mr. Swift. Let's you and I have a chat."

Dunn smoked a Pall Mall. Burt drove.

"You mind if I roll down a window?" I asked.

"I mind," said Dunn.

Hardass.

"Let me fill you in on a few details, Mr. Swift. Are you listening?"

"I'm listening."

"Good. I'm only going to say this once. I don't have to say it at all. I'm being nice. We could simply sweep you under the rug if we wanted. Am I clear?"

"You're clear."

"Good." Dunn rolled the window down just long enough to flick out his cigarette butt. He lit another immediately. I tried to breathe as little as possible.

Burt turned his head, talked and drove at the same time. "I've been telling Agent Dunn here that you're a reasonable sort, Charlie. A good guy."

"I appreciate that, Burt."

"Mr. Swift, your presence jeopardizes an ongoing investigation. That's all you need to know." Dunn puffed hard, blew smoke, not quite at me but close. "I suggest you go far away while you have the opportunity. We're interested in bigger fish than you right now, but later on when we're mopping up, who knows who'll get caught in the net?"

If Jeffers was using his bank to ship currency offshore for Beggar, no wonder the Feds were watching him. I guessed they didn't want a two-bit gunman gumming up the works. I was out of my league, but I was never one to scatter just because some pencil-neck said *Boo*.

"I appreciate your concerns, Agent Dunn." This sounded like the right way to talk to his type. "But I have some responsibilities. I can't just skip town."

Burt frowned at me in the rearview mirror. He wanted us all to be pals.

Dunn shook his head like he was real disappointed. "Your loyalty to Stan is admirable but misplaced. He's all washed up. Orlando's done with him. It's done with you too."

That was probably true, but I had to know. "Where's Stan now?"

Dunn raised an eyebrow. "Well, if you don't know, I certainly don't either. If I were Stan, I'd be on the next jet to Costa Rica."

Could be, I had to admit to myself. Or maybe he was under a parking lot somewhere. A strong possibility, if Beggar got ahold of him. But the fact was not even the Feds were interested in Stan. Like Dunn had said, Stan was washed up, and I was washed up with him.

So what the hell was I doing? Looking for a guy who was maybe dead but certainly wasn't my boss anymore. The monkey cage had burned. The kingdom had fallen, the king banished. I should just empty my safe deposit box and split.

Burt drove us back to my car in silence.

As I climbed out of the backseat, Dunn said, "I think we understand each other."

I nodded. Burt walked me back to my car.

"Sorry about all that, Charlie, but Feds, you know?" He shrugged. "My hands were tied."

"Forget about it," I said. "But I might call you later. I have some questions."

"Jesus, Charlie, didn't you hear the guy? I mean, Stan's been good to me, but that's all finished. Game over."

"It ain't game over, Burt. It might be two outs, bottom of the ninth, and I might be swinging a toothpick instead of a Louisville Slugger, but you better remember how you afforded to put Burt Jr. through Stanford."

I held his gaze just long enough so he'd know I was serious. Then I gave his shoulder a squeeze, softened my tone a little. "I just need some closure. You answer a few questions, and I'm out of your hair that much sooner."

He chewed his lip but nodded. "Sure, Charlie. No promises, but call me. I'll tell you what I know, which isn't a whole damn lot."

"Thanks."

I got back in my car and watched Burt and Agent Dunn pull away before I retrieved the tape recorder.

I pushed play.

Tina: "What's that?"

Snorting sounds.

Tina: "I wish you wouldn't do that. It's bad for you."

Jeffers: "Not now, Tina."

Shuffling sounds, moving.

Jeffers: "If you're worried about my health, you should keep people from pushing their way in here and punching me in the face."

Tina: "What are you going to do?"

Jeffers: "I've got to call Beggar."

Tina: "Why?"

Jeffers: "I've got to tell him something. Do you know what he'll do? He'll sic that pet killer of his on me. Mercury."

Tina: "Your best protection is to get those books."

Jeffers (shouting): "Well for Christ's sake. Go after Swift. He's got the damn things. That's why I pulled the gun on him. Don't you think I want the books?"

Tina: "Calm down, Alan. Don't worry about Swift. I'll tell Styles to—"

The sound warped, and the tape ground to a halt. The damn batteries had worn down. I smacked the recorder with the palm of my hand but couldn't bring it back to life. Figures. Just when I needed the thing.

First things first. I couldn't keep driving around with Beggar's ledgers in the back of my car. That was just asking for trouble. I thought about leaving them with Ma or Marcie or Danny, but anyone I gave them to became an instant target.

I drove to the airport, parked in the short-term lot.

I found a row of lockers in one of the terminals, picked one at random and dropped in a few coins. I stashed the gym bag with the ledgers inside and locked it up tight. I put the locker key on my own key ring, hoping it would blend in. It looked exactly like I was trying to hide an airport locker key on my key ring.

I left the airport and headed back toward the city without

any clear idea of where I was going. I'd already decided I needed some help but wasn't sure who to call. Bob was dead, Benny was missing in action, and I'd heard Lou Morgan cash it in over the phone. I'd have to look outside the monkey cage for a friend.

I pulled off the Beltway and found a convenience store with a pay phone. I bought a cup of black coffee inside to make change. At the pay phone, I dialed Jimmy the Fix, and he answered after two rings.

"What it is?"

"Jimmy, it's Charlie Swift."

The pause was only a second, but considering my circumstances, it was a lifetime. In that pause, I rehashed my relationship with Jimmy the Fix. We'd always been on good terms, worked together a few times. As one of Stan's most trusted boys, Jimmy was usually in on the know. I knew he was good people, and I was sure he thought the same of me. But while we were on the same side, we weren't exactly peers. He was administrative, in on big decisions. He handled a lot of business for Stan. I was a dumb gun monkey that played Monopoly and made people bleed when they got out of line. So there I was in the middle of this eternal pause while Jimmy the Fix decided if I was worth the time of day.

When the pause at last ground to a halt, Jimmy said, "I don't know where Stan is, Charlie."

"I'm sorry to hear that."

"It's been tough," said Jimmy. "I'm surprised to hear from you. You sound healthy. Good."

He meant I didn't sound like I'd been shot dead by hired killers.

"I need some help," I said.

He *tsked* on his end. "I'm in a pretty precarious position

here. So far Beggar thinks I might be useful. He's leaving me alone."

"He told you that?"

"It's implied."

"Is it?"

"Yeah."

"Why?"

"Because I'm not dead," said Jimmy heatedly. "Like I said, I'm surprised to hear from you. Get out of Orlando. Beggar won't chase you north or west. He just wants all of Stan's old team out of harm's way."

"But not you, huh?"

"A guy's got to survive, Charlie. Why don't you wise up? If Stan's alive, he's hauled ass by now. You should too."

I gripped the phone tight, barely had my voice in control. I took a deep breath, then started in. "I want you to listen to me real good, Jimmy. I haven't done a lot of good things I can be proud of. I'm good with my fists and with a gun, but those aren't the things that make your ma proud or impress a good woman or win you any community service awards. Okay, I'm not a model citizen, and neither are you. We don't try to be, and it ain't profitable anyway. But I got one rule, just one I've been faithful to no matter what. I've always been good to the people that were good to me. If you don't have people like that —if you can't *be* a person like that—then you're never going to have a friend or a moment's rest or a single good night's sleep as long as you live."

It was about the best speech I could muster on short notice, but it expressed a whole wad of twisted, churning feelings I'd had thumping around in my gut since this whole ordeal began. This time Jimmy's pause was deeper and stank of guilt and indecision. I hoped I was pushing Jimmy's buttons in the right places, that he'd remember all the times Stan had stood by his side when the breaks were against him.

"God damn you, Charlie."

And I smiled.

"Okay," said Jimmy. "First thing I'm going to do is ask about the rest of that goon squad you play Monopoly with."

"What about them?"

"Are they accounted for?"

"They're dead, if that's what you mean."

"Not all of them."

"No," I admitted. "I can't find Benny."

"Try harder."

"What are you getting at?"

"I'll give you a second to think about it," said Jimmy.

I didn't need a second. I knew what he meant, and Blade Sanchez's words came back to me. Blade had said he could go to work for Beggar. Sure. That made sense. Before Beggar took over Stan's territory, he'd want to get a few guys on the inside.

"I'll call you after I find Benny," I said.

"Charlie?"

"Yeah?"

"Thanks for reminding me about some things."

"You're welcome."

I hung up the phone, got back in my car.

I drove. My head buzzed. Too much to think about. Time for a quick recap of my situation.

Stan was missing, maybe dead. All my buddies from the monkey cage were dead except for possibly Benny who was maybe a rat. Everyone kept telling me to run, but I had nowhere to go. I had a set of ledgers in an airport locker which could shut down Beggar for life if they fell in the wrong hands. Probably why the Feds were keeping a close eye on Jeffers, who just wanted to shove white powder into his nose and get through the day with as little fuss as possible.

In my corner: A fat guy called Jimmy the Fix. My kid brother with his toy gun. Marcie and a house full of dead art. Burt the cop, who might answer a few questions if he felt like it and if the Feds weren't too far up his ass. Not much of an army.

Anything else?

Oh, yeah. I was hungry. I pulled into Wendy's, ordered a burger value meal, biggie-sized it. I ate it too fast, digested poorly. I was pissed off, my stomach sour.

I went back to the convenience store, went inside for more change. I had calls to make.

NINE

Turns out I wasn't the only guy in town with a kid brother.

In my hunt for Benny, I'd called a topless cocktail waitress named Ruth he shacked up with sometimes. I woke her up, and she gave me an earful. I told her I was looking for Benny, and she gave me another earful.

"He tore out of here like his ass was on fire," she said with her cigarette voice. "Went on the road with that brother of his."

"What's his name?"

"Shane, I think."

"On the road where?"

"Gainesville."

"Why?"

"What are you, a fucking cop?"

"If I have to come over there and smash you in the mouth, you'll wish I was only a cop."

"Tough guy. I meet all the charmers."

"Talk."

"The Shane kid's in some kind of band. They play up and down the state."

"What's the name of the band?"

"Oh, for God's sake." I heard her fumbling around on the other end, rustling some papers. "They call the band Spanklicious, and they're playing at the Handlebar Saloon. Benny said he'd call me later, but he probably won't. He said he'd be back in a couple of days, but I don't believe that either. That's all I know, I swear to God. Can I go back to sleep now?"

"Sure. Got any messages for Benny when I find him?"

"Tell him to drop dead."

I said I could deliver that message no problem.

Gainesville was a college town about thirty-five miles north of Ocala, and when I got there, I found another pay phone, dialed Marcie, and left a message that I might be busy for a day or two. Then I grabbed the phonebook and found the number for the saloon.

I got to the Handlebar Saloon about 10 P.M., which is when the kid on the phone said the band really got cranked up. The Handlebar was in a worn-out chunk of downtown near the railroad tracks and some other buildings that reminded me of Dresden war photos after the bombing. The dirt parking lot across from the saloon held an equal split of pickup trucks and motorcycles. There wasn't any music when I walked in, so either the band was on break or hadn't started yet.

The Handlebar's interior looked like it had taken up the bombing motif. The walls were mostly exposed brick with the occasional graffiti-covered patch of yellowing plaster. The wooden tables and chairs were rickety and mismatched. The patrons were a rough, working-class lot, and I maneuvered through them as unobtrusively as possible. I found the bar and waved over a beer. The fiftyish man who brought it had a canned ham for a face, and the sleeves of his flannel shirt were rolled up, revealing a set of serious looking tattoos. A special forces skull on the right arm, a naked girl riding an atom bomb a la Slim Pickens—except with nipple—on the left.

"I'm looking for the band." I placed a five-dollar bill on the bar for the dollar draft. "Are they on break?"

He nodded past me. "That's them there."

I looked. Three middle-aged men mounted what passed for

the Saloon's stage and grabbed guitars. A fourth sat behind the drum set. This didn't strike me as Shane's band, and I didn't see Benny. The bartender brought my change, and I tried again.

"That's Spanklicious?" I felt like a first-rate jackass saying it.

"That's The Dan Riley Band," he told me. "Spanklicious was the early band. Left about an hour ago."

Shit.

I asked, "Are they playing at the same time tomorrow night?"

"They would've, but we fired them."

I raised an eyebrow.

"Buncha damn noise. You want another beer?"

"Sure."

He refilled my glass and said, "All that jumping around and screaming might be fine for the college kids, but these folks all work for a living. They got enough stress in their lives."

"Do you know where I might get ahold of them? Maybe what hotel they're at?"

"Maureen books the bands. She'll be in tomorrow morning."

"It's important," I said. "Just point me in the right direction."

"Mister, I'm the only one behind the bar, and people need beer. Try tomorrow."

I finished my beer and left as the band cranked up a sluggish version of "Brown-Eyed Girl."

I found the Ramada Inn, got a room.

I kicked off my clothes and flipped on the TV. I needed something mindless to do, so I emptied the guns out of the duffel and began cleaning them. That didn't take long. I flipped through the channels. Shit. I flipped again. Still shit.

Okay. Back to work.

I called Burt. He answered halfway through the first ring. He was still awake, full of coffee and worry.

"Give me your number there."

I gave it to him.

"Give me ten minutes." He hung up.

When he called back, I heard traffic noises in the background.

"It might not be safe to talk on the home phone," said Burt.

"You know I'm looking for Stan, Burt. Let's start with that."

"Look, I have no idea where he is. I'd tell you. Honest."

"What can you tell me?"

"They got people watching Jeffers around the clock," said Burt.

"What for?"

"Easy," said Burt. "The FBI has been putting a case together against Beggar Johnson for three years. Now, they're in a position to shut him down hard. Jeffers was supposed to be getting some accounting ledgers that exposed Beggar's whole operation from Miami to Jacksonville. The Federal boys have Jeffers over a barrel. Either he coughs up the ledgers and testifies against Beggar, or they put him away."

That didn't make any sense. I was the one supposed to be bringing the books. Jeffers knew that. I got suspicious. I mean *more* suspicious. I went to the window and scanned the parking lot through a crack in the drapes. A black Ford Tempo about ten spaces down, maybe some people sitting inside. The darkness made it hard to tell for sure. Could be I had a few Feds on my tail. Maybe they thought I'd lead them to the books.

Or maybe it was Lloyd Mercury, Beggar's big boy, the killer Jeffers seemed so worried about. I tried to recall what he looked like from the one time I'd seen him. It wasn't difficult. You don't forget a guy like that. He looked like a cocked gun ready to go off. Hard, mean, and quick to pounce.

I made a mental note to look over my shoulder once in a while.

"How was Jeffers going to get the ledgers?" I asked.

"Don't know. The FBI doesn't tell me anything," said Burt.

That explained it. They were keeping Burt in the dark on some of the details. Maybe they suspected his loyalty. Maybe he just wasn't important enough to know everything. If I were the Feds, I'd be careful too. I thought about those men with the badges in Toppers. They'd been Feds too. They almost had the books then except for me. I showed up and shot everyone dead.

"Thanks, Burt," I said. "Anything else?"

"Yeah. Sorry to tell you this, but the FBI has frozen a bunch of bank accounts, Jeffers's included." He cleared his throat apologetically. "Yours too. And I wouldn't try getting near your safety deposit box."

That just fucking figured. "Thanks for the heads up."

"If you and Stan pull this thing out of the fire, just remember who was on your team."

"I'll remember."

The Handlebar was open early the next morning, so the third-shift crowd didn't have to wait for normal bar hours to get drunk. I was told Maureen wouldn't be in for an hour, so I retreated to a less dilapidated part of town for coffee. I called Marcie, left her another message. I went back to the Handlebar.

Maureen was a tired, sagging matron who didn't look like she gave two shits about anything or anybody, least of all me. I asked her questions, and she answered, not out of kindness but because she judged it would be more trouble not to. Smart lady.

"Worst mistake I ever made," she said. "God damn punk metal bullshit or whatever they call it. I thought maybe we'd attract a younger crowd, you know? Broaden our appeal a little."

"But the regulars didn't care for them?"

"The regulars wanted to kick the shit out of them. You know what they did when the crowd started booing? Spit on 'em. On everyone in the audience."

"So you gave them the boot?"

Her nod started a ripple through the flab sacks on her face. "They wouldn't have lasted another second, let alone another night."

"I'm not exactly a fan, but I do need to find them. I thought you might know where they're staying."

"I'll tell you what I told the other guy. Talk to Parker. He tends bar for us, and it was his idea to book the band in the first place. I should've fired his scrawny ass too."

"What other guy?"

"He's out there now." Maureen jerked a stubby thumb at the back door. "He came in with the same questions you did, and I told him Parker was in the alley having a smoke."

"Thanks. I better have a look." I headed for the back door.

"Mister, I'd take it slow if I were you. This other fella's about as big as they build 'em."

"I'll be careful."

In the alley, an enormous comic book character was pushing a greasy kid up against a stone wall. He was doing it just right. The kid's feet dangled about a foot off the ground, and the giant had to keep pushing against his chest with the flat of his meaty hand to keep him up there. The big guy was Lou Morgan.

Holy shit.

"New Guy!"

Lou whipped his head around. "Charlie?"

Lou folded the kid in half and jammed him down deep into one of the big alley trash cans. "You stay put, Parker. I got to talk to this guy." He gave the can a loud kick for emphasis.

Parker made a cooperative noise, and Lou threw his arms

around me in an uncomfortably tight bear hug. "Holy fuck, Charlie, I never thought I'd see you again."

"Me?" Funny, but I didn't mind the hug so much. "I thought I heard you die on the phone. How'd you get out in one piece?"

He posed muscle-man style for me. "This is the Lou-man you're talking about. I fought my way out like a fucking champ, that's how."

We traded stories. I told him I was looking for Benny. I told him why.

His face fell, and he shook his head. "Damn. I was hoping to find somebody to tell me what the fuck's going on. You mean Benny's working for Beggar?"

"Looks that way," I said.

"That's a real bummer," he said. "I liked that little guy. He was little but mean and tough, you know? I thought he was cool. Kinda gets you mad to think somebody cool like that would sell you out."

I knew what he meant. I thought about the beers I'd shared with Benny, the times around the Monopoly table in the monkey cage. I started getting hot all up through my face. Sometimes I get so furious about stuff like that my whole body shakes, and I'm doing something harsh without thinking first. My fists tightened, and I started feeling bad for Benny, knowing what I was going to do to him.

Lou threw up his hands. "Then that's all she wrote, man. Might as well go home."

"We'll go home when I say. We find Stan first, and that means we find Benny."

"You're not in charge of me anymore, man. O'Malley's is ashes. The boss has hit the road."

"You got a choice. You're either nobody going no place, or you're one of Stan's boys, and we're on the job."

He put his hands on his hips, exhaled. "Okay, man. You're the boss. But stop fucking calling me New Guy."

"Whatever you say, New Guy."

"The kid in the can's name is Parker. He's about to tell us useful things, aren't you, Parker?"

I stepped around Lou and found Parker in the trash can. "How's it going?"

"A little cramped."

"I'm looking for Spanklicious."

"I know the house," said Parker. "Just get me out of here, okay? And I'll tell you where."

"Don't get me wrong, Parker. I'm not here to rescue you. You tell me what I want to know."

"And you'll get me out of here?"

"Yeah."

"902 Texar. It's a one-story white house. My roommate knows the drummer, and we put them up."

"Are they there now?"

"Maybe. I guess. I don't know. Get me out of here, dude."

"Okay," said Lou. "Let's go get them. Let's find Benny."

I pointed at the trash can. "What about him?"

"We don't need him."

"The second he crawls out of that can, he's going to phone ahead and warn them we're coming."

"Yeah. Okay." He grabbed up the lid of the trash can and clamped it down hard over Parker. The kid's muffled protests caused Lou to pound on the lid. "Shut up in there. We'll let you out when we're done." He scooped up the can by the handle, his biceps rippling without effort.

"Okay, I got him," said Lou. "Let's go."

Lou Morgan was a big, dumb slab of meat good only for throwing punches and taking them. He wasn't somebody I'd normally include in my circle of friends, and we'd only given the lug a job because we didn't want to get our hands dirty throwing deadbeats out of O'Malley's. A towering waste of space.

God, but I was glad to see him.

TEN

I told Lou to leave his Harley Davidson at the Handlebar, and we took my car. We'd stuffed the trash can into the trunk. The trunk wouldn't close, but we kept it tied down with an extension cord I'd found in the backseat.

We parked the car in front of Parker's house and got out. Lou had fetched the trash can out of the trunk and carried it under a huge arm. I decided not to comment. I knocked on the door, but I guess Lou figured four seconds was enough to answer because when nobody let us in, he smashed the door in with one good kick. The wood frame splintered, and the door flew into the living room landing with a heavy *whump*.

Two naked kids pulled apart from each other and scattered. She ran into the bedroom and slammed the door. He bolted for the kitchen in his socks, clutching jeans and T-shirt in his hands.

"I got him." Lou dropped the trash can and pounded out of the room after him.

I tried the bedroom door. It was locked but not as solid as the front door. I leaned into it good just once with my shoulder and it gave. I found her crouched on the other side of the bed with a sheet around her. She was big-eyed and scared, screamed a little when I hauled her up by a skinny arm.

I dropped her on the bed, and she said, "Don't rape me" in a weepy, little kid's voice.

She was maybe seventeen, slight, pale, short bottle-red hair almost burgundy and a gold ring in the nose. Her breasts were pointy fried eggs with raspberry nipples. "I'm not going to rape you, so take it easy. Shoot you in the head or smack you up some maybe, but not rape."

That didn't help much. Her eyes filled with slow tears.

"Aw, shit. Look, calm down, okay?" There was a half-empty bottle of third-rate bourbon on the dresser. I put it in her hands and told her to take a slug.

"I–I don't drink." She pushed the bottle back at me.

"I sure as hell do." I tilted the bottle back. It was cheap, but the harsh warmth coursed into my limbs. Just what the doctor ordered.

"In the first drawer," she said with a little more confidence. "A small wooden box with a butterfly carved on the top."

I found the box and gave it to her.

She opened it and produced a ziplock baggy and some rolling paper. She tried to roll a joint, but her hands shook too badly, and she dropped the paper. She looked up at me.

"Take your time."

"I'll use the pipe," she said. "That's easier." The pipe looked like it'd been carved from a miniature wooden figurine, a dinosaur maybe, or a dragon. She puffed it to life, inhaled deeply, and held it. Her eyes fuzzed over as she finally exhaled. I saw the fear drain out of her a little, and she slumped where she sat on the bed.

I opened a window.

"Is Thomas in some kind of trouble?" she asked.

"That's your boyfriend?"

She shrugged, looked away from me. "We just hang out. Did he do something? Cause if he did, I don't know anything about it."

"Take it easy," I said. "I just need to ask you some questions. What's your name?"

"Lizzy."

"Were you here last night, Lizzy?"

"I'm in and out all the time."

"When the band was here?"

"Spanklicious? The guys had a pretty big party. The cops broke it up after the fight."

"Tell me about it."

"The fight?"

"Yeah."

"Shane's brother got pretty drunk."

Benny. "Go on."

"He kept going on about something that Shane was supposed to do for him, but Shane didn't want to. Shane was all like saying how he was an artist, and Benny was all like telling him how he was ungrateful and everything."

"Uh-huh." I took another swig of the bourbon. "Think for a minute, would you? How about some specifics?"

Lizzy puffed the pipe. "I don't know any. Really." She didn't look at me, puffed the pipe like she was blowing up a life raft.

I grabbed the pipe, yanked it away from her. She frowned and made a noise like a kicked puppy.

"I don't believe you, Lizzy."

Her shoulder slumped and she twisted the sheets between her fingers. Her eyes met mine slowly. "You're not a cop, are you?"

"Do I act like a cop?"

She shook her head.

"Okay then. What was the fight about between Benny and Shane?"

"Who?"

"Benny is the name of Shane's brother. The bald guy."

Her eyes drifted to the pipe. "Uh…"

I gave it back to her. She took a big gulp of smoke, held it, let it out slow, her eyes rolling back in her head. "They fought about the drugs. Not this stuff." She tapped the pipe with a skinny finger. "Major blow. Shane's big bro—Benny—provided a bunch for the party, kept saying he was giving samples. He told Shane he just got some good money and that they were going into business for themselves. He wanted Shane to deal the stuff from the back of his van."

"Why?"

"Because Shane goes around to all these clubs with his band, easy for him to see the right people and sell a lot of the stuff."

"How do you know all this?"

"Me and Shane sort of hooked up for the night, so I was with him. They didn't seem to mind talking in front of me."

"Where are they now?"

"Beats me. The band got fired from the Handlebar, you know."

"I know."

"They probably went on to their next gig."

"Where?"

She shrugged, took another hit from the pipe. I shot back another mouthful of bourbon. It had been a long couple of days. I sat there with Lizzy quietly for a moment, her escaping into her vice, me into mine.

"Would Parker know?"

"Maybe."

I took her by the wrist. "Follow me."

She scurried after, holding the sheet in front of her. We stopped in front of the trash can, and I pried the lid off.

"Man, I really got to take a piss," said Parker. Lou had pretzeled him into the big can pretty good.

"Parker? Oh my God!" Lizzy dropped her sheet and leaned into the can. "Are you okay?"

"I can't feel my legs."

"He'll be fine," I said.

"What's he doing in there?"

"It's like Biosphere."

"What?"

Lou returned through the kitchen. He was breathing heavily and glistening with sweat. "That little naked bastard can run. I chased him six blocks and gave up." He got an eyeful of naked Lizzy and said, "Hope he had time to finish you off, honey. If not, just climb aboard the Lou Morgan express, and he'll take you home."

"What's he talking about?" said Parker.

"It's nothing." Lizzy shot Lou a hard look.

Lou grinned down into the can. "We caught Red here bumping uglies with some guy when we busted in."

"I knew it!" Parker yelled from the bottom of the can. "You cheap little whore. It was Thomas, wasn't it? You've been fucking him."

"Parker, don't. It's not like that." Lizzy erupted in teenage tears.

"Better check her ass for carpet burns," said Lou.

"Sonovafuckshitdamn—I'm going to kill him!" Parker threw a tantrum the best he could in his cramped space, shaking the can and nearly tipping it.

Lizzy ran tearfully and dramatically back into the bedroom and slammed the door. She let out deep moaning sobs between great gulps of air. It was all very moving.

I put my hand on Lou's arm and pushed him gently back. "Give me some room."

He went rigid, resisted for a second, but stepped back. He'd learn. I was still in charge. He was still New Guy in spite of what I'd told Danny.

I looked down at Parker. He had his little fists balled and pounded the sides of the can with feeble rage. His girlfriend was a slut. Things were tough all over.

"Parker."

"Can you believe that shit?" he said. "My own fucking room-mate."

"Parker."

"You bitch." He raised his voice so Lizzy could hear him in the next room. "You fucking cunt!" She launched into her sobs again with renewed vigor.

"Bitch!"

I grabbed a softball trophy off the end table and banged it against the trash can three times hard. "Parker!"

"Holy shit, that's loud."

I asked, "You want out of this can or not?"

"Yes."

"Where's Shane's band playing next?"

"Mudhog Sammy's."

"When?"

"Wednesday night."

Day after tomorrow.

"What about tonight?" I asked.

"They're playing someplace in Ocala. I don't know the name. But I heard Shane say Ocala. Honest Injun."

"You know where they're playing. Think hard."

"I'm telling you straight, dude. I don't know."

"What are you worried about? Ratting out your pal? Forget about it. Your name will never come up." I held up three fingers. "Scout's honor." I nudged Lou.

"Huh? Oh." Lou held up three fingers too.

"I really, really don't know," said Parker.

"If you're lying, Lou's going to bite your legs off and shove them up your ass."

"I'm not lying," said Parker. A little desperation had crept into his voice. "That's all I know. I swear."

I put the lid back on. Tight.

"Come on," I said to Lou. "Let's go."

On the way back to Lou's motorcycle, I noticed the black Ford Tempo again, this time in my rearview mirror. I didn't believe in coincidences. I told Lou.

"Who is it?"

"Feds maybe." Or Mercury.

"Can you lose them?" asked Lou. He craned his neck to get a better look.

"Will you stop that, bonehead. Don't let on like we see them."

"Okay, okay." He sat still, faced forward.

I hit the accelerator, darted between a couple of cars, and cut off a jeep full of college kids who gave me the finger. I took a hard left from the wrong lane, leaving a wake of horn blasts and squealing tires behind. I did the zig-zag routine through a residential neighborhood, and by the time I found a major road again, I was satisfied we'd thrown off our tail.

I said we'd better ditch my car for a while. They knew what it looked like. Lou agreed and suggested I go to the regional airport and find a rental counter. Good idea. Avis had what we needed.

I used a stolen MasterCard and a fake Arkansas driver's license and rented the car under the name Borris Freeman. I wanted an LTD or something comfortable, but Lou had his own idea.

"You can't go slugging around the swamp in some big-ass pimp-mobile."

"I'm not slugging anywhere," I said. "I'm taking the Interstate."

"Four-wheel it, man. Let's ride high in that Suburban." Lou pointed at a ridiculously oversized sports utility vehicle in the fenced rental yard.

"Fuck that."

"I'm a big guy. I need a big ride."

"The thing drinks three miles to the gallon," I said.

"Man, you're renting the car. I got no problem springing for gas."

I gave up. "Fine."

"Righteous."

Idiot.

He didn't look so happy when he filled up the truck in Ocala. Forty-two fifty for regular unleaded. We'd left the Interstate and were heading down State Road 200. Lou stuck a cigar in his mouth, lit it and filled the cab with a thick layer of gray–blue smoke.

"Will you roll down the fucking window? I've only got the two lungs."

He laughed. "Can't take it, huh?" But he rolled it down.

He found a country station on the radio and turned it up a notch too loud.

I turned it back down a little. "Let's take it easy, okay?"

"You don't like the twang?"

"The what?"

"The twang. Country music has that twang."

"Could you clam up for a while? I'm trying to think what to do next."

He shrunk into his cigar, taking slow, sulky puffs.

ELEVEN

We drove around without much of a plan, the Suburban gulping gas like a kid sucking back Kool-Aid. We went into a dozen clubs that advertised live music. I got fed up halfway through the search and started sending Lou inside while I waited in the Chevy. We broke for dinner, didn't rush through our meals. We got back on the road just as aimless as before.

Finally, I steered us into a convenience store, and Lou ripped a phone book out of a booth. We sat in the car and flipped through the listings.

"Dewey's Deck and Landing." Lou showed me the ad. "Says live music."

"Call them."

"Here's the address. It's close. Right off 200."

"The phone's closer."

"It's been a long day, man. I'll buy you a beer."

Good point.

Dewey's was tucked in behind a Pizza Hut and near a small grocery market in a ratty little plaza. The gravel parking lot overflowed. We parked on the grass and had to pony up five bucks each to get in. The cover was for the band, but we found out quick it wasn't Spanklicious.

For one thing, I actually liked the music. I'd never heard Spanklicious, but I didn't think they'd be covering an Ella Fitzgerald tune. The gal on stage wore a long black dress, velvet gloves up to her elbows. Her voice was beautifully dark and raw. The four guys behind her knew what they were doing: horn, bass, guitar, upright piano.

"This ain't them," said Lou. "You want to leave?"

"Let's hear a song," I said. "Let's have a drink."

The music shifted into a hot swing number, and college kids decked out in vintage dresses, pinstriped suits, and wide ties flooded the sunken dance floor in front of the stage. The bar crowd looked wrong. Mixed. The dressed-up kids were there for the music. The frat guys were out of place, and there were a lot of them in white baseball caps, Greek letters on their sweatshirts. They were there just to get drunk, and they were good at it.

Lou muscled his way to the crowded bar. He squeezed between two of the frat kids, jostling them out of the way. They turned to give him some lip, saw his size, and decided to pay closer attention to their drinks.

Lou handed a plastic cup back toward me, and I took it. I tilted the contents back between my lips. It went down cheap and wet, cold and perfect. It *had* been a long day. A long, hard, bad couple of days. I made a mental note to call Ma later. And Marcie.

The college kids were giving Lou a wide berth. The giant leaned back with both elbows spread along the rough wooden bar like he owned the joint, taking up more than his fair share of space considering the crowd. There'd be trouble soon. I knew Lou's type. He wouldn't start anything, but he'd throw his weight around until a drunk-enough kid took a poke at him. He needed to turn some kid's lights out to feel better, like he was in control of something, like his life hadn't just taken a nosedive. That was the type.

"I'm going to ask around," I told him and moved away into the mass of kids.

"About what?" he called after, but I just nodded pretending I'd heard him wrong.

I finished my beer as I reached the far end of the bar. It took me a minute to get the bartender's attention, but he spotted me as the band finished a song I didn't recognize heavy on the horns.

"You know a band called Spanklicious?"

"That's Smoke Up, Johnny." He pointed at the stage, shouting over the racket.

"I mean another band."

"No. You want another?"

"Yeah."

He didn't ask what I was drinking, which was fine since I didn't know. He brought it back too foamy, and I tried again.

"Other places around here have a band tonight?"

"Hell if I know," he said.

I drank, ordered a third, drank it, and ordered another.

I was thinking about the restroom when the girl onstage announced the band was taking a quick break. I circled the dance floor, plying my way through the crowd, found the men's room. The single urinal was mercifully free, so I unzipped and let out some beer.

Someone flushed in one of the stalls. The girl singer came out, fished a lipstick out of her purse and put the purse on the narrow shelf under the mirror. "Don't mind me, *hon.*"

I usually only let sixty-year-old waitresses at truck stops and really fat table-dancers call me hon, but the singer was pretty, and I liked her voice, so I said, "No problem at all, *doll.*"

She glanced at me sideways. Her lips curled into a little smile before she applied her dark lipstick. Her nose was a little too pointy, gave her a hawkish look. "The line for the little girls' room is murder. I had to hold my bladder all the way through Tommy's horn solo." She shook her head like it was the saddest thing in the world. "Nine minute fucking horn solo."

She left as some frat boys came in, and they paused, looking at the front of the restroom door to see if they had the right one. She was gone by the time they figured it out.

I straightened my tie in the mirror, decided I wasn't impressing anyone, and pulled it loose again. I looked at my eyes. Red. Too much beer and not enough sleep.

The singer's purse was still on the shelf. I grabbed it and left the restroom.

On my way back, I spotted Lou still guarding his territory near the bar. He was chatting up a busty coed in sorority letters, the frat guys still glowering over their shoulders at him. It wouldn't be long now.

I had another beer, remembered I had a purse in my hand, and found the singer on the steps that led up to the stage. She was on her way back up, and I asked her to wait a minute.

"I can't talk now," she said curtly. "We're on."

"You left this in the can." I held out the purse.

Her eyes softened. She took a step down. "Thanks. I appreciate it." She grabbed the purse, but I hung on to the other end.

"Do you know a band called Spanklicious?"

"Yeah. They come through every few months. Sounds like somebody throwing glass bottles into a buzz-saw. What do you want to hear them for?"

"I'm not a fan. I'm just looking."

"They usually play at Cafe Blitzkrieg. It's a bottle club on 4th, or was. It burned down—shit—maybe a week, ten days ago. They always got shit bands. I don't think anyplace else in town would have them."

I let go of the purse. "Sorry to trouble you."

She looked at me sort of weird, curious. "No trouble." She took the stage, and the band jerked to life with "Hit that Jive Jack."

When I got back to Lou, he was having some hard words with one of the frat kids. Another came up behind him and broke a beer bottle at the base of his skull. Lou teetered, and the frat guys saw their chance. About eight dove on him. The guy behind the bar yelled. The band played louder, segued into "Sing, Sing, Sing."

Lou kicked out with a big boot and caught one in the stomach. The kid folded good, hit the floor hard. Lou grabbed a fistful of one's shirt and tossed him over the bar. The other guys were landing solid blows into Lou's midsection. They might as well have been punching a dump truck. I moved in to help, but I didn't hurry.

One of the bigger frat guys threw a wooden chair. Lou ducked, and the chair sailed over the railing and down into the dance floor. It obliterated a couple who'd been swing dancing pretty well up till then. All hell broke loose. Screaming. Some afraid. Most angry. A tiny girl heavy with rhinestones scooped up the chair and hurled it back. It landed on a crowded table, spraying beer in every direction. The guys at the table jumped the rail and waded into the swing kids.

The bouncers arrived, two fat guys who didn't know where to start. They looked at Lou. They looked at the brawl on the dance floor. I guess they weren't ambitious enough to tackle Lou, so they headed for the dancers. The band had abandoned the set list and dove into a quirky cover of "Tie a Yellow Ribbon Around the Old Oak Tree."

Lou looked happy. He had a very picturesque dribble of blood in one corner of his mouth, and he planted a fist in the face of anyone who dared come within range. I picked a random kid and popped him in the mouth so I could feel involved.

His buddy aimed a fist at my nose. I turned and took it on the cheek. Then I leaned in with an uppercut that rattled his teeth and made the cartoon songbirds circle his head. He went down.

"That's enough, Lou," I shouted over the din. "Let's go. Cops!" I didn't really see any, but that would get him moving.

"Right behind you, man."

He hammered one last kid on the top of his head with a meaty fist and kicked his limp form under a table, then followed me to the exit. The guy on the door looked nervous, held up a hand wondering how he was going to stop us, figured out he wasn't, and ducked behind the cash register.

In the parking lot, I backed the Suburban into a Mazda by accident in my hurry to leave before the cops arrived. I didn't hear any sirens, but it would be soon now.

"Fuck, man," said Lou. "Watch your driving."

"Thing's the size of a battleship."

I got us away, pointed us toward the Interstate.

"Well, shit," said Lou, who grinned like he'd just won the Nobel Prize for kicking ass. "I guess we showed 'em."

We drove into a cluster of restaurants and hotels where Interstate 75 intersected with 200. I got us a couple of rooms at the Best Western.

In my room, I flipped on the light over the twin sinks, poked at the swollen area under my left eye where the kid had nailed me. I'd had too much beer, gotten careless. A watery punch thrown by some college kid. Should have seen it coming. Stupid.

I flopped down on the bed, grabbed the phone, and dialed Marcie's number. She answered after eleven rings. "Yes? Hello?"

"You sound out of breath."

"I ran in from the garage."

"What're you doing?"

"Working. I have three howler monkeys on ice."

"You have three—what're you doing?"

"I got them from the Sanford Zoo," she said. "They were free. Can you believe it?"

"Dead monkeys. That's quite a deal."

"Ha, ha. You think it's a big joke, but a friend of a friend owns an alternative art gallery in Jacksonville. You know Minnie Shwartz?"

"She owns the gallery?"

"Minnie? No. Minnie owns squat. But she knows Naomi. Naomi runs the gallery."

"Naomi who?"

"Naomi nothing," said Marcie. "It's one of those one word names. Like Cher."

"Or Zorro."

"Hilarious." A pause. "You okay?"

"Holding my own."

"Why'd you call?"

"Just to hear a friendly voice."

"And I'm as good as anyone?" Her question was only half playful.

"You know that ain't true."

"So you like me best, huh?"

"I like you best. What are you going to do with the monkeys?"

"I don't know yet, but I'd better get started before they start going bad."

"You could do one of those see no, hear no, speak no evil things," I suggested.

She laughed. "You're wonderfully silly and cliché. I have to go."

"Be careful. Don't dead animals have parasites or ebola or something?"

"My monkeys are melting."

"Bye, baby."

"Bye."

We hung up.

I thought about calling Ma, but it was getting late. I went back to the mirror and checked my bruise again. Stupid.

I'd bought a toothbrush and some toothpaste and deodorant at the 7-Eleven a block from the hotel. I scrubbed my teeth. I'd forgotten to buy a razor. My stubble was thick and dark.

There was a hard knock on the door. I opened it, and Lou was standing there shirtless with a little syringe sticking out of his upper arm like a stray pub dart. He was red faced, strands of blond hair matted to his forehead. His face was crinkled up like an actor's in a laxative commercial.

"I need you to push it in, man. Make the juice go in."

"Are you on the junk?"

"I think I stuck it in a nerve or something. I can't get my other arm up to push it in." It was true. He tried to bring his other arm around but it froze up halfway like Frankenstein playing the violin.

"If you're shooting junk, I swear I'll fucking put a bullet in your face right now."

"It's not dope, man. It's—It's part of my muscle building regimen."

"Steroids."

"It hurts, man."

"I hear that stuff shrivels your gonads."

"Will you just push it in!"

I took hold of the syringe gently and thumbed down the contents.

"Take it out."

I pulled the syringe out of his arm and dropped it on top of the television.

The arm was his again. He rubbed it, flexed. "Yeah, man.

Yeah!" He slapped his muscles, flexed some more and dropped to the floor where he began doing pushups. "Feel the burn. Ride the burn. Oh, yeah." It didn't look like he was going to let up anytime soon.

"Could you shout slogans and sweat in your own room?"

"It's not even midnight. We got to find Spanklicious." He kept on with the pushups.

"That's a bust. I talked to the girl in the band."

"Too skinny. No rack."

"She said the joint they play in burnt down."

"Burnbabyburnbabyburn—now what?"

"We know where they're going. Tomorrow night."

"Back to Gainesville," said Lou.

"Mudhog Sammy's."

TWELVE

This time the phone book was a bust, and Information stuck me for two quarters so I could find out no place called Mudhog Sammy's existed as far as the phone company was concerned. I parked the Suburban in a pay lot off downtown near the clubs, and Lou and I searched on foot. I didn't think any of the respectable places would inflict Spanklicious on their customers, but we had to start someplace. Since it was a lazy afternoon, nobody much minded taking a few seconds to talk to us, but nobody was much help either.

Finally, an old black man with trumpet player's cheeks pointed us in the right direction. "A place just off Main called Underground. Full of kids. Plays that new clank and crank electro-junk. Maybe that the place. Maybe not. No telling. All them bands look alike. Sound alike. Ask somebody over there."

"Thanks." I pulled a wad of bills from my pants pocket. "Let me take care of you."

"Thanks, no. Just remember where to come back to when you want to hear something good. We got Diesel Joe Jarvis on the ivories tonight."

"We'll keep it in mind."

We found the Underground just off Main down at the rotten end with the homo bars, but it was closed. A sign said they wouldn't open until ten and advertised a band called the Bone Destroyers. We stood on the sidewalk with our hands in our pockets.

"Okay, New Guy," I said. "How do we find these guys?"

"I don't know, but I'm getting hungry."

"Later."

"I'm telling you, man, I get cranky if I don't eat on some kind of regular schedule. I've got to keep my carb level at a certain—"

I tuned him out. Across the street, three dirty teenagers sat on the curb, panhandling the pedestrians. The two girls looked like they might have been pretty under their layers of street grime. The guy had half of his head shaved, and the other half was a green mop, tattoos up and down his arms. He leaned back on his elbows letting the girls do the work.

"Shut up about food," I said to Lou. "Follow me."

I walked up to the kids as I fished the wad of bills out of my pocket again. I peeled off a single and handed it to the first girl. Lou made a noise behind me like I was the dumbest thing on legs.

"God bless you, sir." That must've been what she figured generous people wanted to hear. She made the dollar disappear into her sweater, but kept looking at me, expectant. She knew there was more to it. Smart kid.

I took out a five, held it where they could see it. The other girl paid attention too. The guy still acted like it was none of his business.

"A band called Spanklicious," I said. "Ever heard of them?"

The girls looked at each other. Then the guy said, "They don't play the Underground." He looked away again like that was all I needed to know.

The one girl shrunk into her sweater. The other one was a little older, blond hair tucked up under a Gators ball cap, ring in her nose, another in her left eyebrow. She eyed the five in my hand and tried to turn the guy's comment into useful information. "They wouldn't play downtown. No place around here."

"Where?"

A shrug.

"You know a place called Mudhog Sammy's?"

"No."

I gave her the five and said thanks. Lou started in on me as we walked away.

"Might as well of flushed the six bucks down the toilet."

"I didn't see you coming up with any brilliant ideas," I said.

A voice chased after us as we turned the corner. "Hey, mister."

We looked back. It was the girl in the oversized sweater. She jogged up to us, stopped, looked at us hard for a second. "Are you two cops?"

"No."

"If I ask straight out and you're cops, you have to say so, or it's like entrapment or something, right?"

"Sure."

"I know some more about the Mudhog and the band."

"Tell us."

"I want some money. More than five."

I took the bills out, showed her a picture of Andrew Jackson.

"More."

"How 'bout I squeeze it out of her?" said Lou.

That didn't scare her. She just looked at me.

"Let's hear what you have," I said. "I'll decide what it's worth."

"The Mudhog's out on the Prairie, back in the woods before it gets too swampy. It not like an official kind of place, you know? It was like this old house, and then kids started hanging around a lot. Then some people just sort of set up shop and sold beer but didn't card anyone, and you can usually score some smoke or whatever you want. Maybe on a Saturday night there'll be a couple of hundred kids."

"Keep going. What about the band?"

"They'll be there tonight, but they don't just play. They also deal from the back of their van. I've scored from them a few times."

"How do we know this ain't just a pretty story, so you can tap us for a few bucks?" asked Lou. He said to me, "She saw that wad of dough you had, man. Maybe she figured you looked gullible."

She pushed up the sleeve of her sweater and turned her arm over to show us the tracks. Some of the needle marks looked fairly old. "I get high out there off and on when I can get a ride. That's why I asked if you were cops. I could get in the shit talking to cops."

"What did the van look like?"

"It's been a while."

"Think."

"Not like a new minivan. Bigger. Blue. Dark blue. But you can't miss it. It's got like a really shitty airbrush job of a moon and stars kind of night sky picture on the side."

"Probably has Orange County plates," said Lou.

"Ford or Chevy or what?" I asked her.

"I don't know," she said. "Can I have the money?"

"No. I want directions."

"I told you Paynes Prairie."

"I want a map. You draw it." Lou had a pen, and I ripped down a lost dog sign from a telephone pole. She drew a map on the back.

"That's the worst map I've ever seen," said Lou.

"Label the roads."

"I did," she said.

"That one."

"For fuck's sake, it doesn't have a name. It's a dirt road."

"Then write that. What's it near?"

"There's a bait shack about four miles back," she said.

"Write that down."

She gave me the map, and I handed her two twenties.

"Waitaminute," said Lou. He grabbed her by the arm and pulled her close.

"Ow, that fucking hurts you stupid—"

"Shut up."

She shut up.

"I'd hate to think we paid you good money for nothing," said Lou.

"I told you the truth."

"Yeah, but keep it to yourself. I wouldn't like to hear that you warned them we were coming."

"Don't worry." She jerked her arm away. "Bragging that I talked to you guys won't exactly win me a lot of friends."

We headed out to Paynes Prairie that evening, the girl's map surprisingly accurate. It had been dark about an hour when we passed the bait shack, and I flipped on the Suburban's high beams so we wouldn't miss the dirt road.

"Don't start punching people unless I give the signal," I said.

"It's cool, man." He kissed the knuckles on both hands. "The ladies are ready when you say."

We turned onto the dirt road, which wound its way back into the woods. It was narrow and made of soft sand, so we poked along at twenty miles per hour. Soon, I saw blue lights flashing through the trees, reflecting off low clouds. A lot of lights.

"Aw shit, man." Lou had seen them too. "We might want to forget about this."

I rounded the next bend, and a patrol car blocked the way. More blue lights came up, and officers stepped out of the woods on both sides with shotguns cradled in their arms. One held up a hand, and I stopped the Suburban.

"Let me talk," I told Lou.

I rolled down the window as the deputy came up to my side.
"I.D."

I gave him the fake. He glanced at it a second then handed it
back.

"What're you doing out this way?"

"My daughter," I said. "She took off with some bad kids out
here. My old lady will have my ass if I don't get her back."

He nodded like he'd heard that one before. "A lot of people's
kids are in there. You'll have to call the station later tonight
after we've processed them all. Can't let you through now."

"She supposed to be with some kids in a big blue van with
stars and moons on it. The band, I think. Spanklicious or some
crazy thing. I'm really worried."

He sighed. "Hold on."

He checked with one of the other deputies and returned
shaking his head. "We got a lot of cars, motorcycles, trucks. You
name it. Nobody's listed a van like that. Listen, buddy, I know
you're worried, but we got like eighty kids in cuffs out here,
and the dogs are sniffing for dope now."

"Okay. Thanks."

As I backed out he called after me. "Call the station in the
morning."

We drove back to the bait shack and parked. It was closed, so
I took a leak in the woods around back, then let Lou drive for a
while. I didn't know what to do.

"The cops probably busted the place before the band got
there," said Lou.

"Maybe."

"You know what I think, man? I'll tell you what I think," said
Lou. "I think that's the end of their little mini concert tour.
Right?"

"Right."

"So they'll probably head back for Orlando. Right?"

I didn't know. I didn't know where to go next or what to do. And I didn't have very much faith in Lou's detective skills. "Let's get something to eat. We'll think about it."

This whole trip was starting to feel like a wild goose chase. I missed Marcie. I worried about Ma and Danny. What was going on back in Orlando while I was tromping around in the woods?

Back in civilization, Lou spotted a pizza joint in a strip mall. He pulled in, passed a Christian bookstore, a barber, and slammed on the brakes in front of an all-night Laundromat.

"Shit." My arms flew up to keep my forehead from smacking into the dashboard. "What the hell'd you do that for?"

"Look, man. There! Right over there." He pointed, and I followed his finger with my eyes. At the end of a line of cars between the Laundromat and the pizza place sat a big blue Chevy van with a shitty airbrush painting of a night sky with a crescent moon.

Lou made like he was getting out of the car. "Let's get 'em."

I pulled him back in. "Get who, moron? All we see is a van." I looked around but didn't see Benny. "Okay. Back up into that space." I jerked a thumb behind us. "We'll wait."

We watched for twenty minutes, people going in and out of the restaurant and the laundry, but no one going to the van. Then three kids came out of the pizza place. The fat one thought he was growing a beard, and the blond chick with short hair was cute in a dirty, gutter sort of way.

The third had to be Shane. I'd heard a description, but I didn't need it. He was tall and cocky, good looking in that uncombed way kids are now. His black hair was pulled back in a tight, wet ponytail. His earrings looked like fishing lures. Leather jacket. Yeah. One of those. Young tough.

They took a package wrapped in brown paper from the back

of the van. They looked at their watches, spoke a few words, and Shane tucked the package under his arm, gave his pals the thumbs up. They retreated to the pizza place. He went toward the Laundromat.

"Now can we get him?"

"Hold on," I said. "What's he doing?"

"Washing his undies? What's it matter?"

He went into the Laundromat and took a seat between two lines of washers. It was easy to keep tabs on him. The laundry was well lit, one of those big, floor-to-ceiling windows in front. We watched awhile. Shane just sat there. The other customers filled washers, tended dryers, folded clothes. Shane lit a cigarette.

"Look," said Lou, "let me go in there and drag the little bastard out. I'll ring his bell until he tells us where Benny is."

"Let me try just asking him first. I'm fairly persuasive. You stay here. Come rescue me if I get in trouble?"

"How will I know that?"

"You'll know."

I thought about putting on my shoulder holsters but decided I could handle Shane easy enough without the automatics. I climbed out of the Suburban and gave Lou one last firm look over my shoulder. I needed him to stay put, not cause another scene. If we needed a scene, I'd damn well cause the thing myself.

I entered the Laundromat, stood with hands in pockets, looked the place over. A shriveled lady with white hair sat with her knitting and watched the clothes tumble around in a dryer. A guy in a New Orleans Saints jersey sat under his comb-over, reading the newspaper. A few more patrons scattered around the place. Dirty laundry got clean. Wet laundry got dry. In the middle of it all sat a little piece of shit called Shane, smoking a cigarette like he was doing it a favor, waiting for an opportunity to cause the world some pain.

I sat next to him.

He looked at me. I looked back.

"What's up?" he said.

"Ain't nothing up, Shane. Just thought I'd pay you a visit. You look like a real prick. Anyone ever tell you that?"

"Hey, fuck you, man. I don't need this shit." He patted the package in the seat next to him. "If you want to do business, then let's do business. I'm not here to get jerked around."

"I see." I gave my brain a second to digest what he'd said. "Whatcha got there? Some junk? Spanklicious not selling any albums I bet, so you're pushing a little smack."

"Fucking shut up, man." His eyes pinballed around the room, landed back on me again. "Keep your voice down. This is a private transaction."

"I'm not who you think I am, Shane, and I'm not here to buy your dope. I'm here to find Benny—"

"I don't know no Benny."

"—and I'm here to drop on you like a bag of bowling balls if you don't start coughing up some God damn answers."

"Who the fuck are you?"

"I'm the guy that's been chasing your ridiculous band all over Central Florida. You don't really have any fans, do you? The band's a cover so you can ride around delivering junk."

"Fuck you, asshole. We sold sixteen CDs last week, and I'm all done talking to your sorry ass." He opened his leather jacket and showed me the butt of a pistol sticking out of his waistband. "Now get the hell out of here."

My hand darted into his jacket as he was finishing his tough talk, and I grabbed the pistol, pulled it out. I twirled it in my hand as his eyes widened until I was holding it by the barrel. I lifted it high and brought the butt down on his knee with every-thing I had. The kneecap shifted with a fleshy *thuck*.

Shane fell forward, his hands going to the knee. His cry sounded like an animal. "Ohmyfuckinggod! Ow shit, oh, Christ whatthefuck." He rocked back and forth, his eyes filling with tears. "Oh please, oh please, God."

I stood, got a handful of his jacket in my fist, and pulled him to his feet. He hopped on one leg. "Kid, that's just the begin-ning. You and me are going to have a long, painful talk."

The Laundromat leapt into action around me. Shuffling. The unhappy click and whirl of thumbs on revolver hammers. Bullets sliding into chambers.

"Freeze, motherfucker! Police. Drop the gun right fucking now." It was the guy in the Saints jersey. "Right now! Do it. Drop the gun."

I froze, looked around, but didn't drop the pistol. The little old lady with the knitting needle pointed a magnum at me the size of a howitzer. No less than four of the other Laundromat patrons stood with pistols in hand, ready to make me heavy with lead. I was real unhappy with this turn of events.

"I said drop the gun!"

"Don't be stupid, buddy," said another. "We got you covered on all sides."

"I don't know this asshole," said Shane.

"Nobody's talking to you, fuckwad." To me: "Drop it now!"

Stupid. Stupid. Stupid. "Wait. Just hold on a second. There's been a mistake."

"You're making it now," said the old lady. "Drop the gun, or I'll blow your motherfucking balls off!"

"This ain't my stuff." Shane shook the bag in the air. He was still hopping on one foot. "I'm a musician, you fucks."

Stupid. I was a dumb son of a bitch. Standing there like a putz, holding the wrong end of a revolver.

"Just shoot them both," someone shouted.

The Laundromat's big front window filled with headlights. A V-8 engine roared beyond. Heads turned. An explosion of glass as the Suburban plowed through the front window. The vehicle's big tires bulldozed the shin-high row of brickwork, filling the place with dust, knocking plaster loose from the ceiling. Lou was behind the wheel, grinning like a madman.

Screaming. Orders. One stray gunshot.

He crunched the front bumper into a row of washing machines. They tipped, and warm, foamy water flooded the floor ankle deep. Water lines split open, covered everything in a thick sudsy spray. The guy in the Saints' jersey made a grab for us, slipped, fell face first into the soup.

I leapt over the fallen row of washers toward Lou. I still had a hold on Shane's jacket, but he didn't clear the washers. His ribs smacked into the side of one, and he grunted pain. I dragged him over. The old lady jerked her trigger three times, and the washer sprouted three holes where Shane had been, the slugs making metallic *tanks* as they punched through the side of the machine.

The back door of the Suburban swung open, and Lou shouted, "Move it!"

Gunfire. Shattered glass. The windshield of the Suburban looked like a Braille scream. Lou's head popped back up. He held one of my automatics, aimed high, emptied a clip into a row of dryers. The shots sent the police to the floor. I pulled Shane into the Suburban. "Go, Go, Go!"

Lou backed the thing out fast, but I hadn't closed the door. It snapped off against the wall. Shots chased after us.

"Does that look like an unmarked police car?" Lou motioned with his chin to a beige sedan parked behind us.

I turned. Looked. "Maybe."

Lou threw it into reverse and stomped the gas. He smashed

into the sedan hard, jammed it up against three other cars near it. I grabbed Shane, kept him from bouncing out.

"Let me out of here," he said. "You're fucking nuts."

"Shut up." I pushed him onto the floor. Told him to stay there. Lou put us into drive, jerked the wheel, and tore out of the parking lot. I had to grab a seat belt to keep from sliding out myself.

"We've got to get off the road," I said.

Lou nodded. "Right."

He turned off the street, zig-zagged us into a dark residential neighborhood. In the background: sirens.

"We've got to ditch this tank." I scanned the street for someplace likely.

"I know. I know."

"Wait. Back up."

Lou stopped the car, then backed up, stopped in front of a house with a *For Sale* sign. I hopped out, ran up to one of the front windows, looked in. No furniture. Empty. I ran back to Lou.

"Pull in around back. There's a chain link fence with a gate. Pull in up close to the back of the house." I jumped back into the Suburban. Sirens much closer.

There was a padlock on the gate. Lou pushed through it with the Suburban. I got out again, tossed the broken lock into the bushes, pushed the gate closed. One hinge was loose, but it would look okay from the street.

Lou had parked, gotten out. He had Shane by the collar of his leather jacket. I elbowed a hole through a glass pane of the house's back door, reached in, and unlocked it. We went inside. Everything was dark, hot, and stale. Nobody had been there for a long time.

"Keep him here," I told Lou.

"I got him."

Shane didn't say anything. I guessed he'd wised up some. He still limped.

I went through to the empty living room and peeked through a crack in the heavy drapes. Blue lights flashed with red down the street, edged closer, passed the house. I waited five minutes, and they came back the other way. This time two patrol cars, one following the other fast. I waited fifteen more minutes but didn't see any more signs they were still searching the area.

I had Shane's gun stuck in my pants, so I pulled it out and looked at it in the sliver of light that slid in through the crack in the drapes. I don't think it had ever been fired. The light sliced through the room and fell across Shane's face. He looked young. Two big men had grabbed him away, spirited him into the darkness. He looked scared.

THIRTEEN

Shane opened his mouth to protest, but a quick, hard look from me shut him up. I told Lou to search him, and he found a cell phone in the kid's jacket pocket. It was one of those little kind, and Lou flipped it open, saying, "Kirk to *Enterprise*."

I took the cell phone and handed it to Shane. "Call Benny."

"What?"

"Call your brother."

"I don't—"

I slapped him hard across the face. Tears welled in his eyes.

"Don't give me that shit. You dial him up right now. I'll tell you what to say."

"Okay, okay." He dialed.

I said, "Tell him this address. Tell him to come here, you understand? Something went wrong with your drug deal, and you need him to come here. Tell me you understand."

"Sure. I understand."

We waited.

"Hello, Benny?"

I cocked his pistol and put the barrel against Shane's temple.

"Yeah, it's me," said Shane. "I need your help. I had some problems with the drop."

Benny's voice screeched on the other end, and Shane pulled the phone away from his ear some.

"Take it easy, Benny. No, I can't go into it right now." Shane glanced at me, and I nodded. He gave Benny the address. Shane said, "Hurry."

❖

Benny showed up twenty minutes later. I had Lou stand behind the door and open it. I stood out of sight on the other side. We made Shane stand in front of the door about ten feet inside the house where Benny could see him. Shane still favored the bad knee.

The door creaked open, and Benny walked in. It never occurred to him for a second he was about to get his head handed to him.

"What the hell's this?" Benny asked Shane. "Somebody forget the light bill?"

He took three more steps in, and I spoke up. "We've been looking all over the place for you, Benny."

Benny started at my voice, turned to look. His eyes needed a second to adjust, then he saw it was me. "Oh, hell."

He made for the door, but one of Lou's big hands fell on his shoulder.

"Charlie, you got to let me explain. I know it looks bad, me splitting town just when everything's turning sour, but I can explain, I tell you."

"There'll be a time for that," I assured him. "First things first. You know the routine."

"Charlie, please."

I slapped a strip of duct tape over his mouth.

We used the rest of the roll to tie Shane to a staircase.

I thought maybe I'd tie Benny to a chair, but there wasn't a single stick of furniture in the house. Lou and I took Benny into the bathroom, because the shower curtain rod was surprisingly sturdy. We tied his hands up to the rod with strips of rag we'd found under the kitchen sink. He looked scared, the blood gone from his face.

He worked his mouth behind the tape like he wanted to ask us something, but I shook my head no. Talking would come later. After we softened him up.

I worked the ribs for a little while, my knuckles biting hard into Benny's side. He took the shots with whimpering grunts. I worked my way into a good rhythm, trying not to give any spot particular attention, spreading the punches around his whole torso. I stopped for a few seconds to shed my jacket, handed it to Lou, glimpsed his face. He looked a little sick. He liked to fight, but this wasn't a fight.

Benny cried a little, and I let up.

I pulled the tape off with one quick jerk. "Where's Stan?"

He drew a wheezing breath, like ice skates on a chalkboard. I turned the shower on him, gave him a blast of cold water. He leaned into it, letting it wash over his face, hanging limply from the curtain rod.

"Okay," I said. "Let's hear it."

"How much do you want to know?"

"Start when the Earth cooled, and I'll tell you when to stop."

"It was Beggar Johnson," began Benny. The water beaded on his bald head, dripped down and streaked his face, soaked his mustache. "He came to me with an offer. It wasn't like I had a choice, Charlie."

"That's bullshit."

"No, Charlie, no bullshit. Really. Beggar said Stan was finished in Orlando. Young blood was coming in to take over the territory. The old man might go soft or he might go hard, but he was going. That's how Beggar put it. He said my future was in my own hands. If I cooperated, it would go easier for everyone. Geez, Charlie. I mean, well, shit. I got a life, right. What am I supposed to do? Stand up to Beggar Johnson?"

"You could have come to me or Bob or any of us."

"I thought of that. I really did, but Beggar had Sanchez with him. They made it look like the whole team was bailing out, going over to Beggar. I got scared."

"You sold out."

"It's not like that." Benny tugged at his bindings. "They're cutting off the circulation."

I shook my head, sat on the edge of the tub. "Stan was good to us, like a dad, Benny."

"There's more, Charlie."

"What?"

"You're not going to like it," he said.

"Talk."

"Stan was…" Benny shook his head, groping for the words. "Something was wrong with him, Charlie."

"Shut up. What do you know about it?"

"He's a good man, but he wasn't sharp anymore. He wasn't all there."

"I said shut up." My fists balled.

"I'm not saying he's senile…just, I don't know. Old fashioned. Beggar could see he wasn't running the show right."

I got all hot up through my face. I couldn't see how to tell Benny how wrong he was. I had to *make* him understand. My teeth clenched. My fists came up.

"My arms. Can you untie—"

"Ungrateful fuck."

"They're numb."

I grabbed a fistful of his shirt, held him so he wouldn't swing while I was hitting. I started punching again, short jabs with the other fist. One, two, three—

"Wait—"

Six, seven, eight—

"I just want—"

Ten, eleven, twelve—

"My arms. I can't feel—"

I kept punching, lost count.

Benny sobbed, yelled. "Okay. What do you want? I'll tell you already."

I stopped. I was sweating good, nearly punched out. What did I want?

"I'm going to get some air," said Lou. New Guy looked green and confused.

"You stay," I barked. God damn stack of muscles. Couldn't he stomach to watch a pro work? Lou didn't argue. I let go of Benny. "Stan. What happened to him? Where is he?"

"I don't know. For God's sake, Charlie. I don't."

"You must want another pasting."

"Charlie." Lou tugged at my sleeve like some little kid. "He's had enough, man. He doesn't know."

I swatted him away. "You listen to me, New Guy. You understand this. Everything was good. Stan did what he did, and we did our job. It was perfect. And when somebody came along to ruin it, this rat bastard didn't stand up. He didn't stand up for Stan or for you or for me. He turned on his own, and that's the unforgivable sin."

"There's a place, Charlie," said Benny. "I heard some talk between Beggar and that killer of his."

"Mercury."

"Yeah. A warehouse in Bithlo, out of the way. I heard them talking about it. I don't know if Stan's there, but they were talking about how out of the way it was, like maybe it was a good place to hide something or somebody."

Benny leaned pathetically against the shower tile. He was covered with sweat and bruises. A little ragged moan crawled out of him.

For a second, I felt bad for him and reached for the shower knob to give him another cold bath. Then I thought about Stan, what I would do if I even found him. Everything had been good. Now it was shit. My hand veered toward the hot knob.

At first, Benny was grateful. He lapped at the water, let it soak him, run down his chin. But the spray heated quickly. Benny's eyes got big with realization. And then the hot hit him full on.

"Shit! Fucking turn it off." He hollered, twitched, tried to twist away from the spray. "Ow, fucking shit, you're killing me!"

"Come on," I told Lou.

He went out ahead of me. I pulled the bathroom door shut, Benny still yelling for us to come get him. He'd be a little pink, that's all. The hot water would run out soon, and he'd just be wet and prune-skinned. But his pleas for mercy followed us into the hall.

Lou looked at me like I'd just fucked his pet bunny up the ass, but he didn't say anything. He needed out for a while, so I thought of an errand for him.

"Can you hot-wire a car?"

He nodded. "I used to do repossessions."

"Get us something. They'll pick us up in two seconds if we go out in the Suburban. I'd like to be out of here before daybreak. Try to be discreet."

"Okay." He looked at the bathroom door then back at me again. "You going to be okay here, man?"

"Me? Yeah. I'll be fine. He's not going anywhere."

"If you're going to work him over again, do it while I'm gone."

I waved him away. "Sure."

He left out the back.

I put my ear to the bathroom door. Benny had shut up his screaming. Probably the water had turned cold, or maybe he'd passed out. I had some thinking to do, so I went outside and sat in the front seat of the Suburban with the window down. I thought about turning on the radio but didn't want to risk the noise.

I closed my eyes, replayed the fiasco at the Laundromat. Shane was a two-bit pusher. He thought I'd been at the Laundromat to make a buy. I looked in the backseat, thinking maybe the paper package had flown out when the door had come off or during one of Lou's sharp turns. But it was right there on the floor. I grabbed it, tore it open. Three fat kilos of snow-white powder. I took a closer look at the wrappings. The brown paper was a grocery bag from a Piggly Wiggly. The inside layer was the sports section of *The Orlando Sentinel*.

I figured Shane's band had been ferrying the stuff all around the state. It looked like Benny had gotten little bro in on the act, and I resolved to take Danny's Buck Rogers gun away from him. We'd have another loud talk about college.

I slunk back into the house, back into the bathroom. The water had turned ice cold, and I shut it off. Benny's weight had bent the curtain rod enough so he could rest his knees against the side of the tub. His eyes were shut, and he maintained a low, steady whine, a whimper. I couldn't tell if he was dreaming he was in hell or awake for the real thing.

I untied his hands, pulled him down. His arms flopped dead to his sides like two sleeves full of Spam. He groaned again. I let him down on the floor, sat down next to him, brushed the wet hair out of his eyes.

"Benny."

His head rolled toward me without the eyes opening.

"Sorry, Benny."

His face scrunched. "It hurts. My ribs."

"I know. I'm sorry."

"It hurts." His voice was a whisper, the hiss of a knife sliding into its sheath.

"Bob's dead, Benny, and I barely know New Guy. Why didn't you come to me? I'd have done anything if you'd just come to me."

"I tried...I was too scared."

"Tell me."

He coughed, and his whole body wracked. He faded, and I thought he'd gone out on me. "Benny."

I exhaled long, rubbed my temples. I must've hurt him more than I'd meant. I felt along his ribs, and he sucked breath. I tried with a lighter touch. I might have broken a couple. Maybe a punctured lung, internal bleeding. He was groggy.

"I hit you," said Benny. "I'm sorry. I called Beggar after Bob and I left your mother's house and told him you were taking the books to Stan, and he said I'd better get them or be sorry."

"It's okay."

"So I went to your apartment. I waited in the shrubs, and when you came out I hit you." He coughed, red flecks on his lips. "I guess the joke was on me. I grabbed the briefcase, but it was empty."

"Just take it easy."

"It's cold." Benny's eyes were glassy, unfocused.

"It's okay." I sat on the bathroom floor and pulled his head into my lap. "It'll be okay."

I pinched his nose between thumb and forefinger, put my other hand over his mouth. He went stiff, feebly tried to wiggle free, but there wasn't much left in him. I felt him give, go slack under my touch, and that was all.

I pulled down the drapes in the master bedroom and wrapped him, dragged him to the hall closet, and put him inside on the floor under the shelves. I had to fold him up to make him fit, put him in a sitting position with his knees up to his chest.

I took one of the rags we'd used to tie him and wiped the

place down, made sure I covered all the fixtures in the bathroom and all the doorknobs. I didn't want to leave any prints. I circled the house twice, once inside and once out, to make sure we hadn't left anything.

Then I went to Shane. He sat like a shrunken ball up against the stairs. The duct tape was twisted and stretched where he'd tried to pull free. He must've heard everything that had happened to his brother. He looked at me like I was the devil. I cocked his pistol, lifted it, aimed it at his forehead. Shane was a loose end. He shook. Tears in his eyes. I felt something hot and wet on my face. Tears there too. Everything had gotten so fucked up. How did it happen?

I lowered the pistol.

I fetched the package of coke, spilled half of it in front of Shane. "If you call the police, you'll have to explain that. If I were you, I'd just get out of here, understand? Keep pulling at that tape, and you'll get free. Benny was…just business. He screwed up."

I couldn't tell if Shane understood or not. It didn't matter. I went outside and sat on the back steps. The night was cool. I huddled inside my jacket, and the tears came quick and hot down my face. I let it out, put my face in my hands, my shoulders heaving up and down. I was a mess of tears and sweat and snot. I made the low whimpering sound of a wounded animal.

An hour later, Lou pulled into the backyard, driving one of those updated Volkswagen Beetles. It was electric green. Lou opened the door, looked like a giant climbing out of a clown car.

"This is what you got?"

"I figured it was the thing most opposite of a Suburban. Inconspicuous."

"You're a regular James Bond."

"I also stole a license plate off a Dodge up on blocks two houses over for when the Bug's reported stolen."

"Good. Help me get the stuff."

We took everything out of the Suburban and jammed it into the backseat of the Bug. I checked under the Suburban's seats and went through the whole thing, but it looked like we'd gotten it all. I wiped it down with the rag.

"Anything new?" Lou asked.

"I'll tell you on the road."

"What about the kid?"

"It's been taken care of."

He didn't ask about Benny.

FOURTEEN

We ditched the VW about a half-mile from where I'd left my car. We walked in silence, Lou all sullen. I dropped him at his motorcycle and sent him back to Orlando with some instructions. I needed him to keep an eye on some people.

"How will I get hold of you?" he asked.

I gave him Ma's number and waved bye. The Harley thundered away like the end of the world. I found a phone at an Exxon station. Time to put Benny's information to use.

I dialed Jimmy's number. He answered in one ring but sounded sleepy. I apologized for ruining his nap.

"Hookman, what's the latest?"

Almost nobody called me Hook or Hookman anymore. "I got a lead, Jimmy."

"What is it?"

"I don't want to talk about it on the phone."

"Nobody ever does."

"It's important."

"Okay, Charlie-boy. Make the drive. I'll be waiting."

The drive from Gainesville to Wedgewood, the golf course community on the edge of Orlando where Jimmy lived, took just a hair over two hours. I wanted this to be over quick. If Stan were on ice in the warehouse Benny had told me about, then I needed Jimmy's help to bust in and grab Stan out of there—dead or alive.

Wedgewood was an up-and-coming community with gleaming white houses that all looked more or less the same with cookie-cutter lawns. But it was near good schools, safe and clean. A place where the residents didn't have to worry about guys like me and Jimmy. I parked in the driveway behind his Cadillac.

I knocked, and he let me in with a smile and a nod. He was still a great big fat tub of goo.

"Hey, Charlie, come on in." Jimmy waved me into his living room. A ten-year-old kid sat watching *The Wizard of Oz* on video. It was near the beginning of the film, and the house had just landed on the witch. "That's my son, Jimmy Jr. Say hi to Charlie, Junior."

The kid turned, gave me a wave, then glued his eyes back to the tube.

"The tin man's my favorite," I said.

"I like the monkeys," said the kid.

"The what?"

"The monkeys."

"What for?"

"They fly."

"They only fly when the witch tells them to. How about the lion?"

"He can't fly."

"There's more important things than flying, kid."

"You look like shit, Charlie," said Jimmy.

"I had a long night." It was true. I was wrung out, no sleep.

"Come on. I got coffee."

I followed Jimmy into the kitchen and slumped at his table. He poured me some coffee in a *World's Greatest Dad* mug. Jimmy sat across from me. His mug said *100% Italian*. For a second it was like we were two buddies, maybe getting ready to hit the golf links, maybe going fishing. But I forgot all that when Jimmy raised an eyebrow, cleared his throat. Time to get down to business.

"I might know where Stan is."

Jimmy's face was blank. "Yeah?"

"I found Benny. If Beggar has Stan, Benny had an idea where they might have stashed him."

"Where's Benny now?"

"He's not in the picture anymore," I said.

He knew better than to ask more about it. I told him about the warehouse in Bithlo. Jimmy nodded, said he knew the place. That made sense, since Jimmy was in charge of moving stolen goods in and out of the city. I didn't know too much about that end of the operation, but I'd heard there were warehouses and storage sheds all over the city full of hot televisions, car radios, leather jackets, tires, compact discs and booze.

"Charlie."

"Yeah?"

Jimmy cleared his throat, fiddled with his coffee mug. "All that stuff you said about sticking by Stan. That's all true, so I'm going to help you, okay? But there's more. Another reason I'm going to help you."

"What?"

"Larry Cartwright."

Another of Stan's lieutenants. "What about Larry Cartwright?"

"He's dead."

"How?"

"What's it matter? I called his house, his office, and his cell phone like maybe five hundred times. Nobody's seen him. Pretty clear to me Beggar's trimming the fat. I don't feel as safe as I did last time we talked."

Good. I hated to be a hardass, but trouble for Jimmy meant he was more on my side.

"There's more," said Jimmy. "We got to face up to the fact that Stan might be past saving."

I was painfully aware of that possibility but didn't say anything.

"There's something you don't know about." Jimmy lowered his voice and leaned forward. For a moment the house was dead quiet, only the sound of singing munchkins coming from the other room. "The stash."

"What the hell's the stash?"

"Money," said Jimmy. "So much money not even God knows how much."

"I have no fucking idea what you're talking about."

"Forgive me, Charlie, but Beggar was right about a couple of things. Orlando *is* a juicy territory. We were raking in money hand over fist, so much we didn't know what to do with it. Well, we can't have the Feds and the IRS and everyone breathing down our backs all the time, right? We can only launder the money so fast, and we could only make so many trips to safe deposit boxes without getting people suspicious. So Stan just started stockpiling the cash. He didn't know how to get rid of it or launder it any faster."

"How long's this been going on?"

"Four, maybe five years," said Jimmy. "Cash just kept arriving in suitcases and trunks and trucks."

I shook my head, closed my eyes tight trying to get the dragon's horde image of all that money out of my head. "What's this got to do with finding Stan?"

"I'm just saying we might not find Stan. He might not be findable. In which case we got to look out for ourselves." Jimmy's eyes darted toward the living room where his son still watched the movie. "We got families to think about. A big stack of cash could set us up in the Bahamas, Spain, Australia."

I chewed my bottom lip while thinking about it. "We look for Stan. Maybe we find some other things along the way. Fine. But one thing at a time."

Jimmy put up his hands. "Fair enough."

"Now what?" I asked.

"I think I know a way to get us close to that warehouse. I got to make some calls."

"Okay. You got any medical tape? Maybe some iodine?"

"You okay?"

"Just a scrape."

"In the bathroom down the hall, under the sink," said Jimmy. "Take what you need."

In the bathroom, I peeled off the old bandage where the bullet had grazed my side. It was crusty with dried blood, but from what I could see it looked okay. I flushed the bandage. I cleaned the wound, taped on a new bandage. I looked at myself in the mirror. I looked beat. And old. I thought about Jimmy's fairy story, the stash of money. Maybe I should just get out of town. Maybe I'd take Marcie. I wondered offhand where my *National Geographic* was.

I just wanted to sit someplace with a drink. With Marcie. Yeah, she was nice, a good one. She knew all about me and didn't mind. But I had to finish what I was doing. There was something about quitting in the middle and running off without knowing what happened that didn't sit right in my gut.

I splashed water on my face, dried myself, went back out to the living room.

On the television, Dorothy was skipping along the yellow brick road. She looked confident; she didn't know the score. Oz was in color, but Kansas was real.

Jimmy came out of the kitchen, his coffee mug leading the way. In his other hand he held a pastry the size of a hubcap. No wonder he was a blimp. "I got it all straight, Charlie. I got one of my boys dropping off a truck. We'll slip in like it's a regular delivery. Just sit tight. I got to get some stuff." And he was gone again.

Jimmy Jr. still had his eyes glued to the movie. He was sitting real close to the TV. Ma would have told him to move back or he'd go blind.

"How's the movie, kid?"

"Good."

"What you want to be when you grow up?"

He turned, spared me another quick glance. "A paleontologist."

"A pa–paleo—a what?"

"A paleontologist."

"That's pretty good, kid. When I was your age I either wanted to be a cowboy or a robot."

"Which did you choose?"

Hilarious fucking kid.

Jimmy came back with a tote bag, and he'd changed into a sweatshirt and sweatpants. He told his son to behave while he was gone, and then we were in the parking lot next to a big yellow truck which used to be a moving van. You could still see where the word *Ryder* had been spray-painted over, and I asked Jimmy if the truck was hot.

"They're not looking for it anymore," he said, and that was good enough.

I shrugged into my shoulder holsters. We climbed into the truck. Jimmy cranked the ignition.

"How is it an important guy like you is driving a truck?" I said it with a straight face, but he knew I was ribbing him.

He shrugged, scrunching his chins into fleshy wads. Jimmy had been living the soft life, and he bulged pretty good under his Florida Gator sweats. He was one of these career wise guys that was always shoving a bratwurst down his face, and whenever the sun came out, he'd sweat barbecue sauce.

Jimmy said, "I like to keep a hand in." He looked back at his house. "I just hate leaving Junior on short notice. I guess it's okay leaving him with Maria—that's my house girl. Maria. It's been a while since I been on a run, you know? I fix up deals, right? It's been ten years since I drove a truck or waved a piece around or any of that crap. I do most of my work over the phone. I fix deals."

"You fix deals," I acknowledged.

We drove.

"What's in the truck now?" I asked.

"Nike sneakers and Zippo lighters."

We drove east toward Bithlo, past the junkyards and the trailer parks, to the very edge of Stan's crumbling kingdom.

"You ever think about getting out of this business?" I asked him.

Jimmy's mouth hung open, and he looked at me like I had three heads. "What do you mean?"

"What the hell do you think I mean?"

"Think too much about that kind of stuff, and you'll go batty."

I guess what I really wanted was to find Stan and have him tell me everything was going to be okay. Either we'd kick Beggar Johnson's ass back to Miami somehow, or Stan would give me the okay to get the hell out of town. I didn't feel right without Stan telling me what to do. That wasn't easy to admit, but it was true.

Jimmy smelled a buck. I shook my head and laughed to myself over the notion of a secret stash of money.

"What's funny?" asked Jimmy.

"Nothing. How are you fixed for artillery?"

"Why?"

"Just in case."

"I got a snub-nose .38 on my ankle."

"Get it up around your waist. Tuck it in your pants."

"I'm wearing sweats. It'll fall down."

"Tuck it in your underwear too."

He did like I said and grimaced, sucking in a sharp gasp of breath.

"What's wrong?"

"The metal's cold."

"It'll warm up."

We drove more.

I kept a casual eye on the rearview mirror, and about ten minutes into the trip I saw something I didn't like. I said, "Jimmy, let's stop for some coffee and a muffin. What do you say?"

He looked at me sideways. "Now?"

"Yeah. How about it?"

"I guess," said Jimmy.

Some ambitious redneck had built a sandwich shop up against a Chevron station, so Jimmy pulled off the side of the two-lane highway and parked the truck. We took a booth in the sandwich shop. A teenage waitress with a Southern accent as thick as a slab of ham took our order for two coffees and a cheese Danish for Jimmy.

Jimmy poured sugar into his coffee and kept pouring. I thought maybe he'd dozed off, but he cut the flow and dumped about two cows' worth of milk in after it.

"What are you making, cake batter?"

"Lay off."

"Don't get defensive."

"Okay," said Jimmy. "What gives?"

"We're being followed. Don't look around. Eat your Danish."

He took half the thing in the first bite and said, "Bring me up to speed."

"Mutt and Jeff in a black Ford Tempo."

"Since when?"

"Since Gainesville. I thought I'd given them the shake."

"Maybe not," said Jimmy.

"They're at the pay phone across from the pumps, waiting for us and pretending to make a call."

Jimmy raised an eyebrow. "You sure?"

"No." It *looked* like the same car.

"We got to be sure."

"I know."

Jimmy frowned. "We can't lose them in the moving van."

"No."

"Well, shit."

"Let's pay for this and get going."

"What about our buddies?" Jimmy asked.

"Like you said. We need to be sure."

We drove for a while. The jokers in the Tempo stayed at a discreet distance, but they were definitely tailing us. They probably thought they were doing a good job.

"Pull into that Burger King up there," I said. "I'll get to the bottom of this shit."

FIFTEEN

After Jimmy parked the moving van, I told him to sit in a window seat inside the Burger King so our shadows could keep an eye on him from the parking lot. I sat with him for a minute.

"What if they're Feds?" asked Jimmy.

I'd thought of that, but it seemed more likely the Tempo on our tail were Beggar's boys trying to track down those ledgers. I'd been thinking a lot about Alan Jeffers. He knew I had the books. I was supposed to bring them to him, but it looked like he was turning rat, willing to hand over the books to the FBI. But if that were the case, why hadn't Agent Dunn put the squeeze on me? I kept chewing that question over in my mind, but only one answer even came close to making sense.

Jeffers was playing both sides. He told the FBI he was trying to get the books for them, and he told Beggar he was doing the same thing for him. In the middle sat Alan Jeffers, thumbing coke up his nose and wondering how he was going to pull his ass out of the meat-grinder.

So I didn't think they were Feds following me, because Alan Jeffers hadn't told them they should. I didn't take the time to explain all this to Jimmy. I just told him to trust me.

"I'll be back. Stay in the window where they can see you."

"What for?"

"Because you're decoy-boy."

"What're you going to do?"

"Just wait."

Jimmy looked worried as I left him.

I high-stepped it out the other side of the restaurant and circled behind. From between two Dumpsters, I could see the goons in the Tempo. They smoked cigarettes and watched Jimmy through the window. I watched for a minute, but they didn't look like they suspected anything. I continued my wide circle behind the gas station, all the time keeping an eye on the Tempo, but they didn't notice me. I ducked into the gas station.

Inside, I bought a cheap pocketknife, a thick, souvenir Florida State Seminoles throw pillow, and a roll of duct tape. You can do abso-fucking-lutely anything with duct tape. Astronauts should take a dozen rolls on every shuttle mission.

The girl behind the register raised an eyebrow.

"Don't ask."

I locked myself in the men's room around the side of the gas station. A quick glance on the way in told me Tweedle Dee and Tweedle Dum were still keeping watch on the Burger King. I cut a slit down the side of the Seminole throw pillow. I fished one of the automatics out of my shoulder holster and jammed it into the pillow, where it nested tightly in the heart of the stuffing. I wrapped the pillow in duct tape and kept wrapping until I'd used half the roll. The whole thing was now a tight wad of stuffing armored with several layers of tape. I dropped the knife into my pants pocket and threw away the rest of the tape.

The pillow looked like a misshapen, armadillo-skinned football. I tucked it under my arm and headed for the Tempo. They were either amateurs, or they let themselves get too comfortable watching Jimmy through the BK window. In any case, I came upon them and swung open the back door on the passenger side without any resistance. I slid into the backseat and slammed the door as they jerked around frowning at the surprise of me.

"What in the hell—"

"Shaddup." I pulled the automatic out of the pillow and showed it to them. "Keep still, and do like I tell you. Get your hands up where I can see them."

They put their hands up on the steering wheel and dash-board. "I don't know who you think you are, but—"

"You're even dumber than you look." I let him feel the auto-matic's cool metal on the back of his neck. He was the one in the passenger side. Clearly another low-forehead type in a cheap suit and three-dollar haircut. The guy behind the wheel was a stick figure with one of those Don Juan skinny mustaches and an overbite that gave him a rat look. "You just talk when I tell you, and we can all be chums."

Before some passerby phoned the law, I brought the auto-matic down and stuffed it back in the pillow, keeping a loose finger on the trigger. Both of them faced forward waiting for me to speak. They didn't look particularly worried, so I knew this wasn't their first picnic. I'd need to get tough.

The one with the cheap haircut *tsked* at me. He was taking the hard line. "Pal, I think you need to reconsider your posi-tion. If you knew who we—"

I pulled the pistol out of the pillow again and smacked the barrel across the base of his skull. He grunted, bent forward and stayed there, moaning softly and rubbing his new lump.

"You dipshit," said the other, "you just assaulted a federal officer. That's five years hard time. You want to try for more?"

"What the fuck are you talking about?"

"Okay, now listen." He said the words slowly, like he was talking to a dog or a retard. "I'm going to go into my jacket for my badge. No funny stuff. I promise."

I pointed the gun at him. "Slow."

He came out with the standard-issue billfold, flipped it open. A badge. An ID that said he was FBI Agent Nicholas Styles. He nodded at his buddy in the passenger seat. "He's Agent Novak. He'd show you his ID too, but he's not feeling so well."

God damn. They *were* Feds.

"Now, how about handing over that gun, Swift? It's really your only option."

"Just hold on a second." I'd really stepped in it this time. I had to think.

"The longer you wait, the worse it gets for you, Swift," said Styles. "Just hand me the gun."

"I said shut up a minute."

Novak groaned. The knot on the back of his head was swelling good and quick.

"He might have a concussion."

"So what?"

"So if he sustains some sort of serious injury because you prevented me from getting him to a doctor, and then he dies, I guess you can tack on a murder charge."

I knew I hadn't hit him hard enough for that, but I was getting flustered. I had to get control of the situation again. People were going in and out of the gas station, and I remembered I was waving a pistol around. I stuck it back in the pillow.

"What's it going to be, Swift?"

I decided I should be the one asking questions. "What are you tailing me for?"

"Orders."

"You can do better than that."

"How many times do I have to say it?" asked Styles. "We're the FBI. We don't answer to cheap hoods."

"I don't care if you're J. Edgar Hoover in a ball gown," I said. "Did Agent Dunn put you on my tail?" Dunn had warned me to skip town. Maybe he'd set these two jerks the task of making sure I left.

At the mention of Dunn's name Novak lifted his head, and he and Styles looked at each other a moment. It wasn't much, but it was enough to tell me something was going on.

"Of course," said Styles. "Orders from Dunn. Who else?"

Who else? Good question.

I said, "Okay. Call Dunn. We'll wait for him. I'll surrender to him. Nice and quiet." It wasn't much of a bluff, but I'd sensed some kind of chink in the armor at the mention of Dunn's name. I had to see how they'd react.

Novak spoke first, but not to me. To Styles. "Nick, we can't call Dunn. He'll—"

"Quiet!" Styles shifted his eyes from me to Novak and back. "Enough of your double-talk, Swift. Stalling for time won't help you."

I nodded to myself, tried not to let my smile show. They might've been big-shot FBI agents, but they were basically still cops, and like all cops they'd come to depend on people falling into line whenever they flashed their badges. I'd seen past the badge, and I saw only a couple of jokers trying to pull a bluff.

"You don't have orders to tail me at all, do you?"

"Don't be moronic, Swift."

"Doing a little overtime work, eh boys?" I smiled openly now. "What did you think? That I'd lead you to those ledgers?"

Novak groaned louder.

"Can't you see he's hurt?" said Styles.

"Too bad."

Novak really groaned this time, and I leaned forward to tell him to put a sock in it. He twisted suddenly in his seat and reached over at me. He grabbed my wrist with one hand, went for the gun-pillow with the other. What happened next was strictly reflex.

I squeezed the automatic's trigger inside the pillow, and the stuffing dulled the report to a thick *fwup*. The .45 slug tore through the back of the seat and found a home in Novak's back. He wheezed, twitched once, and fell over his folded hands on the dash like he'd fallen asleep at prayer.

"Shit!" The blood drained from Styles's face. I thought he might be sick. "God, Swift, what'd you do?"

"The same thing that's going to happen to you if you don't answer some questions." I had to keep talking tough, had to keep control of the situation, but inside my guts churned. What *had* I done?

"Jesus, Swift." He was shaking his head, looking at his buddy. "Don't kill me, okay?" He started breathing hard and sniffling. I thought he was ready to start the waterworks.

"Knock it off," I said. "Think hard and answer my question."

"What fucking question?" He voice was strained. He talked to me, but his eyes stayed on Novak.

"Why are you tailing me? I know Dunn didn't put you up to it, so don't try to tell me he did. I can smell it every time you lie."

"Like you said. We wanted the ledgers."

"Why?"

"Why? What do you mean why, you son of a bitch? They outline Beggar Johnson's whole operation. Whoever has those ledgers has Beggar by the throat."

"So if I have them, I guess I'm pretty big shit."

"You'd get Beggar's attention, that's for sure."

"That's all I wanted to know."

I pulled the trigger, and the automatic belched inside the pillow, spit lead and stuffing at Styles. He fell over the steering wheel dead.

I kept telling myself I had to do it. I was already up to my neck for killing Novak. I might have gotten away with the four agents I'd popped in Toppers, but Novak had been different. Styles had seen me. If I let Styles go, I'd have every cop in the state on my ass within an hour. This was how I explained it all to myself. This was how I tried to convince myself I was still in control of the situation.

So why were my hands shaking so much when I reached inside Styles's jacket and then Novak's? I pulled out their badges and slipped them into my jacket pocket. It wasn't that I wanted some morbid souvenir. I just knew these guys would be found sooner or later. Maybe the gas station owner would notice the car had been there a while. A couple of dead bodies would cause a fuss, but a couple of dead FBI guys would set off alarms all over the place. I figured I could toss the badges in a Dumpster down the road.

I climbed out of the Tempo, closed the door, looked all around, over my shoulder. As far as I could tell, nobody had taken notice of me or seen what I'd done.

I walked back toward the Burger King, feet leaden, arms rubbery. How had everything gone so horribly down the shitter? I felt overwhelmed, that I was screwing this all up, leaving a trail of bodies a blind man could follow. Any minute now the Feds would swoop down on me with the handcuffs or Beggar's boys would come along and throw a sack over me.

Forget it. I'd had enough.

I went into the Burger King. "Let's go," I said to Jimmy.

"What happened?"

I started walking out, motioned for him to follow.

"Take me back to my car."

"What? Why?"

"I'm tired."

He saw my duct tape pillow. "What the hell's that?"

I ignored his question. "I'm going home. You were right. Stan's dead or gone."

"We don't know that." Jimmy waddled after me, out of the Burger King and into the parking lot. "What about the warehouse?"

"Forget it."

"Forget it?"

"That's right." I climbed into the moving van's passenger seat and waited for Jimmy to drive. He hauled himself into the van's cab with a grunt and settled his gut behind the wheel.

I made it clear I didn't want to talk. He drove back to his house where my car was parked. I got out and walked around to his side of the van, and he rolled down the window.

"Sorry, Jimmy. But this was all crazy from the beginning. I should've just taken everybody's advice and disappeared. We can't help Stan. You should go too, Jimmy, or you'll end up like Larry Cartwright and Bob Tate. Take your kid and go. There's no magic stash of money, and only God can help Stan now."

"Sheesh, Charlie, I don't know what to say. Call if you hear something."

"I won't. I'm leaving town."

"I mean it," said Jimmy. "Just get some rest. Things will settle down."

"Sure, Jimmy."

I got in my car and drove away.

I pulled up in front of my apartment slowly. I hadn't been there in a while, but somebody might still be waiting around to do me some harm. I got out and climbed the stairs, my eyes darting into every shadow. Seemed safe enough. I went inside with guns drawn, but there was no need. All clear.

I went to grab my green duffel bag and remembered it was full of incriminating accounting ledgers in an airport locker. I took a big red Samsonite suitcase from underneath the bed and put it on top. Opened it. I shoved in about a week's worth of shirts and underwear and socks. An extra pair of shoes. I put in two more suits, tried to fold them in easy so they wouldn't wrinkle too bad. I saw my *National Geographic* on the table and tossed it in. The rest of my stuff could rot. I almost packed my toothbrush when I remembered I hadn't used it in a while.

I went into the bathroom and brushed my teeth. It occurred to me I was greasy and messed up. I stripped out of my smelly clothes and let them drop on the bathroom floor. I kept my revolver close by on the sink just in case. The shower was warm. I just stood in the hot water a long time, maybe twenty minutes. It felt like the best thing in the world. When the hot water started losing strength, I shut off the shower and stepped out. The wound on my side had started to scab okay, so I didn't bandage it again.

I looked at my bed. Tempting. No. I'd fooled around long enough. Time to get the hell out of Dodge. Everything else could go to hell. I toweled off, climbed into a dark gray suit, and strapped my guns back on. I grabbed my suitcase.

Adios, fuckers.

I put my hand on the doorknob.

The phone rang.

The little guy in my head who tries to keep me out of trouble shouted *don't pick it up, dumbass*.

I picked it up.

"Yeah?"

A brief pause, then: "Charlie?"

"Marcie?"

"Oh, Charlie. For God's sake where have you been?" She sounded frazzled. "I've been calling and calling."

"What's wrong? Are you okay?"

"No, I mean, I am now. But I need you."

"Slow down. What is it?"

"Not on the phone. Come over."

I glanced at my suitcase. "I'm right in the middle of something here, hon."

"CHARLIE, COME OVER RIGHT FUCKING NOW!"

"Okay, okay. Take it easy. Just calm down. I'm on my way."

"I'm sorry. I didn't mean to yell. Just please come over."

"Okay. It'll be okay. I'll fix it." I didn't know what it was yet, but I'd fix it.

I hung up after promising about twenty more times that I was on my way. I checked my guns, and everything was go. I got back in my Buick and headed for Marcie's house at top speed.

Halfway there I realized I hadn't brought the suitcase.

SIXTEEN

Marcie was waiting for me on the front porch, sitting on the top step, her elbows resting on her knees, a gin and tonic the size of a fireman's bucket cupped in her little pink hands. On first glance she looked like she was just enjoying a well-deserved drink after a tough day's work.

As I walked closer I saw a different story. Her hair was messed up. The top two buttons of her blouse had been torn off. Her bottom lip was swollen and purple.

I looked down at her, touched her lip gently with two fingers. I was shaking, not with fear this time but with anger. "Who did this?"

"I don't know his name." Her voice was a little loose. Probably not her first gin and tonic. Probably not her last.

"What did he look like? What did he want?" I'd find him. I'd find whoever did this and plant him in the ground six feet under.

Marcie raised an eyebrow. "You want to know what he looked like?" She curled a finger at me. "Follow me."

I followed. She led me through the kitchen and out to the garage where she kept her giant, dead polar bear.

She pointed at the dead body on the floor. "That's what he looks like. Familiar?"

"What the fuck happened?"

"I—" Her voice caught. When she started talking again, she didn't sound so casual. "He came in looking for you, came to the door and—he pushed me in, it was so f-fast—" She began crying, moved forward into my arms. I hugged. She hugged back tight, burying her face into my chest. I stroked her hair.

I recognized the guy bleeding on the floor. Vincent, one of the goons who worked for Beggar. He'd been there when I'd passed off Sanchez's body as Rollo Kramer. I didn't think it would help Marcie to know his name, so I just kept hugging.

Abruptly, she pushed back from me, wiped the tears from her eyes. She frowned then laughed. "I hate you seeing me like this." She sniffed. "Damn it, I feel like such a little idiot."

"It's okay."

"It's not okay. I'm too old to act like some little crybaby bitch." She squared her shoulders, took a long pull at her gin and tonic. And just like that she was a rock, totally in control of herself, confident. At least that's the show she was putting on. I'd seen past that to the fragile woman behind the tough shell. I'd seen it, if only for a few seconds.

I put on a pot of coffee, and we sat at the kitchen table. When it was ready, I poured myself a cup. I offered her some, but she shook her head and fixed herself another gin and tonic. I thought about telling her to ease up, but then I figured she probably knew what she was doing.

"Let's hear about it," I said.

"Sure." She took one more big gulp before starting.

"I was just sitting around watching television," said Marcie. "I was hoping you'd call, actually. There was a knock on the door, and I saw him through the peephole. I'd never seen him before, so I asked who he was through the door. He said he was a friend of yours and he had a message for me. I was so eager to get the message I didn't even stop to think it was a trick."

She slapped the palm of her hand against her forehead. "Stupid. I can't believe I was so dumb."

"It's okay."

"Will you stop saying it's okay? It's not fucking okay. It was stupid. I wasn't born yesterday, you know. I know how things work."

Right.

She jumped back into her story. Once the guy had gotten inside, he grabbed her. She tried to get away, but he convinced her to cooperate by getting rough. That's where the torn buttons and purple lip came in. She'd had too much experience with tough guys from her marriage to Rollo, so she knew she'd have to play along or get another knuckle job. But she was still thinking, her mind always working.

The tough guy came straight out and said he was looking for a set of accounting books, and he had a pretty good idea that Marcie's boyfriend had hidden them with her someplace.

I cringed inwardly. That's almost what had happened. I'd almost left the books parked under a raccoon in Marcie's freezer.

The guy asked Marcie if she'd heard of Beggar Johnson.

She'd said she had.

Then he asked her if she knew what Beggar would have him do to her if she jerked us around.

Marcie said she knew.

"Okay, then," the guy had said. "Now be a good girl and take me to those books, and I can let you get back to your life."

"But I knew it didn't work that way," said Marcie. "These kind of guys use you up until there's nothing left you can do for them. Then they get rid of you. So I kept thinking how was I going to get myself out of this mess. I told him the books were in the garage. I figured I could get ahold of a rake or a hammer or something, maybe hit him in the head or…I don't know what I was thinking really, but I had to try something."

She was right, of course. Vincent almost certainly had instructions to get rid of Marcie after he'd found the books. I sipped my coffee.

"So we go into the garage." Marcie finished her drink, started chewing the ice. "But the guy must've sensed I was getting ready to try something, or maybe he was just the suspicious type. He grabbed me and pulled me behind him, said he wanted to go in first—except the garage is dark. He felt along the wall for the light switch, and when he didn't find it, I told him there was a string hanging down from the ceiling to turn on the lights."

Suddenly I knew how this story was going to end, and I couldn't help smiling to myself.

Marcie saw me, and her lips curled into a smile too. She was trying to be serious about telling me what happened, but her knowing that I knew what was coming made it morbidly funny, and we were both grinning big as she told me what happened.

"So he takes these careful steps forward into the dark garage so he doesn't walk into something," said Marcie. "And he's swinging his hand back and forth trying to catch the string. When he finally gets it, he says 'got it' like he's so proud of himself." Marcie giggled, but tears rimmed her eye. "And then he jerked that string." She laughed hard now, had to catch her breath before she could continue. "And then—and then he saw the bear, and he screamed—" Big laughs now, her whole body shaking. "I mean, like a little girl, he's screaming. He backs right into me, our feet tangle up, and we both go down in a pile. But he drops the gun." Her laughter trailed off. "I scrambled after it. He tried to grab at my legs, hold me back, but I'd already grabbed the gun. It was heavy."

No laughter now at all. Her face was blank. "And he lunged for me, and I pulled the trigger, and just like that he was dead. He fell over, blood spreading on his chest." She heaved a big sigh. "One minute he was walking and talking, and the next he was just meat, like something I'd brought home from the zoo to stuff and mount."

"I'm sorry, Marcie. It's my fault. I put you in a bad position."

"You sure as hell did." She tried to make a joke out of it, and the smile returned to her lips for a split second, but it couldn't hang on, and her face was blank again.

This was why guys like me and Bob Tate and even Rollo Kramer always lost wives and girlfriends. We were walking danger zones, and everyone around us suffered. Then I had a bad thought and I told Marcie I had to use the kitchen phone.

I dialed Ma, and Danny picked up after three rings. "Yo."

"Danny, it's Charlie."

"Jesus, Charlie, where the hell you been? Some guy named Lou Morgan's been ringing the phone off the hook for you."

"Later," I said. "Right now I want to know what's going on over there."

"Over here? Nothing. Amber and I are watching television, and Ma—"

"What's Amber doing there?"

"You said to stick around the house and keep an eye on Ma," Danny reminded me. "Since I couldn't go to Amber's place, she came here."

"Listen to me. I want you to tell Ma to pack a suitcase. No, make that two suitcases."

"Huh? What for? Charlie, what's going on?"

"We're playing it safe. That's all. Put Ma on the phone."

I heard Danny yell at Ma to come in the living room. I waited. She picked up after a few seconds.

"Charlie?"

"Ma, pack up whatever you think is important and get to the airport. I want you to stay with Aunt Irene, okay?" Aunt Irene was Ma's younger sister.

"Is there trouble, Charlie?" Ma sounded suddenly sharp. She walked around all day doing her old lady act, but when the heat was on she knew better than to argue. Ma wasn't stupid.

"There might be, Ma. I'm sorry. Better if you're in Michigan with Irene."

"I understand. You make it right while I'm gone."

"Sure, Ma. Put Danny back on will you?"

"Charlie?"

"Yes?"

"You're my son."

"I know, Ma."

"Be careful."

"I will."

She put Danny back on the phone.

"What do I do?" he asked.

"I want you out of there in thirty minutes. Call me here right before you leave so I'll know you're away." I told him Marcie's number. "You got that?"

"Right. Thirty minutes. I'm on it."

"Good. I got to go." I started to hang up.

"Charlie, wait."

"What?"

"What about this Morgan guy? He keeps calling for you."

Shit. I'd forgotten all about Lou. Marcie kept a pen and a basket of scrap paper near the phone. I picked out a piece and grabbed the pen. "Did he leave a number?"

"Sure."

"Give."

Danny told me the number, and I wrote. I didn't recognize it.

"Thanks, Danny. Call ahead and book a flight into Detroit while Ma's packing."

"Check. Call you in thirty."

We hung up, and I felt a little better. Marcie had almost been killed because of her association with me. I didn't want any of Beggar's goons showing up to Ma's house because they thought I might have hidden the ledgers there. But if they did, I wanted Ma long gone. I didn't tell Danny or Ma, but I sort of had the idea Ma would run out the clock in Michigan. Orlando was all done with the Swift family.

Marcie must have had similar notions, because she came out of her bedroom with a suitcase in each hand, pantyhose streaming from the bags where she hadn't zipped them up all the way.

I scrunched my face at her. "What the hell's this?"

"What does it look like? I'm getting out of here."

"What? Where?"

"Someplace where my getting killed doesn't happen," she said. She threw the suitcases down hard, went into the bedroom, and came back again with a garment bag. "I still have the five thousand from Rollo. I'll call after I find someplace, arrange for a real estate agent to dump the house on someone."

"Marcie."

"Maybe I'll go to New Mexico. I've always wanted to try the desert."

"Marcie."

"I could try stuffing prairie dogs. Oh, buffalo! I could do a lot with a buffalo."

"Marcie!" She stopped, looked at me. I spread my hands, my face a raw question mark. "What about me?" And as soon as the question left my mouth, I felt like some little kid left out in the cold, standing there the first day of kindergarten as my mom pulled away in the car.

"You? What about *you*?" Marcie threw her garment bag down on the other bags, kicked the whole pile of luggage with a savage grunt. "You. All those guys working for Beggar are you. Rollo, he was you too. I married him. Where'd that get me? And it was you that tried to kill me today. It was you I shot dead. That's what about you!"

"Okay, okay." I was nodding my head up and down fast while she was talking, trying to show real hard I understood what she meant. "I don't blame you. But I'm going to fix it. I'm going to wipe the whole slate clean, and we can go anyplace you want and start over."

"Bullshit."

"No. Really." I moved forward quick, grabbed up both of her hands between mine, searched her eyes with my own. "We haven't known each other long, but I want to be with you. I'm going to do some things, set them right, but when that's finished I'm starting all over. I won't have anything. I want to have you."

She sighed, heavy and tired. "You're such a corny dumbass."

"It's all true."

"What's this stuff you need to set right?"

"Stan." And as soon as I said it, I knew I'd go all the way. It wasn't a loose end I could live with.

"He's probably dead, you know." Marcie wasn't trying to be insensitive, just frank.

"I know. But I have to know what happened. And I have to do what I can about it. He was like a dad. What if it was your dad?"

She nodded, chewed her lip thinking about it, looked down at her shoes. "I understand." Then she looked back up at me, hard, that toughness coming back into her eyes. "But I'll be damned if I'm going to sit around this house and wait for some wise guy to come and put a bullet in my head."

"No." I took out my rapidly dwindling roll of cash, peeled off a wad of fifties, and handed her the bills. "Get a hotel, a good one."

"Where?"

"Near the airport. We might be leaving in a hurry."

"Okay." She made the money disappear into her blouse, and we stepped toward each other. We hugged long and with the relief of decisions made. She knew where she stood now, and I knew what I had to do.

She broke the embrace and said, "Come on. You've got to help me before you go."

I followed her into the garage, and she picked up the dead guy by the ankles. "Get the other end, will you?"

I gripped him under the shoulders and lifted. "This is how we met, isn't it?" I grinned.

She batted her eyes at me. "You're so fucking romantic."

"What are we going to do with this bastard?"

"Get him over to my worktable," she said. "I'll cut up some trash bags to put around him. We'll wrap the whole thing in duct tape. You can do *anything* with duct tape."

It was then I knew I was in love with her.

SEVENTEEN

By the time we finished wrapping up the corpse, Danny called. He said Ma had a flight in ninety minutes, and they were making for the airport. I said I had an errand, but I'd meet him back at Ma's house after. We wished each other luck.

Marcie and I dumped the guy's body in a shopping center Dumpster about ten miles away. I covered him over with trash and cardboard boxes. Nobody saw us. I took Marcie home.

She kissed me on the cheek as I left. "The Airport Hilton. Hurry and finish your business, or I'll leave your ass here."

I scooped her close and gave her a more serious kiss square on the lips. She hugged back, and our tongues met. She pulled away breathless. "That was nice, but you still have to hurry."

She left in her Volvo, and I headed for Ma's. When I got there, the driveway was empty. Ma hadn't had a car for a few years. Danny must have still been on his way back from the airport. I let myself in, found a Pepsi in the refrigerator, and opened it. I sat at the kitchen table, sipped cola and waited.

I remembered Lou and snapped my fingers, leapt to my feet, and went into the living room, grabbed the phone and sat in Dad's old chair by the window. I dialed, and Lou answered in two rings. "Yeah?"

"What's up, New Guy?"

"Stop calling me that."

I ignored his request. "What did you find out?"

"I went to Stan's like you said. Nice house, locked up tighter than a drum, but I figured this is a special case so I broke in a bedroom window."

"Good."

"Didn't find anything though. I went through the whole place twice. Nobody's there."

"Any signs of a struggle?"

"Hell if I know. What are the signs of a struggle nowadays?"

"Blood," I said. "Bullet holes. Furniture knocked over. Use your imagination."

"Nope. Nothing like that."

That's what I'd figured. I'd given up trying to call, and I'd been pretty sure Lou wouldn't find anything, but I had to be certain. I'd have felt pretty stupid tear-assing all over the state looking for Stan if he were lying dead in his own living room the whole time.

"Where are you, by the way?" I asked.

"Phone booth near the ABC Liquor on Goldenrod," said Lou.

"The whole time?"

"Back and forth. Another fifteen minutes I'd have been on my way to the Arby's across the street."

Whatever. "You know what to do next?"

"I remember."

"Keep your distance when you get over there." I wanted Lou to get over to Heathrow and keep an eye on Jeffers's house. With Feds and Beggar's men coming and going, it seemed like a good idea to know what was going on.

"Don't worry. Later, man."

"Later, New Guy."

"Don't call me New—"

I hung up.

I didn't like waiting, but there wasn't any choice. I needed to see Danny. I started poking around the living room. The house was strangely quiet without Danny shouting at me or Ma throwing together some grub in the kitchen. I opened the hall closet and found Dad's collection of *National Geographic*. They were lined up in order, seventeen years' worth, only the one with the Polynesian article missing. I pulled a few down and scanned through them until I found one that talked about the Yucatan Peninsula. It had maps and large color photographs of the pyramids.

I was about halfway through it when Danny and Amber pulled into Ma's driveway. I set the magazine aside and opened the door for them. Danny walked in, leading Amber by the hand.

They immediately started with the questions, but I told them that would have to wait until later.

"You guys got to get out of here. There's people probably looking for me right now. You don't want to be with me if they find me."

"Let me help," said Danny. "If you're really in that much trouble, you could use an extra hand."

I squeezed his shoulder, smiled at him. He was a good kid. "I know I can count on you, but it's more important you take care of this." I'd taken the airport locker key off my ring. I gave it to him. "You keep that someplace hidden."

He shoved it in the pocket of his jeans. "I'll think of someplace later."

"Not too much later. You got a place to stay?"

"He can stay with me," said Amber.

I thought about that a second. Sure. That should work. "Sounds good. I'm sure Danny has no objection."

They smiled at each other. Amber blushed. Danny just beamed like he had the world in his pocket. I didn't blame him. She was a good catch. I handed Amber the *National Geographic* with the Mexico stuff and told her to write her phone number on the cover.

"Go pack," I told Danny. He started up the stairs, and I

grabbed his arm. "Pack like you're not coming back. Understand?"

He nodded and took the stairs two a time.

While he was gone, I turned to Amber. "You know Ma and I have been trying to get him back in school."

"I know."

"Do you think you can have any better luck with him than we have?"

Amber smiled big, and somewhere a chorus of violins played. "Oh, he's going back to school. He just doesn't know it yet."

"You're a good girl."

Danny came back down with a tote bag over his shoulder. He assured me nothing would happen to the key as long as he was on the job. He thought he was still auditioning for the monkey cage. Amber would cure him of that. He grabbed me up in a big bear hug, and I hugged back. Amber kissed me on the cheek and squeezed my arm.

"Enough with the mush," I said. "You two get out of here."

I watched them pull out of the driveway, disappear down the block. I went inside and picked up the phone again, dialed Jimmy the Fix. He picked up after five rings.

I asked, "You still have that moving van?"

I tried to convince Jimmy to drive in like we were making a routine delivery.

He frowned at my plan. "I went out there and had a look yesterday after I dropped you off. This isn't a warehouse on the normal delivery route. There's a guard on the gate, but I've never seen him before. I don't know what's going on in there."

"We'll figure something out." I was beyond worrying about it. I just wanted to get on with things.

We passed the Burger King next to the gas station where I'd

deep-sixed the G-men. The car wasn't there anymore. There wasn't any sign that anything had happened at all. We continued into the sticks, a little past Bithlo. Boondocks.

"Who's your favorite character from *The Wizard of Oz*?" I asked Jimmy as the moving van approached the chain-link gate in front of the warehouse.

I thought he'd balk at the question, but he answered lightly. "The wizard, I guess. Except he's stupid to get in the balloon at the end."

I raised an eyebrow, and a smile crept across my face. "He's just going home."

"Home." Jimmy said the word like it had taken a crap in his mouth. "That's what you leave so you can make good. The wizard's got the whole Emerald City under his thumb, and he gives it up to float off with some skirt and her dog. You ever been to Kansas? It's like elevator music with grass."

"Here we go," I said as we got to the gate. I noticed my duct tape pillow still in the floor of the van. I grabbed it, slid one of my automatics inside. There was still enough stuffing to muffle my shots.

I ducked as he pulled the moving van through the gate, and when he stopped, I slipped out the passenger side, closing the van door quietly behind me. By the time I made it around the back of the van, the guard on the gate was at Jimmy's window. He must've been squatting behind a tree or something, because I hadn't seen him on the way through. I had the gun-pillow handy and took about four steps before the guard saw me and swung a serious-looking 12-gauge in my direction. I brought the pillow up and squeezed two shots into his belly before he could fire. Pillow stuffing flew ahead of me with each shot like a cartoon snowstorm. He fell hard, his shotgun dropping to the gravel road.

Jimmy stuck his head out the van window. "Get him into the shrubs."

I dragged Mr. Dead into the bushes by his heels. I checked his pockets for extra shotgun shells but didn't find any. I picked up the shotgun and climbed back into the passenger seat. "Drive."

I checked the shotgun's load. It held six double-ought shells. The pillow was about out of stuffing, so it was past its prime as a silencer. I tossed it out the window and returned the automatic to its shoulder holster. I pulled a pair of latex gloves out of my pants pocket and put them on.

Jimmy parked the van in front of the warehouse, and when nobody came out to squirt lead at us, I told him to keep his revolver loose and wait.

"Anybody comes at you, cut loose on them with your .38," I said to Jimmy. "Don't follow me in there, or I'll shoot you by mistake. Got it?"

Jimmy nodded. He looked pale.

"Just stay here and protect yourself." I tried to sound reassuring. "I'll be doing the rough work."

"Right."

I kept the shotgun low and strolled up to the loading dock door nice and casual, like Avon calling. I tried the knob. It was unlocked, so I went in. A short hall. One end opened into the warehouse, a maze of crates and boxes. The other end of the hall ended at an office. I started toward it, and a young man emerged in denim and flannel. He was just out of his teens, fair-haired, thin. He had a half-eaten sandwich in his fist and chewed earnestly. He spotted me and the 12-gauge and froze.

I brought the shotgun up slowly, pointed it at his chest. "Nice and easy." I tried to keep the tension out of my voice and was surprised to succeed. "Back into the office." He nodded, and I followed him in.

A square, wooden table dominated the center of the little office, and three men in work clothes sat around it. Denim, more flannel, work boots, feed caps. They started pushing away from the table at the sight of me, but sat still again when I kicked the door closed and pumped a shell into the shotgun's chamber.

The table was covered with empty potato chip bags and playing cards. "On break, huh boys?"

They didn't say anything.

"Anyone carrying a gun?"

They shook their heads.

I lifted my chin at the fair-haired kid with the sandwich. "What're you all doing here?"

He licked his lips and darted his eyes at his buddies. No help there. He looked back at me and said, "We're waiting to close the place up. Everyone else went home."

I looked at their faces. One scared, one angry, two blank. One of those office phones with buttons for an intercom hung on the wall. I ripped it down and tossed it in the corner.

"Where's your boss?" I asked the kid.

His eyes darted to his buddies again.

"I didn't ask them, kid. I asked you." I didn't quite point the shotgun at him, but I held it up and reminded him it was there.

"Upstairs," he said. "There's a spiral staircase across the warehouse, and he's got the big office up there."

"What's his name?"

"Norman," said the kid.

I knew that name. The other guy from the parking garage.

"Who's with him?"

"Frank and Emery."

I didn't know them; it didn't matter.

"Anyone else?"

"No."

"What about an old man?"

"Not that I've seen."

"Guns?"

The kid's mouth hung open, and he shrugged. He looked anxious at not being able to answer.

One of his pals jumped in to help out. He was older, a salt-and-pepper beard and a green John Deere cap. "I'd guess so, partner. I sure never seen 'em lift anything when the trucks come in."

"What trucks?"

"We've been loading trucks all day, cardboard boxes. Couldn't tell you what's in 'em. But that's all we do. Just lift and move."

I nodded slowly, letting the silence stretch, letting them sweat a little. Finally, I said, "Count to sixty, then get out of here. Don't come back. Don't even look back. There's a world of shit coming down. You understand?"

They nodded.

I backed out of the room and closed the door. I threaded my way through the warehouse and found the spiral staircase at the rear. Halfway up the stairs I heard the distant *pop pop pop* of a pistol outside. Jimmy. I grit my teeth. He'd have to be on his own.

I double-timed it up the stairs, and just as I hit the landing, one of Norman's goons erupted from the office with a pistol in his hand. They must've heard the shots, because he came out looking for trouble and leveled his piece at me.

The shotgun bucked in my hands, and the double-ought pellets tore across his chest, a grease splatter of ruby geysers on his white shirt and striped tie. He stumbled back two halting steps, teetered for balance, then fell forward. I rushed the office door hoping to catch Norman and his other man before they could get their ducks in a row.

Once inside, events slowed. I no longer had surprise on my side, so I had to choose my targets carefully. I didn't see faces, only arms and legs and hands holding guns as I took in the situation instantly. And somewhere, in the distant reaches of the lump of rock I laughingly called a brain, I realized I'd made a terrible mistake. If I'd had one of my automatics in each hand like usual, I'd have been able to take them both. But I could only point the shotgun at one.

Norman stood behind the desk. He went for something in the top drawer. The man on my left was too close. He stuck a revolver in my face, and I saw the chamber turn in slow motion as he squeezed the trigger. I didn't have time to do anything but slap my left hand over the end of the barrel, my fingers closing over the gun, pushing it away.

The bullet tore through my palm and exited the back of my hand as I fought down a wave of nausea. I pointed the shotgun in his general direction the best I could with one hand and blasted him in the knee. He collapsed, screaming from the bottom of his throat.

I dropped the shotgun and turned on Norman as I drew the .38 from my belly holster.

He was faster.

He fired twice and one bullet whizzed past my ear, the second taking off a chunk of my right earlobe. I ducked, unloading all six bullets at him. Four slugs tore through a stack of file folders on his desk, sending papers leaping into the air. The fifth caught him low in the belly, the last in the center of his chest. Norman fell stiffly across his desk, rolled off it and landed hard on a large cardboard box. The man with the destroyed kneecap was still screaming.

I shuffled over to him, turned the pistol around in my hand. Three swift strikes with the butt of the pistol at the base of his skull finished him. The room smelled like copper and gunpowder. I was about to throw up but kept it in. I was a bloody mess. My own blood on the left hand, his in my right from the pistol whipping. The fingers of my left glove filled with blood. I found the restroom and grabbed a wad of paper towels to slow the bleeding from my palm.

My head was light, my throat dry.

Back in the office, I searched the desk, didn't know what I was looking for. I'd come for answers and found bodies. I kicked the guy off the cardboard box and looked inside. Plastic bags wrapped in tight bundles. I grabbed a letter opener from the desk, ripped into one of the packages. A bundle of cash, old bills.

Stan wasn't here, and I hadn't found out dick.

Outside, I found Jimmy by the moving van, two of the warehouse workers dead at his feet. One was the fair-haired kid.

Jimmy got an eyeful of me. "Christ, Charlie. You okay?"

I ignored the question, still looking at the dead men. "What happened here?"

"They tried to make a run for it," said Jimmy. "Two others got away, but I nailed these two."

He sounded proud of himself, and I didn't bother to set him straight. Dumb son of a bitch.

"I'll call about a doctor," said Jimmy. "I think I know somebody safe."

He went into the warehouse.

I leaned against the van, my good hand holding me up. My stomach convulsed, and I tried to heave, but nothing would come up. I was sweating all over, and the pain was beginning to finally seep into my wounded hand.

I crawled into the front seat of the moving van and rested my head against the cool glass of the passenger window. Blood gushed with every heartbeat. My vision was going fuzzy.

Jimmy stormed out of the warehouse, his big belly quivering each time his foot hit the ground. It looked like he had an armload of shredded cabbage. He got right up in my face. "It's here, Charlie boy. We found it. It's here!"

I worked my mouth at him, tried to ask him what he was talking about. Stan? Had he found Stan? He was floating away from me. Blood trickled warmly from my ear and down my neck.

"You're fine, Charlie. I got you," said Jimmy. "You hang tough. We'll get you a doctor."

I could barely keep my eyes open, and I drifted off, dreaming of Jimmy in a balloon, dreaming I had wings.

EIGHTEEN

My instinct was to jerk free of the tubes and restraints, but I couldn't remember the last time an instinct had done me any good. I didn't have the strength anyway.

I pried open my eyes. It didn't help. Everything was a uniform blur. I blinked a few times, shook my head. My eyesight began to clear. The hospital room took shape around me. I had a tube in my arm and another in my nose. My hands were tied to the railings of the hospital bed. A thick bandage kept my left hand together. The hospital room looked like any other. I was alone. I let my head fall back on the pillow.

Marcie came into the room, saw my eyes open, and gasped. "That's just typical. I sit in here for five hours, and then you wake up the two minutes I go for a root beer."

I smiled weakly. "Hello." I was damn glad to see her, and my heart did a little flip-flop. She came closer, sitting on the edge of the bed.

"I'm glad you're here," I said.

She smiled, put her hand on my arm.

I tugged at the restraints around my wrists. "Get these off, will you?"

"The doctor said—"

"Marcie."

"Oh, fine." She untied me.

I scratched my ear. Relief.

"Don't pick at it." She frowned.

"It itches." I'd never have back the chunk of earlobe I'd lost in the warehouse shootout. I didn't think I'd miss it. But my ear was wrapped awkwardly in gauze, and it itched like hell.

She shook her head at my hand. "That's a shame. Now your head isn't symmetrical." She touched my wounded hand lightly. "Hey, do you know what stigmata are?"

"Something you get in your eye."

She snorted.

I took a look at my hand. Sooner or later, I'd have to take a peek under the bandage, but I wasn't eager. It seemed to ache in a dull, distant sort of way, and I suddenly understood I must've been full of dope, or it would've hurt a lot more. No wonder I'd been out cold. I mentioned this with a laugh to Marcie.

"Laugh it up, hotshot," said Marcie. "Painkillers aren't the only reason. You lost a lot of blood. When your friend called, I checked out of the hotel and drove straight here. You'd already finished surgery. I brought you something to cheer you up." She placed a stuffed rodent on the sheet over my chest. It looked at me cross-eyed, its tongue hanging out the side of its mouth. Lunacy.

"You thought a retarded rat would cheer me up?"

"It's a chinchilla. And it's supposed to be whimsical."

"Sorry. I love it. Really."

"Smartass. At least you're regaining your senses."

The memory came flooding back. Jimmy had arranged a doctor, and by the time he'd raced me to the hospital in the moving van, I was out of my head and drenched in my own blood. It was all fuzzy after that, a patchwork of memories involving doctors and nurses and people shining lights in my eyes, people who wanted blood and urine and whatever else they could get. Before I went under, I told Jimmy to call Marcie at the Hilton.

"Baby, thanks for coming." Had I said that already?

"Wild horses and all that." She ran a finger down the tube

that led to my arm. "Want me to hook this to a bottle of Chivas?"

"I don't think I should mix it with the dope." I was a little worried. I didn't handle narcotics well. God knew what I might do or say.

She turned serious, not a lot, not too somber. She just altered her tone enough to get my attention. "You were lucky, Charlie. It's just your hand. The doctor says you'll be able to use it again after physical therapy."

"Yeah."

Marcie was too supportive to harass me in my condition, but the look etched on her face said I was a dumbass. Considering the tubes in my nose and arm, I couldn't really argue. I wanted to tell her again it would all be over soon, but I wasn't sure even I believed that anymore. This sort of hospital visit had been one of the reasons she'd packed her bags. I mentally vowed to make it all up to her.

But at the moment, all I could do was lie there and soak in juice from a tube. I shouldn't have worried. Marcie was strong in the way that women who've been kicked around are strong, and there would come a time when she'd kick my ass for putting her through this. But not now, not while I was flat on my back.

She asked, "Can I get you anything?"

"Maybe a magazine."

"What do you want?"

"I don't know. A *National Geographic*."

"You got it. There's a Books-a-Million near here. Anything else?"

"I'm okay. Maybe flip on the TV before you leave."

She flipped on the TV to a shampoo commercial.

"Any particular channel?"

"I'll just watch whatever comes on here," I said.

"See you later, hon. Try not to freak out the nurses." She kissed my forehead and left.

The commercial ended, and a show called *The View* came on. Four mouthy broads started yakking it up. God, help me. At the end of the segment, the announcer said, "Coming up next: Know your vagina."

Holy shit.

I fished around desperately for the remote control, but it was nowhere in sight. I hit the nurse call button.

"Yes?" came a crisp voice.

"Drugs," I croaked into the intercom.

I felt stronger after my nap. A nurse came in with some Tupperware and demanded urine.

"I can't move," I said. I could still feel the painkillers coursing through my veins with giddy potency. "I hate to ask, but could you put that between my legs?"

Without comment, the nurse pulled back the covers. When she saw the chinchilla perched on my crotch, she half screamed before slapping a hand over her mouth.

I giggled like an idiot.

"Hilarious," she said, holding out the plastic jug within easy reach. "I see we're feeling better. Now how about a specimen?"

"I don't feel very productive right now."

"I understand," she said reasonably. "I'll come back with the catheter."

"Wait!" I waved her over. "Give me the jug. I already got enough tubes sticking in me."

She handed it over and said she'd be back for it in a little bit. I put it under the sheet and wedged it between my legs. I was feeling some pressure to perform. If I didn't squeeze out a little high-test...well, I'd rather have another bullet in the other hand.

I positioned myself and grunted. Nothing. I grunted harder. More nothing.

Jimmy walked in. "Hey, Charlie-boy. Sheesh! You don't look so good."

"Yeah...I...uhhhh." A couple of sad dribbles into the jug. I felt a cold sweat break out over my eyebrows and behind my ears. I was bone dry.

Jimmy frowned. "You want me to call a nurse?"

"No."

"You're turning all red."

"No!"

"But you look like you're gonna fucking rupture—"

"Uhhh. Arhh!" I got off a couple of good squirts and brought out the jug. The nurse must've had her piss-radar on, because that's when she walked in.

I handed her the jug, and she held it up to the light with disdain. Jimmy scooted in next to her, so he could squint at my piss for himself.

"Sheesh, Charlie-boy, if you were a horse, they'd shoot you."

The nurse swirled it around in the jug, still examining it closely.

Jimmy said, "Sniff the cork, why don't you?"

She scowled and left.

Jimmy shook his head. "If that's how you look when you're taking a leak, I'd hate to be around when you're dropping a log."

"Don't worry. You're not invited."

Jimmy produced a toilet bag from under the bed and dropped it on my lap. "I thought you'd need a few things. Toothbrush, whatever. Maybe one or two other useful things."

I unzipped the leather bag and looked in. Jimmy had smuggled in my .38 revolver, and some extra shells rolled around the bottom of the bag. Good. I'd been feeling a little naked. I zipped the bag back up and tucked the whole package under my pillow.

"Thanks, Jimmy."

"The rest of your stuff's in the trunk of Marcie's car. She's nice, Charlie. You done good."

"Sure."

He looked at the door, then spoke in a hushed tone. "We checked you into the hospital as Ian Janus. Marcie thought of the name." He shrugged. "The doctor's name is Garrity. I had to slip him some big bills, so you owe me, but Stan's used him before when we needed to keep something on the QT. Our story is you had a mishap with a power tool out in the workshop."

I nodded. "Good." Doctors and hospitals were required by law to notify the police when anybody stumbled in with a bullet wound.

"We had to grease two of the nurses too," said Jimmy. "I think they've worked with the doctor before. Still, you're not gonna want to stick around here too long."

"I'm way ahead of you. As soon as I can walk okay, I'm out of here."

"The doc said he'd be along in a few minutes. He should okay you to check out."

"Good."

Jimmy held up a paper sack where I could see it, then set it down next to my bed. We looked at each other a minute. I waited for him to start.

"Like I said, we found it," said Jimmy. "I couldn't have done it without you."

I wondered what the hell he was talking about, so I asked, "What the hell are you talking about?"

He frowned at me, then lowered his voice. "The stash,

Hookman. The cash. I told you. We found it. All of it. The whole enchilada. That's why Beggar's men were guarding the place."

"What?"

"You've done your part," said Jimmy. "So while you were in surgery, I went back and dumped all the lighters and tennis shoes out of the moving van. All those cardboard boxes were filled with cash. Ones, twenties, fives, hundreds. It's all mixed up. A big mess, but don't worry. You rest, and I'll sort it out."

I couldn't believe it. Jimmy's Flying Dutchman stash of money had been real. But what about Stan? I asked Jimmy if he'd seen anything of the old man.

"Not a clue, buddy. Sorry."

I'd figured as much.

"Listen, Charlie. I think we need to face reality. Either Stan's run for the hills a long time ago already or…" He trailed off. We both knew the other option.

"I need to get back to Jimmy Jr.," said Jimmy. "Maria's probably drinking all my liquor, and God knows what all's happened since I been gone. And I got to get some things in order before the shit hits the fan. I just wanted to check in before I split."

"I appreciate everything, Jimmy. Get back to your kid."

He pointed at me and winked again, then was gone.

I settled back into my pillow, wondering what to do with myself. My hand was sore, but not quite enough to call the nurse for drugs, although I wanted some. The TV was off. I still couldn't find the remote control.

When the doctor finally showed up, my hand was throbbing so badly, I thought my eyes would pop. The doctor had a nurse in tow—the same one who'd made off with my urine—and he looked at what I presumed was my chart, grunting and wrinkling his brow like he was reading VCR recording instructions.

"Well, well, Mr. Janus, how's the hand?"

"Like it should be replaced with a hook."

"Don't worry. I'll prescribe some painkillers." He patted the pockets of his lab coat. "Nurse, fetch me a prescription pad please."

She left.

"Listen, are you feeling okay, or what?" Doctor Garrity's composure faltered. "I mean, are you okay to check out? Do you feel up to it?"

"Yeah. Is there a problem?"

He grimaced. "Let's just say next shift will look at things a little closer. We don't want any hard questions. At least, I don't."

"Right. What about the hand?"

"You'll need to get your local doctor to check on it in about a week. Eventually the stitches will have to come out. The ear too. I hope you'll find somebody that won't feel the need to call me and follow up."

"I know the drill."

"I have some things to tell you. To help you get the hand back into shape after it's healed. It might never be exactly as it used to be, but you'll get use out of it again."

Great.

He asked, "Do you need me to call you a taxi after we check you out?"

"Somebody's coming to get me."

I popped two of the painkillers. Marcie pointed her Volvo toward Ma's house, and I dozed off in about three seconds flat. I woke up when we stopped for gas. I offered to pump.

"I'll pump it," she said. "You don't even know what planet you're on."

"I told you I'm not good with drugs."

It was well after dinner when we arrived at Ma's house. My

car was in the driveway, and Marcie told me Jimmy had arranged it.

"What are we doing here?"

"Charlie, you said to come here." A hint of exasperation.

I didn't remember telling her that, but my hand felt okay.

I checked the mail on the way in. There was one envelope. I put it in my jacket pocket for later.

"I'll get the bags," said Marcie.

"Leave them for later."

We went inside, and I stood there in the hall, looking around and wondering what to do next.

Marcie touched my shoulder lightly. "Charlie?"

"Go get the hotel room again. Watch out nobody's following you."

"Okay."

"I'm going to do some things here."

"Oh?"

"I'll be along. I just need to tie up some loose ends."

"Okay." She looked at me funny. "Are you okay? Can you drive?"

"Yeah, I'm fine." Maybe.

She kissed me, and I remembered she was there in time to kiss back and make it convincing. It was hard to listen to her. My head wanted to think about something else. It just wasn't sure what yet.

I stood and watched her pull away in the Volvo, waved. Back in the house, I made coffee and settled into Dad's chair. The house was dead silent. My hand throbbed a relentless rhythm in time with my heartbeat.

NINETEEN

The house was big and quiet after Marcie left.

My ear hurt.

My hand hurt.

There wasn't really much that felt good.

I knew I wasn't in any shape to drive, not yet.

I hobbled up the stairs, thought about calling Ma in Michigan, but let it go. Okay. I was exhausted. Nothing much to do now except pop one of my delicious prescription pain pills and take a nap. Funny, but it was my ear that hurt the most.

For some reason, I wasn't taking the bullet through my hand too seriously. Then I tried to grab a water glass without thinking. I fumbled it. It shattered on the bathroom tile. It took me twenty minutes to sweep it up, because I couldn't hold the broom and dustpan right. I looked at the hand with renewed worry. It wouldn't be any good for a pistol, not until I got it back in shape.

But for pain, there was no beating the ear. It throbbed along with my heartbeat. I thought about doubling the dose, but the doc had already impressed upon me that a single pill was more than enough to knock me on my ass. I shucked my clothes. As per instructions, I crawled into bed before taking the pill. It took me a few minutes to adjust myself so my ear and hand were both comfortable, an elaborate arrangement of pillows and blankets.

I slipped into narcotic dreams.

I was back in Toppers, the firefight with the bartenders and the badge-men. I spun on my opponents with a pistol in each hand, but they weren't the automatics. I held a pair of revolvers.

The chambers spun and spun, getting nowhere fast. The pistols were slippery, and I had to concentrate to keep from dropping them. I couldn't pull the triggers. I was too weak, or they were jammed.

Bullets riddled my body. No pain. No blood. It was like they were shooting me with those suction-cup-tipped rubber darts from toy guns. I laughed at them and threw my pistols down. They were too hard to hold anyway. My palms were red and sticky.

I stumbled toward the guys behind the bar. My plan: pull off their limbs with my bare hands and juggle them like a circus act. But they all climbed into the little Volkswagen Bug behind the bar. There was a lot of room back there. The Bug was painted like a clown car.

My hands were sticky.

I grabbed a bottle of scotch off the bar and tried to pour it over my hands. Nothing came out. Another bottle. Same result. I started breaking bottles, looking for liquid. Then I couldn't grab the bottles. I was all thumbs. Every time I grabbed for a bottle, it shot away and shattered until the whole bar echoed with the shriek of flying glass. The glass—

My eyes opened.

—broke.

At least, I thought my eyes had opened. I blinked. I thought I had blinked. I wasn't sure. My head was still heavy with painkillers. The noise of glass. I was still dreaming. I tried to sit up. It wasn't fun. Or easy. The glass. It wasn't a dream.

Somebody was in the house.

A surge of adrenaline. Not a mighty surge. Frankly, a relatively feeble surge, but enough to swing my feet over the side of the bed. I shook my head, rubbed my eyes. Wake up, asshole. Somebody was in the house.

I fumbled along the nightstand, knocked over the alarm

clock. A racket. Loud. Where were my pistols? Where had Marcie stashed the bags? I'd told her to leave them in the car. Brilliant. My hand found my British commando knife on the nightstand. Okay. Better than nothing. I drew the blade, tossed the sheath aside. I stood, went to my bedroom door, cocked an ear. Nothing.

I remembered I was naked.

It's hard to repel a home invasion with any measure of confidence when your schlong is hanging out. I felt around on the floor until my fingers crept across my boxers. I climbed into them, nearly losing my balance. That would have to do for wardrobe.

I cracked open the door, took a look into the hall. Dark. I listened. Quiet.

I'd been dreaming. That was it. No breaking glass. No one in the house. Maybe if I hurried back to bed I could still get some of the benefit from the pain pill. Maybe I could dream about something better than—

I saw the flashlight at the bottom of the stairs, the beam playing over the far wall and across the front door. I froze, and realizing that I froze told me how screwed up I was. Snap out of it, Charlie.

I darted across the hall to Ma's room before the flashlight turned the corner and headed up the stairs. From there, I would be able to see if the intruder turned into my room when he came up the stairs, or if he went to Danny's or Ma's. It would give me a few extra seconds to get ready for him. He'd probably be armed. I'd need to get close to use the knife.

They started up the stairs. Two of them in dark pants and pullovers. No masks, but too dark to make out faces. One stabbed ahead with the flashlight. The dark, heavy object in the other's hand was obviously a piece. I saw more as they came up.

Middle aged. Ruddy complexions. Black, thick, Omar Sharif mustaches. One was bald, the other was on his way. I thought they looked familiar, but it was still too dark.

I kept track of them through the crack. The one with the flashlight eased into my room, pushing the door open slowly. The other one broke off toward me.

I backed up behind Ma's big cedar wardrobe. If he went through the room, he'd have to go past me. I'd get him on the blind side. I'd have to be quick with the knife. If I didn't get a hand over his mouth right away, he'd call in the other one. I didn't think I was up to taking both at once with only the knife.

Ma's door creaked open. The hinges squealed, not so bad truthfully, but it sounded like screaming amid the night's deep stillness. The intruder moved into the room. I heard him shuffle around, open the wardrobe right next to me and paw through it. He was searching.

He closed the wardrobe, and when he moved by with his back to me, I pounced. I forced my bad hand to cup his mouth. It hurt, but I clamped down tight. I brought the knife from underneath so I could get him under the ribs.

His free hand shot up to pry at the fingers over his mouth. That was reflex. His gun hand twisted down to block the knife thrust. That was professional. He'd known where the blade would be coming. I could tell by the moves these weren't neighborhood cat burglars. Our wrists knocked together, and I gave up on putting the knife in him. But I had the leverage and a little surprise left. I spun him around and smashed his hand against the wardrobe, a little more loudly than I liked. Once, twice I smacked his wrist against the cedar until he dropped the pistol. He found his feet and pushed back, pinned me against the wall. Some of the air whooshed out of me. I'd been slow, standing wrong. He twisted. Caught my knife wrist with his free hand. We pulled at each other.

The skin between my thumb and forefinger wedged into his mouth. He bit down. Hard. Blood spilled down my hand, between his teeth. My blood. I winced, flinched, jerked the hand away.

The guy's mouth was free. "Eddie!"

I punched him full in the kidney. He grunted, spun away. I aimed another blow at the side of his head. He turned with that one too, and it glanced off.

The other guy exploded into the room. He stuck the flashlight in my face, and I lost vision. I felt two rapid fists in my gut. I tried to exhale with the blows, but my reflexes were off. I backed away, trying to blink my eyesight back into focus. I took a shot on the chin, and sparks went off behind my eyes. My knees went gooey. The last blow on the side of my head sealed the deal. I fell a long, long way into swirling blackness. The long, dark slide into nothing.

Shag carpeting underneath.

My head hurt.

My gut hurt.

Everything that had already hurt now hurt worse.

My eyes popped open. I was flat on my back in Ma's room. The bald one sat in a little wooden chair four feet from me, his pistol pointed lazily at my head. His face looked like it had been spanked by a shovel, a nose broken and rebroken with regularity over the years. I guess they didn't want to risk the overhead light, but they'd snapped on the little lamp next to Ma's bed. The room was a shambles, drawers opened and dumped out, the mattress half off the bed. The sounds of less-than-gentle searching floated in from the hall.

In the light, I had a better look at my guest.

"Hello, Teddy. I'd have had you in for coffee if you'd just knocked." I'd meant to sound nonchalant, but my voice was rough.

Teddy chuckled. "You fucked up real good, Hookman."

Teddy. And the other one—Eddie. I'd heard him call out to Eddie. The Minelli brothers. Eddie was half of a set of twins, which meant Freddy was dicking around someplace, probably in the car keeping watch.

The boys were professional head busters and almost always worked as a trio. I knew these guys, strictly freelance. Once, Stan had sent me and the rest of the boys from the monkey cage over to break up a picket line at Disney. Stan figured we needed some extra help and had hired the Minelli brothers. So I'd seen their work firsthand, knew they were tough customers.

"Why don't you tell me how I fucked up, Teddy."

"You got something what ain't yours."

The books again.

Teddy raised his voice, called out to his brother. "He's awake, Eddie."

Eddie came in, chewing his gum like it was a meaningful relationship. "Word up, Ted."

"Shut up talking like that. You find it?"

"Naw. Buncha regular house shit, clothes and whatnot. One pretty fly set of golf clubs."

"I'll *fly* you, idiot. I told you, stop talking like a mooli."

"Get with the times, home boy."

"I don't want you watching no more MTV. It's fucking up your brain." Teddy turned his ire on me. "Okay, Charlie sport, you know the routine. You either tell us, or we mash you into hamburger, and then you tell us."

"I don't know what you're talking about." Playing dumb wouldn't help, of course, but you had to go through the steps.

"He's dissing you, Teddy," said Eddie.

Teddy frowned at his brother. To me he said, "I'm giving you one last chance."

I didn't answer. I was trying to think of something I could do or say to keep the Minelli boys from stomping my balls.

Teddy nodded at his brother. "Get his attention."

Eddie put the heel of his boot into the palm of my wounded hand, twisted, bore down hard with all his weight, grinning like a sadistic moron.

Pain lanced up my arm, past my elbow to my shoulder. It felt like I was being sliced open with a laser. Sweat broke out on my forehead, chest, under my arms. I fought hard to keep my face straight, didn't show the hurt.

"You should open an acupressure clinic, Eddie," I said, proud to keep my voice steady. "You have a soft touch, like a little girl's."

Teddy chuckled. "Now he's dissing *you*, Eddie."

Eddie scowled at his older brother and kicked me in the head.

"Never mind," said Teddy. "Old Charlie's a pro. Go get the stuff out of the car, the extra battery and the clips. We'll put a few volts through him, see if that loosens his tongue."

"Dope," said Eddie. "Real dope."

"Just get the fucking stuff."

Eddie left. Teddy leaned toward me, pulled a silencer out of his pocket, and screwed it on the end of his pistol. "This is a damn shame," Teddy said in a low voice. "How'd you let this happen? A pro like you. Look at you. You're a mess."

"Stan know you're here?" Half my brain carried on the conversation. The other half started piecing together some kind of strategy. I gathered strength. Something would have to happen soon while Eddie was out of the house.

"Nobody's seen Stan. Probably split town. He don't fuck up like you. You should know better than to take something away from a job."

"My...head. I..." My breath came in short gasps.

"That kick Eddie gave you rattled your brains."

"Uh..." My head rolled to one side. My eyes rolled up.

Teddy kicked my feet. "None of that, asshole. We need you awake, so we can find that stuff."

"Stuff is in...the..." My voice was barely a whisper.

"What?" Teddy leaned closer, nudged me again with his shoe. "Speak up for Christ's sake."

I mumbled, an inaudible rasp between my lips.

"Son of a bitch." Teddy knelt next to me, leaned over.

I sat up as hard and as fast as I could, thrust my head forward and smashed it into Teddy's nose. I heard the cartilage snap, but didn't spend any time congratulating myself.

Teddy brought the pistol around. I blocked it with my bad hand, ignoring the agony. The pistol sneezed out a bullet, which shattered an antique perfume bottle on Ma's dresser. I aimed a kick at his balls but missed. My foot landed in his belly, and he deflated like a set of bagpipes, fell on the floor next to me and let go of the pistol.

I got my good hand around his throat and cut off his air. I brought my knee up twice with all my strength, landing two more blows to his gut. He turned red, then purple. Teddy's struggles were perfunctory now. I held on until he was done. Then I rolled away gasping for breath, my heart drumming a mambo.

Eddie came into the bedroom, car battery and cables in his arms. I grabbed the pistol off the shag before he processed what was going on.

"Shit." Eddie dropped his torture kit and made for the stairs.

I popped a slug into his thigh.

He fell, rolled, his hand darting into his jacket and coming out with some sort of atomic pistol the size of a rocket launcher. If he pulled the trigger on that thing, he'd wake up the world. Patrol cars would be here in two seconds.

I squeezed the trigger three times fast, and the silencer dulled each shot to a high-pitched *poot*. A little red-dot triangle sprung up across Eddie's chest. He fell back, his lifeless head knocking against the floor.

I quickly checked both Minelli brothers.

I checked the window in the hall. Nobody parked on the street. I looked out Ma's bedroom window toward the back. A long, dark sedan in the alley. I couldn't see if anyone was in it or not. I watched for a minute, almost gave up. Then I saw the cigarette, the orange pinpoint flaring in the darkness on the driver's side.

Freddy.

There was no good way to approach him without being seen, and I needed to get some answers out of him.

First things first.

I went back into my room, put on my robe, stepped into my slippers. I looked for where Marcie might have stashed my pistols. Clueless. It must have still been in the car like I thought. I'd have to call her. Later. I'd call later.

I went down to the kitchen and put on a pot of coffee, threw some bacon and eggs into a skillet. Set the burner on medium-low.

I went up to Danny's room and found his Daisy air rifle under the bed. I pumped it up, made sure it had a pellet, then went back to Ma's room, stepping over Teddy to get to the window. I opened the window quietly, poked out the screen. Nothing from the sedan. Freddy still having a smoke.

I dragged Teddy over to the window.

"Ever see *Weekend at Bernie's*?" I asked Teddy's carcass.

I propped Teddy's body up to the window. I aimed the air rifle over his shoulder at the sedan. I shot the window. The pellet bounced off the glass, and Freddy's cigarette went dark. I pulled the air gun back into the house and peeked over Teddy's shoulder.

Freddy rolled down his window and stuck his head out, craning his neck to get a look at the house. The half-moon cast a pale light on his face.

I pushed Teddy from behind, made like he was stretching out the window. I took his arm and waved it at Freddy in a *come-here* motion. I must've still had some of the medication in my veins, because I started giggling. I pulled Teddy back in and dropped him on the floor. I ran downstairs and waited in the dark kitchen with Teddy's silenced pistol in my fist.

When Freddy came through the door, I flipped on the light switch.

He went stiff, his eyes big. He saw me and the pistol, a bad combination. Freddy looked like his twin brother Eddie, except less dead and more scared.

I said, "Hello, Freddy. I want you to take out your piece nice and slow. Two fingers. Twitch funny, and I make you go bye-bye."

He nodded, pulled out his gun in slow motion. It was another of those damn cannons like his brother's.

"What the hell are those?"

"A .410 gauge revolver. Shoots slugs or shot."

"A bit much, isn't it?"

He shrugged.

"Put it on the floor."

He did.

"Now kick it over here."

He did.

"Thanks."

I shot him in the kneecap. *Poot.*

He screamed and went down, blood soaking through his pants. He backed up against the door, squirming on the ground, blubbering and sweating and looking like he was going to vomit any second.

"Calm down, Freddy."

He wasn't listening, kept crying and screaming and trying to hold his knee together, the blood oozing between his fingers.

I picked up his gun and put it in the pocket of my robe. Then I poured myself some coffee. I scraped the eggs and bacon onto a plate, grabbed a fork, and had a seat at the kitchen table. Freddy cut down on the blubbering. He watched as I ate bacon, sipped coffee.

"Where's Eddie and Teddy?" His voice was whimpery.

"They're not going to help you."

"Fuck you, man."

I wiped my mouth with a paper napkin. "I'm not in a very good mood right now, Freddy. Your brothers were going to hook me up to a car battery and shoot electricity through my gonads. I'm not at all pleased with the Minelli boys right now."

"Tough shit."

"I want to know what your job was. I want answers, and I'm tired of fucking around."

"Lick my asshole."

I set the coffee cup down and picked up the pistol. I shot him in the heel. He yelled again, squeezed his eyes shut tight. He rocked back and forth groaning through his teeth.

"Start talking."

"You fucking fuck fuck fuck—"

"Freddy!"

"Beggar got tired of waiting for Jeffers to come up with his books, so he told Lloyd to take care of it."

"Mercury?"

"Yeah. That's why Stan told you to hit Toppers. Myron made a deal to deliver the books to the Feds."

"Why?"

"The FBI had Myron on drug trafficking charges, but they said they'd let him off if he helped put Beggar away. It was bad timing for Beggar, because he was right in the middle of taking over Orlando. Beggar wanted the books back quick. He told Stan he'd go easy on him if Stan helped get the books back."

"What happened?"

"You should know. Stan played us funny, told you to take the books to him instead of Jeffers like you were supposed to. When Beggar got word, he didn't like it. He decided to drop the hammer on everybody hard before things got more out of hand than they already were."

I nodded. "That's a good story. Very informative."

I finished the eggs, sipped coffee. "What do you mean Beggar *got word*? How?"

"Somebody told him. The little bald guy."

"Benny."

"Yeah." Freddy didn't look good. His heel and knee bubbled blood. "All I know is Jeffers is crapping his shorts. And Beggar's not too happy either."

"But you don't know anything more about Stan?"

"No."

"What about Mercury? He up to anything else I should know about?"

"No."

"What were you going to do with the books after you got them from me?"

"Take them to Mercury."

"Where is he?"

"He's moved his office into the back of Red Sky," said Freddy.

"The punk dance club downtown?"

"Yeah."

"What was he going to pay you?"

"Twenty thousand."

"That's a lot just to grab a couple of accounting ledgers," I said.

"He knew we'd have to get them away from you."

I picked up the phone and took it to Freddy.

"My leg really hurts."

"That's a shame," I said.

"I need a doctor."

"Later. Right now you're doing me a favor. You want to be on my good side, right, Freddy?"

"Sure." He swallowed hard.

"Tell me Mercury's number."

"It's in my pocket."

"Get it out," I said. "Slowly."

He did and read me the number.

I dialed it.

"Yeah?" a voice answered.

"Get Mercury."

"Who the hell's this?"

"Minelli."

"Wait."

I put my hand over the phone and told Freddy, "Tell him you're coming over first thing in the morning, early. Tell him to have the money. Fuck this up, and you'll see Teddy and Eddie again real soon."

He nodded and took the phone. "Mr. Mercury? Sorry about the hour. Huh? Yeah, we got them. We want to come over in the morning—early. What? In the morning is better. We're sort of on a schedule." He shot me the okay sign. "Teddy? He's gassing up the car. He told me to call you and said you should bring the payment. Okay. Bye."

He handed me the phone, and I hung it up.

"I fixed you up," said Freddy.

"Yeah."

"Just like you wanted," said Freddy. His voice cracked. He knew he was close to being done. "He'll meet you down at the club. In the morning. With the money."

I looked out the kitchen window. Dark.

I lifted the pistol, reminded myself what the Minelli brothers were preparing to do to me.

"I don't think I'll ever walk the same." Freddy pretended not to see the gun, looked at his leg. He was breaking my heart.

"Here," I said. "I'll take care of it."

The pistol bucked in my hand. Freddy's eyes were wide, mouth hanging open. He fell face first into a pool of his own blood, a hole in the center of his forehead.

I went upstairs and took a shower.

TWENTY

After my shower, I tended my hand, fresh bandages. I needed to be alert, so I couldn't risk a pain pill. Instead, I swallowed a half-dozen aspirin. I put on jeans, a tan pullover, and fished my navy pea coat out of the closet. I hadn't bothered with the thermostat, and the house held a deep chill.

I dialed the Hilton and asked for Marcie Kramer's room.

"Where have you been?" Marcie's voice blared harsh through the phone. She didn't sound sleepy at all, more like she'd been awake, waiting.

"I got tied up."

"I tried to call. It rang like a million times."

"Sorry." I must have been zonked on the pain pills. I was just lucky to come around enough to hear the break-in. "Listen, stay put, okay?"

"What about you?"

"I have to clean up some things here."

We made some goodbye noises at each other and hung up.

I tore the tags out of two sets of sheets and wrapped up the Minelli brothers. The blood started soaking through right away, except for Teddy, because I'd choked him. I cut up a whole box of garbage bags and wrapped the bodies in a second layer in plastic.

I searched the whole house and garage, but couldn't find any duct tape. I wished vaguely Marcie was there to help with the bodies. She was a good hand.

I put each brother over my shoulder and carried them to the alley one at a time. Freddy'd left the sedan keys in the ignition.

I grabbed them, unlocked the trunk, and filled it full of Minelli.

The blood on the kitchen floor was the worst of the mess. I mopped quickly, then threw the mop and bucket in the trunk with the boys. The rest of the mess would keep for later.

My guns were still missing in action, so I gathered up the two .410 cannons the Minellis had carried and educated myself. They were olive-green revolvers with one-inch barrels. Each held six .410 shotgun shells, solid lead slugs. They'd put a good hole in a guy, but really they were pretty stupid guns. Still, I didn't have any more ammunition for the .32 automatic with the silencer, so I put one of the cannons in each front pocket of the pea coat. They hung heavy, looked suspicious.

I filled a to-go cup with the rest of the coffee and drove the sedan to a shopping center twelve miles away. I pulled around back, parked, made sure no one was around. I heaved the bodies into the Dumpster, closed the lid, looked around again. All clear. So long Eddie, Freddy, and Teddy.

I'd spent a lot of time lately dumping bodies, and I wasn't happy about it.

Dawn cracked over the horizon.

I pointed the sedan toward downtown Orlando.

Mercury had sent the Minelli boys to put the snatch on the ledgers and put a couple of .410 slugs into my much-loved and tender body. It was my intention to get some answers out of him by any means possible. And Stan. I had to know about Stan.

I stopped at a gas station, bought a small can, filled it with unleaded.

I drove downtown and parked on the street in front of Mercury's club, Red Sky, where the punk kids came to knock against each other and call it dancing. I emptied the gas can into the backseat, punched in the car's cigarette lighter. When it popped, I grabbed it and tossed it in the backseat. The gas caught immediately, and the car went up in flames. I put my hands in my pockets and walked away like it was none of my business.

Faces came to shop windows. A couple big gorillas in shiny wise-guy suits stepped out of the club and watched the car burn. I ducked down the alley and headed for the back of the club. Behind me, I heard the car explode. In the distance, a woman screamed.

In the alley behind the club, I found the back door to the place. I'd been here dozens of times before, when Stan had sent me to collect protection from the club's old owner, so I knew the layout of the place fairly well.

I didn't want to walk in on a party, so I pulled over an empty metal trash can and used it to boost myself up and look in Mercury's office window. It was empty. I pushed at the glass, but the window was locked. I climbed down and drew back a foot, ready to kick in the door, but I stopped myself. I tried the knob. It was open. I pushed the door in with an ugly metallic squeal of hinges.

Nobody came to investigate.

The office was like I remembered it, and if Mercury had any ideas for decorating the place, he hadn't implemented them yet. I searched the room, the top of his desk, not thoroughly, just to see if anything looked important. Nothing did. I scouted behind the heavy curtain that hid the bar. That would be my spot.

Sirens in the distance, fire trucks.

I cracked open the door, looked down the hall past the restrooms into the club. There wasn't much to see. The sirens were right in front of the club now. I heard footsteps at the far end of the hall, so I closed the door. I took my place behind the curtain, drew one of the Minelli cannons, and stood ready.

Three hoods shuffled into the room with Mercury. I watched

them from the crack in the curtain. I'd been doing a lot of sneaking around lately. The hoods were typical low-forehead bruisers: polo shirts, bellies hanging over chinos, gold chains. Fifty-dollar haircuts on ten-dollar heads. The bulges under their windbreakers made them dangerous.

Only Lloyd Mercury stood out, lithe and sharp, straight and lean as a knife blade. He moved with the graceful and deadly precision of a jungle cat.

One said, "Hey boss, let's get a drink. How 'bout a pitcher of Bloody Marys? Me and Lenny had a late night." I saw him start for my spot.

My heart stopped a second to see what was going on. *Pay no attention to the man behind the curtain.*

"Don't even start," Mercury told his henchman. "I need you straight when the Minelli brothers arrive. Freddy didn't quite sound right on the phone. I have a strange feeling."

"What about that fire?"

"I don't know. Vandals. Kids maybe?"

"It just seems kind of funny, that's all."

Mercury scratched his chin. "Okay. You and Dale stay out front and watch the street. Lenny, check the kitchen. And leave the box here."

The one called Lenny handed Mercury a metal box, which he in turn put in the bottom drawer of his desk. The box looked just big enough to hold twenty thousand if the bills were large. My escape money.

When Mercury's boys had gone, I stepped out from behind the curtain and made sure Mercury saw I was pointing a gun at him.

He startled maybe a tenth of a second before a slow, thin smile spread across his face. "Hello, Swift."

"Let's keep it quiet. We need to have a little conversation without Lenny and the others."

"If you like."

"Get your hands on the desk."

He put them on the desk, palms down.

I backed up to the door, looked in the hall. All clear. I closed it again and locked it.

"Tell me about Alan Jeffers."

"What about him?"

"Don't fuck with me. I already killed three guys this morning."

He nodded, looked at me carefully. "You got the Minelli brothers." It wasn't a question.

I shrugged. "It got messy."

"Who was that on the phone?"

"Freddy."

I saw him thinking, then his smile grew. "Well played."

"Jeffers," I prompted.

"What's to tell?"

"Tell it like a little story. I want details."

He shrugged, keeping his hands on the desk, fingers spread. "Once upon a time there was a crime boss named Beggar Johnson. He had an accountant write columns of numbers of everything he did illegally into little books. One of Beggar's men-at-arms—Myron—betrayed him. The evil FBI had cast a spell over Myron to snatch the books away from Arthur."

"Arthur?"

"Arthur Angus," said Mercury. "Beggar's accountant."

That explained the initials A.A. on the briefcase. "Keep talking."

"So this disloyal Myron person made off with the secret books to the faraway land of Orlando, where he sought refuge with his kinsman, Kyle Donovan, owner and operator of the dubious establishment known as Toppers. Here he was to meet with federal agents to turn over his prize and keep himself out of the terrible big house."

"I asked you about Jeffers."

"Patience." Mercury's smile never budged. "I'm getting to him."

"Okay then."

"The FBI, being creatures of habit, cast the same spell over Alan Jeffers that they cast over Myron. They told Jeffers he couldn't very well be able to enjoy his house and his nice car and his time-share in Boca or be able to put his MBA from Rutgers to any good use if he landed himself in a federal penitentiary. To appease the government men, Jeffers promised to sacrifice these books once they came into his possession."

"I know all this already."

"Indeed. But did you know that the FBI agents who cornered Jeffers and threatened him with jail were in fact suspended?"

"What do you mean?"

"Suspended," repeated Mercury. "From duty. It seems they were under suspicion for taking bribes. They figured, I think, that their careers as G-men were over, and decided to fund their retirement by extorting money from Beggar. Their names are—"

"Styles and Novak," I said.

Mercury's smile faltered only a second. "I underestimated you, Mr. Swift. I see you're keeping abreast of current events."

"I get around."

"Then you probably know the name of the third officer who was suspended."

I frowned, decided to take a guess. "Dunn."

Mercury laughed. "That Boy Scout? Hardly. I see you don't quite have all the details, do you?"

"Why don't you fill me in?"

"I believe you remember Jeffers's attractive assistant Tina."

My eyes went big. "She's an agent?"

"She weaseled her way into Jeffers's good graces as part of a legitimate undercover investigation. Once she learned there was a buck to be made from blackmailing Beggar, she conned Styles and Novak into going along with her. They figured Beggar would pay a cool million to stay out of jail and keep his organization intact."

That explained just about everything. If Tina and her chums were running a sting on Jeffers, then she wouldn't have told Dunn about my bringing the books that morning. That's why Dunn didn't search my car or demand the books, didn't even ask me about them. And Jeffers thought Tina, Styles, and Novak represented the FBI. He'd hand the books right over to Tina if he could just get his hands on them. He'd be too afraid to do anything else.

"You look a little worried," said Mercury.

"I'm just figuring some things out."

"You don't like my story?"

"Keep going. You're telling it good."

"There's really not that much more to it," said Mercury. "Except for one small matter. Beggar still doesn't have his ledgers. You have them. This will not do."

"What do you propose we do about it?"

"In this desk is a metal box," said Beggar. "In the metal box is twenty thousand dollars in cash. It was meant for the Minelli brothers. They are no longer in a position to spend it. How about I hand it over to you?"

"In exchange for what?"

"Two things." He held up one finger. "First, you immediately hand over those accounting ledgers. We can tuck them in a nice safe spot and finally stop worrying about them." He held up another finger. "Second, you leave town. We don't care where you go, but go far and don't come back. Beggar doesn't want any of Stan's old crew cluttering up the place."

I looked at him a second, still pointing the gun. Lloyd Mercury was one slick number. And because of that I didn't trust him, not an inch. He'd put a slug in my back the first chance he got in spite of whatever agreement we made now. And I never forgot for a second what Bob Tate looked like with that bullet hole in his head. Mercury had done that, or at least ordered it.

"No deal," I said. "But since I'm the one holding the gun, I guess I'll take that metal box anyway."

The doorknob rattled. Mercury and I both froze, looked at each other.

A knock. "Boss? What's up?" Lenny.

Mercury's smug smile widened just a little.

Lenny tried the knob again. "Hey, boss."

Mercury was so fast, I wasn't even sure what was happening at first. He heaved out of his seat, grabbing my wrists, pointing the gun away from him. "Lenny!" he yelled.

The door creaked with impact. A shoulder or a boot trying to bust it down.

I twisted away from Mercury, aimed at the center of the door and fired. The .410 slug bullied through the door, splintered wood, left a hole the size of a softball. I heard a groan on the other side, the thud of impact as a body slid against the door and to the floor. I looked at the gun. Not bad.

Mercury flipped his desk over at me. I stepped back, fired twice more. Huge chunks of desk exploded into the air as dust and splinters. My new favorite gun.

Feet pounded down the hall. Gunfire. Bullets ripped through the door, whizzed past my ears.

Time to go.

I fired the last three shots to buy a little time as I stepped through the back door. Two into the hall door, one into the desk. I didn't think I hit anything, but the gun made a fine racket. I stuffed the spent revolver into the pea coat and ran full speed down the alley. I took the first turn. Zigged. Zagged. A look over my shoulder. Nobody following. The bus station was five blocks away, and there were always a couple of cabs out front.

I ducked into the station, approached a long line of pay phones. The bus station was deserted, only the guy behind the window was there, and he seemed more interested in CNN on his little television.

I needed some help and thought of Jimmy. Maybe he was still in town. I dropped in the coins, dialed his number.

It rang and rang and rang.

The cab dropped me at Ma's. I kicked at the dust on the sidewalk for a moment, shoved my hands in my pockets. I looked both ways. The neighborhood was dead still, no kids playing, no dogs or birds, nothing.

I walked toward the house and froze at the bottom of the steps. Someone sat in the front porch swing. I went for my gun but stopped, hand on the pistol butt. For a second I thought I was imagining him, looking at a ghost.

He sat with his hands folded in his lap.

Stan.

He stood. I took a step back.

"Stan?"

"How's it going, kid?"

Anger and confusion and relief all mixed together. He stood there like the last couple of days were nothing. "I've been looking everyplace for you."

He just started talking like we were back in the monkey cage. "I got a job for you, Charlie. You up for it?"

"Up for it?" I blinked at him. "Up for what?"

"I got a job for you."

"Stan, where have you been? What's going on?"

It was like he was looking right past me, putting on some crime-boss act instead of just being Stan. Like he was spilling out lines he'd rehearsed in the mirror.

"I need you to give those books to me," he said. "Once I have those books, I'm in the clear. Beggar won't dare move in on Orlando. I'll have him by the fucking balls." He handed me a scrap of paper with a phone number on it. "You call me at that number when you get the books. You're a good kid, Charlie. I know you been saving those books for me."

Was he out of his mind? Bob Tate was dead. And Benny and Sanchez. Cartwright too. Jimmy had skipped town. There was nothing left to Stan except old bones. He was an empty suit, a king without a kingdom. "Stan, I've been looking all over to find you, but there's nothing left. Orlando is over for us. I'm sorry."

From somewhere in his little frame, he tapped a store of rage. "You listen to me, Hogan. Nothing's over till I say it's over! Get it? Now are you with me or against me?"

"Stan."

"Dammit, answer me. It's a simple question. I need to know who's on my side."

"Stan, please."

"What's it going to be?" he shouted.

"Stan, I'm not Thumbs Hogan."

"What?"

"You called me Hogan. Thumbs has been dead for years."

"No, I didn't." He wasn't shouting now. He stared at me, half-confused. "I didn't do that. What are you saying? You saying I don't know what I'm talking about?"

"No, Stan." I felt sick in my gut. "My mistake."

"You call that number." He turned and suddenly seemed weak and small as he hobbled down the porch steps. "I'll be waiting."

He walked down the street half a block and climbed into a red Pontiac. His driver was waiting.

I stood still, watched the car glide away through the neighborhood, turn and vanish through the trees, back the way it had come, maybe all the way back to 1955 when Stan had a straight back and a strong voice and a head full of hair, back when his word was law.

I thought about what he'd said to me. It didn't matter, a conversation between two people who didn't exist anymore.

TWENTY-ONE

To hell with all this.

What did Stan expect? What did he think I could do? All I wanted was to find him and help him, make sure he got away okay. Stan had delusions that he could get back on top again. I didn't want to think of the old man as slipping, as losing his mind, but he wasn't facing reality. I was. In my reality, the best I could do was save my own neck, go off someplace with Marcie and maybe have a life. I went in the house.

Inside, the faint sulfur of gunfire still hung in the air.

As I was putting on another pot of coffee, the urgent, pan-icked thought that Lloyd Mercury was in the house washed over me. I froze, listening for some sign of him. Instantly, I felt ridiculous. I wasn't used to fear getting me like that, crawling under my skin. It was a new feeling, and I didn't like it.

I poured coffee. Drank. Thought. Frowned.

Soon Mercury would come for me. Or maybe he'd send men. And if he found me like this, beat up, one handed, I'd be toast in two seconds flat. I wouldn't catch him by surprise again, and I wasn't good enough to take him straight out. It hurt to admit that, but, again, I was facing reality. Beggar Johnson paid top dollar for his hired killers. The plan: pack up and run.

I rolled the plan around on my tongue and swallowed it. Digested it.

Okay. Enough with the horseshit. It was go time.

I wasn't going to bother going back to my apartment for my packed suitcase, but Ma's spare luggage was too flowery. I found a Nike tote bag in Danny's closet. I had a few articles of clothing around Ma's house, some T-shirts and jeans. I twisted the silencer off the .32 automatic and packed both along with the knives. I threw in the empty .410 pistol and kept the loaded one in my pea coat in case I wanted to shoot down a jumbo jet.

Now I had to make things permanent. This wasn't a vacation trip I was leaving on. Ma wasn't coming back. I wasn't coming back. I never wanted to be within Beggar's reach again. I wanted to go someplace nobody knew me. The big start-over.

Finish.

Shopping.

At Joey's Gun & Outdoor Supply, I bought a hundred rounds of .32 ammunition and a black leather shoulder holster. I didn't see any kind of holster which could possibly accommodate the Minelli revolvers, but I got a hundred .410 shells. I pondered over the various kinds of shot, wondering at the different patterns, maybe something good for blasting away into a crowd, but I decided I didn't know anything about it. Besides, I liked the way the enormous lead slugs tore through everything in their paths.

My next stop was ABC Liquor. I bought twelve bottles of the absolute cheapest and most alcoholic brandy they had.

My hand hurt. I broke a pain pill in half, took it dry.

Thirty minutes later, I was half-loopy but still able to function.

Supermarket: Candles. Kitchen matches. Charcoal lighter fluid. Rubbing alcohol. Cigarettes.

I took all my shopping back to the house. I found a dusty ashtray under the kitchen sink, cleaned it, and put it in the living room on the lamp stand next to the empty liquor cabinet. When Dad had been alive, it was kept full of Cutty Sark. I lit three of the cigarettes and set them in the ashtray to burn. I opened ten of the brandy bottles and emptied them onto the carpeting around the lamp stand, poured a trail to the drapes, dumped the remains into Dad's chair. It was old and would burn well.

I pulled my car out of the garage and parked it on the street. Back in the garage I dumped the bag of old rags under the barbecue grill. I emptied the charcoal lighter fluid onto the rags, let them soak. I relocated anything even remotely flammable next to the grill. I thought about the Halloween costumes Danny had when he was a kid but was sure they'd been thrown out long ago.

In the kitchen, I turned on all the stove burners.

I was using my injured hand too much. I took the other half of the pain pill.

Upstairs I made sure I had everything I wanted, went downstairs, put the Nike tote in the trunk of the Buick.

Back inside: I threw an apron and two hand towels on the stove burners. Into the living room, struck a fistful of the kitchen matches and scattered them on the carpet. The brandy caught. I watched for a moment as the flames spread, crawled toward the curtains, leapt up the wall.

I grabbed the *National Geographic* with Amber's number on the cover. I also found the jacket I'd worn home from the hospital and grabbed it too. An envelope fell out of the pocket. It was the piece of mail that had been in Ma's mailbox. I stuck it in my back pocket.

I left the house through the garage, paused to drop a match on the rags.

I got in the Buick and drove a block away, parked, got out of the car, and watched.

It wasn't much of an arson job, but I'd avoided using gasoline or something else obvious. Maybe it would pass muster. Maybe not. Ma was insured.

It didn't look like much at first, but then the smoke came. Some windows popped out. Flames lapped from within. I couldn't have explained to anyone why this was a good idea, but I knew it was. Fire, the great cleanser. Pushing me forward, burning bridges behind.

Neighbors came out of their houses. I didn't wait for the sirens. I cranked up the car, drove.

I'd been fucking up in every direction, starting with the stupid way I'd handled the Rollo Kramer job and what I'd done with Sanchez. What I was doing now might not have been smart, but it was decisive. Permanent. No going back. Stan had always said lead, follow, or get out of the way, but do *something*. I laughed at the burning house. This was something all right.

I took another pain pill.

Maybe I hadn't done a damn thing right, but I was sure as hell giving myself a clean slate.

And Ma was better off in Michigan. The house wasn't safe anymore. I didn't want her there by herself. And it was full of papers, photo albums, a trail. I couldn't have anyone coming after me or using Ma to try to find me. Maybe my solution was a little harsh.

I giggled.

A song running around my brain, the one 'bout the lion sleeping in the jungle.

The pain pills, I realized. I was off my rocker.

The Tokens, that was group. "The Lion Sleeps Tonight." I hummed it loud.

I put about five miles between me and the fire, then pulled into a gas station to fill up. I reached into my back pocket for my wallet and came out with the letter. I took a good look at it for the first time. It didn't have a stamp or a postmark. There wasn't even an address, just CHARLIE SWIFT on the front in block letters. I tore it open and read.

> *Mr. Swift,*
>
> *You've made things very difficult for me and my friends. I want those accounting ledgers, and I want them soon. Your brother wouldn't cooperate, but the young lady was more forthcoming. We convinced her to tell us everything she knew. We know the ledgers are in a locker someplace. Call me at Jeffers's home and tell me where, and I promise no harm will come to young Amber. I don't know what she is to you, but I believe she's very important to your brother. Try anything foolish, and you won't see her again. Believe me, Swift, I'm at the end of my rope, so don't push me. Just do what you're told. I'll be waiting for your phone call.*
>
> *—Tina*

My heart dropped into my stomach. I ran to the car and got the *National Geographic* with Amber's phone number. I found a pay phone quickly and dialed. Sixteen rings, no answer. I looked her up in the phonebook, scribbled down the address.

I fractured every known traffic law getting to Amber's apartment complex. Her place was on the second floor. I ran up the stairs three at a time. A yellow strip of police tape stretched across her door. I tore it down and went inside.

Inside, a few sticks of furniture overturned. A dark stain in the center of the carpet. The place was small, so I went through it fast. Nobody there. I sat on the couch, flexing my sore hand and thinking hard.

I picked up the phone and called Burt Remington. His answering machine came on after four rings, and I hung up without leaving a message. I tried him at the police station, and the operator put me through to his desk.

"I've been trying to call you," said Burt. "Did you know your brother's in the hospital?"

"He's alive?"

"In bad shape, but yeah."

I melted against the couch with relief. "What happened, Burt?"

"It was at his girlfriend's place."

"Amber," I said. "I'm here now."

"You're not supposed to be there. It's a crime scene. It's sealed."

"Can it, Burt. I want to know what fucking happened."

"Okay. Calm down. The neighbors heard gunshots and phoned us. A patrol car went over to investigate, and they found Danny on the floor. The apartment door was wide open. Danny'd been shot, and he was bleeding pretty bad. The officers at the scene phoned for the paramedics, and he was taken to County General. He's there now. I'm told he's recovering okay."

"I'm on my way."

"Whoa, Charlie, hold on. That might not be good for you, to be seen around there."

"Is he under arrest or something?"

"No. He had this enormous fucking gun, but it was purchased legally and registered, so it's a straight case of self-defense."

I'll be damned. "Then what's the problem?"

"Well, nobody believes it was a simple break-in. I managed to call off my boys, but the Feds are a different story. Agent Dunn keeps showing up around Danny's room. I think he's hoping to catch you there. Dunn is crazy pissed. There's been some strange, bad shit going on."

"I'll worry about Dunn."

"Charlie?"

"What is it, Burt?"

"What's going to happen?"

"Don't worry," I said. "It's all going to be over soon."

Danny opened his eyes, saw me, and grinned weakly. He had the usual array of tubes in his arms. I'd sent the nurse out so I could talk to him.

I said, "Hey, Bro."

"Hey." His voice was barely above a whisper.

"What happened?"

"They came in so quick." Danny swallowed hard, closed his eyes. "I had my gun out, fired." He shook his head. "It was no good. I didn't even know what was happening."

"How many?"

"Three. I'm not sure. It was all confused. Three, I think."

"One was a woman, sharp features, short black hair?"

"Yes."

Tina.

"Do you remember anything?" I asked.

"They shot me, Charlie. I was so scared. I thought I was going to die."

A lump rose in my throat. "I know. I'm sorry. Try to remember."

"I was trying to stay awake, trying to get up and help. Amber was—"

"Go on. It's okay."

"She was screaming. Oh God, screaming and begging for them to let her go. The woman said they'd take her someplace out of the way. She said it wasn't safe to stay in Orlando."

"Where?"

"I don't know. Oh, God."

"It's okay, Danny." I grabbed his hand, squeezed.

"You've got to get her back, Charlie."

"I will."

Tears streamed from the corners of his eyes. "Please. You've got to find her, get her back for me. I'm begging you."

"I will," I said. "I'll find her. I'll fix everything."

Outside the hospital room, I found a water fountain. My hands shook, breathing turned heavy. Danny. My brother. Almost dead.

I took a pill, found the elevator, went down.

In the parking lot, Agent Dunn stood next to my Buick waiting for me. I stopped in front of him, and we looked at each other for a second. He lit a cigarette, puffed.

"I'm getting pretty damn tired of never knowing what the hell's going on," he said.

"Sorry."

"I told you to get out of town."

"I've been trying."

"Maybe I should take you downtown, question you there."

"I don't have time for that," I said. "How about I make you an offer?"

He gave me a curious look. "Like what?"

"Like maybe I help you solve some of your problems."

"Really? This is just absolutely fucking fascinating. And what are my problems per se?"

"You've got three rogue agents for one thing," I said.

"It's only one now. We found two of them shot, but you wouldn't know anything about that, would you?"

I shrugged. "I know I can get Beggar Johnson's accounting ledgers for you."

That made him stop puffing his cigarette.

"Where are they?" he asked.

"That's not how it works. You've got to get out of my way and let me do what I need to do. I'll send you the books. Beggar's no friend of mine. Put him in jail, or don't. It's all the same to me. But I don't have time to mess with you right now."

He considered, then stepped aside. "Sure. Why not?"

I got in my Buick, but he grabbed the door before I could close it. "I'm not going along with this because I trust you. I don't. I'm going along with this because this case is already so fucked up, I don't see how it could hurt." He handed me a business card. "But if you're on the level, I can be reached at this number."

I took it, and he stepped back. I closed the door and drove away.

I went back to Amber's apartment complex, parked the Buick, and grabbed my tote bag. I'd made sure to park as far away from Amber's apartment as possible. I was a little tired of people following me, and I wanted to finish my business without any of Beggar's men or the Feds on my tail.

I zigzagged my way through the buildings and found Danny's Impala. I threw my luggage in the backseat and found the keys under the floor mat.

I'd been holding the steering wheel too tight from stress, and it made my hand hurt. I wanted another pill bad. I resisted and drove.

I knocked on Jeffers's door, but he didn't answer. His Lexus was in the driveway, so I tried again. Tired of waiting, I tried the knob. It turned, and I pushed my way in. Nobody in this town locked up anymore.

In the hall, I passed a bathroom. A radio sat on the back of the toilet, country music, turned up loud. I kept walking.

Into the kitchen. A little TV on the counter blared *I Love Lucy* at me. *Whaaaaaa, Ricky!*

I remembered where his office was. Jeffers wasn't in it, but his stereo was up almost all the way. Steve Miller Band blaring "Jungle Love."

The living room, another TV. This time MSNBC's constant flow of misery. The Middle East blah blah blah. Washington blah blah blah. The economy blah blah blah.

I felt another giggle stirring in my gut, looking to rear its ugly head. I pushed it down. Not now. Find Jeffers.

In the corner of my eye, I caught a little flash of movement through the French doors leading out back. My hand drifted into the pocket of the pea coat, closed around the butt of my Minelli cannon. I ducked behind a curtain, looked through the French doors to the backyard. Jeffers had a pool, and I wondered if I was walking in on the *Sunset Boulevard* scene with Jeffers facedown in the pool like William Holden.

Jeffers stood stripped to the waist. He was sagging and pale, a few tennis muscles covered by a layer of prosperity. His back was to me. He danced a silly, drunken middle-aged dance. A little portable radio sat next to an empty gin bottle. Jeffers was having a little party for himself. The radio and gin bottle perched on a glass table with a mirror and a mound of white powder.

Jeffers was barefoot, and his slacks were soaked to the knees, where he'd evidently braved the first step or two into the swimming pool. I turned down the TV, so I could hear what he was dancing to. Some oldies bubblegum pop.

I opened the French doors and stepped outside. I kept my fist around the Minelli cannon but didn't haul it out.

Jeffers heard somebody behind him and spun quickly.

"Tina?"

"Nope."

He looked terrible, dark heavy bags under the eyes, skin sallow and clammy. His hair was a matted, greasy mess. I didn't believe he'd bathed recently or gotten much sleep. I assumed the tumbler of clear liquid in his fist was gin.

His glassy, bloodshot eyes focused on me with effort. "It's you."

"It's me."

"Where've you been, for Christ's sake?"

The song on the radio segued into "Sugar Shack."

I decided Jeffers wouldn't appreciate all of the real and gritty drama in its entirety, so I boiled it down for him.

"I'm looking for Tina."

"She was looking for you too," said Jeffers. He was looking dead at me but not focusing too well. "She got tired of waiting and left."

"To go where?"

"Oh, my God. Oh, oh, oooooh." He trailed off into a sad, throaty moan and slumped into the lawn chair next to the table.

"Jeffers."

"I've messed it all up," he said. "Oh, God why can't I die? Look at me. How come I don't die?" He started crying, a long, high-pitched feeble blubbering.

"Knock it off," I said. "Answer my question."

He kept on crying and groped for the mirror with the cocaine. He curled his arm around it lovingly, drew it to him, pushed his face down into the powder.

"Stop that."

He sniffed, tears dropping from his face at the same time, clumping in the white powder. He pressed his whole face into it, snorting and crying and writhing, coughing out sobs and sniffing in the powder when he could take a breath.

"Stop that. You look like a retard. Stop it."

"I need it." *Sniff.*

"You don't need it. This isn't helping."

"I need it, need need need it. Oooooh, please oh please." His face was still down on the table. He scooped the powder onto him with both hands, into his eyes, mouth, on his cheeks like he was trying to burrow into it, hide like an ostrich.

I grabbed him under the arms, pulled him out of the chair.

He went limp, dead weight, cried at full volume like an infant. His skin was slippery. I pulled him to the edge of the pool, dropped him. Moans.

"Sorry about this," I said.

I dunked him into the cold water. In and out, in and out. I kept that up for a while until he shouted at me between dunks.

"Okay, okay. Stop."

I pulled him away from the pool, let him lie on the grass. He was still crying, just a little, but it wasn't the out-of-control tantrum like before. He was spent now, defeated, but I could talk to him.

"Oh, Tina. I wish Tina were here."

"Me too," I said. "She could make us some coffee."

"She was so much more than a coffee maker."

Whatever.

"Oh, God, where is everybody?"

"I don't know." I turned one of the pool chairs around, sat looking down at him lying sprawled on the grass, eyes crunched up, lips pulled back in a feral grimace. "Tina's undercover FBI, you know."

Jeffers picked his head up, looked at me like I was Sherlock Holmes or a Martian or God. "How did you know about that?"

"Just tell me where you think she might have gone." *You dumb shit.*

"I don't know I don't know I don't know." He shook his head back and forth in the grass as he spoke.

"Guess."

"She just left. Went away and never came back. I *need* her."

"You don't need her. Straighten up and think for a minute, will you?"

"She said she had a plan. She said we'd get the money and leave this place, just be together, her and me."

Deluded asshole.

"They fired me from the bank," said Jeffers. "Froze my accounts."

There was a lot of that going around.

"Where's Tina's room?" I asked.

"Tina's gone. Gone gone gone gone—"

"Where's her *room*?"

"Past my office. All the way at the end of the hall."

I left Jeffers on the grass, found Tina's room.

She'd cleaned it out quickly. Naked hangers in the closet along with a suitcase-sized emptiness between some old boxes. Nothing helpful in the boxes. Her dresser drawers were empty. I looked under the bed. Nothing there. I kicked over the waste-paper basket near the bed, and a stack of papers fell out. Credit card bills. Visa. Sears. Phone bills. Junk mail.

I went back into the kitchen, rummaged the fridge and found a can of light beer. My hand hurt again. It was too soon to take another pain pill. I took one anyway, washed it down with the beer. I took a stool. Sat there. Thought. Scratched my head. Drank the beer.

I went back to Tina's room and picked the old phone bill out of the trash can. There were no local calls listed. I guess they'd be on Jeffers's bill. This statement was for a calling card. Tina had made twenty-two calls to Spring City, Tennessee.

I went back to Jeffers. He was passed out. I shook him awake, and he opened his eyes flinching at the daylight.

"What is it?"

"Did Tina ever say anything about Tennessee?"

"She has some family there, I think. A brother? Tom. Yeah. Good old Brother Tom."

"Get straight," I advised him. "Go someplace. Do you have a relative you can stay with? A brother or something?"

"I don't know. Let me think."

"Don't think too long. Agent Dunn might lose his patience and come for you here. Lay low for a while or don't. Whatever. I'm going. I have work to do."

"No."

"No what?"

"Please." He started misting up again. "Don't leave me. Please. I can't die. I'm trying to die, but I won't die."

"You'll die," I said.

"I used to be a banker." He started crying again.

"We all used to be something."

On the way back through the house, I used Jeffers's phone, called the airlines, asked questions, wrote down the appropriate information. Then I called Marcie at her hotel room.

"Charlie!" She practically shouted into the phone. "I'm getting pretty God damn tired of sitting in this hotel room."

"Shut up and listen. There's a flight leaving for Acapulco in fifty-one minutes. Go get a ticket."

"What about you?"

"I'll catch up when I can."

"When?"

"Maybe a day. Maybe two."

Maybe never.

TWENTY-TWO

Time to drive.

The concrete snarl of Orlando's tangled road cluster faded away as I took the turnpike to I-75 and aimed the Impala north. The Florida–Georgia state line put itself behind me, then Atlanta, and I branched off toward Chattanooga.

Spring City was a small town along Highway 27 surrounded by low mountains. The temperature had dipped considerably during my trek north, and the sharp wind hissed and whistled through the cracks and creases in the convertible's top. I'd driven all the way wearing my pea coat and with the heat on.

The dead, flat sky was a uniform gray.

I'd made decent time, stopping only four times to fill up with gas or coffee or take a piss. I didn't want to risk driving such a distance on pain pills, so my stomach burned with too much aspirin.

At the local Days Inn, I asked for a room and checked in under the name Peter Tork. I wanted something around back, away from the traffic noise. They gave me 126.

I pulled into a service station, hopped out of the car near a pay phone. The wind bit into me immediately, and I pulled the pea coat tight.

I unfolded the phone bill I'd salvaged from Tina's trash can, dropped the coins into the slot, and dialed the number. It rang three times.

"Hello?"

"Hello," I said. "Is Tina there?"

"Who can I tell her is calling?" A Southern accent, not too thick.

"I'm an old friend from Florida. Pete." It seemed plausible enough when I'd rehearsed it, but coming out of my mouth, it sounded pretty weak.

"She ain't been there long enough to make old friends."

"Is this her brother Tom?"

"This is her *husband* Tom."

Bingo. She told Jeffers it was her brother. Sure. That made sense. Hussy with a badge.

"Oops. My mistake." I chuckled. Kept it light. "She said to give her a visit if I was ever in the neighborhood."

"She ain't here right now. Went out."

"Whoa, just my luck, huh? And the sky looks like snow too."

"She's out right now. Like I said. She went up the mountain. Won't be back for a while."

I didn't know exactly what "up the mountain" entailed, but it sounded like I was in for a wait.

"I'm at the Days Inn, room number one-two-six," I said.

"You'd better just call back."

"That's not going to work. I need you to take a message."

"Listen, mister, I got things to do and—"

"That's not going to cut it, Tom." I put a little heat in my voice. "Now I want you to get a pen and a piece of paper, and I want you to write this down. Are you listening?"

"Yeah."

"Tell Tina I brought some things she wanted."

He went quiet on his end, and I tried to puzzle whether he was in on it or just confused.

"Okay," said Tom. "I think I got your message. I'll tell her when she gets in."

"Thanks, Tom. I appreciate the help."

I hung up.

I felt pretty smug about my little performance as I got back in the car. I'd simultaneously made contact with the kidnappers and let them know they weren't as clever as they thought. I'd found out where they were and who they were, and I had what they wanted.

Very soon now I would shoot them all stone cold dead and send Amber home to Danny.

The cold was bad on my hand. I finally relented, took a pain pill, and sat in the car until it took effect. I bought a bottle of beer in the service station to help push it down.

I pulled into the rental car place in case Tina had seen the Impala.

Here's what I said to the guy behind the counter: "Gimme a car."

His look was so funny.

"What kind of ride do you need, bud?"

Bud.

"I'm not sure," I said. "Just something comfortable. Price isn't a problem."

"How about a nice mid-size?"

Wow, this guy had bad teeth. Wait? What was it Tom had said? Up the mountain. That sounded fairly rugged.

"Do you have a Suburban?"

Bad Teeth shouted into the back room, "Hey, Leanne, we still got that red Suburban?"

A female voice floated out of the back room, country accent like Minnie Pearl. "No. That big feller took it."

"What big fellow?"

"You know. With all the hair and muscles smoking that god-awful cee-gar. Looked like Fabian?"

"Fabian?"

"Like on the romance book covers."

"Lord, woman," said Bad Teeth. "That's Fabio."

"Well, he had muscles."

"Lou Morgan." I felt my face twisting up into a huge grin. "Was his name Lou Morgan?"

Holy shit. I'd forgotten all about New Guy. I was losing my mind. He must have followed Tina up here on his own.

The woman stuck her head out of the back room. She was wrinkled and flannel. "That's it. You know him?"

"I know him."

"Well, he got the Suburban."

I'll be damned. The big, dumb sonovabitch. He'd found his way to Spring City and was hot on Tina's trail. The town was small, but I still didn't have time to drive around looking for him. But it sure would have been nice to have some backup. Even if it was Fabian. I laughed.

"Mister?" Bad Teeth was giving me the fish eye.

"What else you got in a four wheel drive?"

"You going up the mountain?"

"Abso-fucking-lutely straight up the mountain."

That earned me a bad look, but he filled out the paperwork on a white Chevy Silverado. He said I could leave the Impala around back.

"And how will you be paying for this?"

I threw down a Visa card.

He ran it through the machine and smiled as he handed it back to me. "Thanks for your business, and have a good day, Mr. Minelli."

I sat in the Chevy and watched the doors to my hotel room. I was parked a respectable distance away but close enough to see anyone approach.

After leaving the rental place, I ran a few last-minute errands. I'd found a Wal-Mart and bought a thermos, filled it with coffee later at the same convenience store I'd been to earlier.

Waiting in the truck was a three-hour deal. I'd sucked back most of the coffee and pissed behind the Chevy four times.

Another pain pill.

It was well after dark when they finally appeared.

Tina wasn't with them, but this was the group all right. They parked the car two spaces down from the room, a dirty red Camaro a few years old. They piled out, three of them, and stood shuffling with indecision in the parking lot, hands deep in flannel coats, steam trailing from their mouths in the cold. The looked at each other nervously. Hesitation. Amateurs. Good. I wasn't looking for a challenge. Two must've been local. Feed caps, baggy trousers, scuffed boots, three-day beards. One was tall and fat. The other was short and fat.

The third guy was out of place, the only one wearing a wool, gray overcoat and wingtips. He had a tie. Neat haircut. Red hair. Ex-military maybe.

Or maybe FBI. Dunn would be sad to learn that another of his sheep had deserted the flock.

When they took the iron police battering ram from the back of the Camaro, I figured I'd guessed right. He was clearly in charge and directed the two locals to charge the door with the battering ram while he pulled his revolver.

This made me laugh. I'd left the door unlocked.

They smashed down the door on the first try. It flew open, and they followed, all three crowded in. The locals dropped the battering ram, drew pistols. I couldn't see them once they were inside, but I imagined them standing there with idiot looks on their mugs. They'd spot the page and pick it up, realize what it was, turn it over, see my note.

This isn't how we do business. Now go home and wait for a call.

I laughed at the looks I knew must've been on their faces.

They were so dumb, and I was so smart. They should elect me president of the world.

The trio emerged from the motel room, shoulders slumped, faces confused. The guy I thought might be the agent signaled them back into the Camaro. They drove.

I followed.

The agent was the only one I worried might spot me, so I kept as far back as I dared. It wasn't any trouble. I followed them through the little town, climbing steadily through the hills. Soon I was on a looping zigzag, the beginning of the slow, back-and-forth climb. I was finally going up the mountain. I was glad I had the truck, although the Camaro seemed to be doing fine.

The climb was steep and dark, and I was the only vehicle behind the Camaro now. I felt fairly conspicuous, but there was nothing to do but keep going.

Up the mountain.

Into the darkness.

And the snow started falling.

Up the mountain might as well have been a different world. After climbing a thousand feet or so, the road leveled off, and the socioeconomic difference between up the mountain and down the mountain became clear. Down the mountain meant civilization. Up the mountain was the frontier.

Almost completely dark except for moon and headlights. The Camaro led the way.

To the left or right or above, the occasional cabin or mobile home twinkled in the night. I passed a poorly lit shack nestled among the evergreens just off the road. A sign out front said: *Store.* The sky was a panorama of black velvet. It was peaceful and quiet and cold. The snow came heavier.

The Camaro slowed, turned up a steep gravel driveway. I

followed the wandering path with my eyes, and it ended at a surprisingly elegant, two-story house lit well by outside floods. I kept driving.

Two miles later I passed what might have been a service station, with a single-wide mobile home right next to it. I pulled into the dirt lot. The single-wide had neon beer signs in the window. A sign out front declared *Top of the Mountain Tavern*. Impossible. There must've been zoning laws against such a thing. It couldn't be a tavern.

I went in.

It was.

The little trailer tavern was close and hot and heavy with a layer of tobacco smoke.

They had an itty-bitty pool table jammed up under where there should have been a dining room table. A jukebox played a country song I didn't know. A bar. The patrons looked like guys you'd imagine drinking beer in a single-wide. I went to the bathroom. It was the first barroom bathroom I'd ever been in that actually had a bath.

I wanted to give Tina and her partners some time to settle down. They'd be all wound up now, waiting for the phone to ring, and that would make it hard for me to spy on them. I grabbed a barstool and ordered coffee.

The bartender was skinny and greasy, a pack of cigarettes rolled up in his T-shirt. "This ain't Denny's. It's a drinking establishment."

"A beer then."

"Draft or bottle."

"Draft. Light."

He nodded and returned a moment later with a foamy mug. I popped a pill, chased it with the beer.

On the jukebox, George Jones let everyone know that he

stopped loving her today. I ordered another beer and made myself take this one slow. I didn't know the next two songs, and I'd had enough of the Top of the Mountain Tavern. I paid for the beers and went outside.

The truck had a half-inch layer of snow on it. It was still coming down. I was freezing.

Back inside I asked the bartender if he sold half-pint flasks of Chivas.

"We got Jim Beam."

"I'll take it."

I sat in the cab of the truck and twisted the top off the Jim Beam. It burned its way down my throat, spread to my arms, all through my chest. I cranked up the truck. Turned on the heat.

I drove back to the kidnapper's house and parked the truck at the bottom of the hill. Even with the headlights out, they couldn't fail to spot me coming up the driveway. I parked a quarter mile away and started up the slope at a slow march. There was a good blanket of snow underfoot now, and it crunched clean and hard with each step. The moon filtered through the sparse evergreens, cast everything in an other-worldly glow. I buttoned the pea coat, took another hit of the Jim Beam, headed for the smear of light at the top of the hill.

TWENTY-THREE

Near the end of my hike, my cheeks were frozen. The slight wind made my eyes tear. My hands were relatively warm in the pea coat's pockets, but my injured ear burned in the freezing temperature. I tilted the flat bottle of Jim Beam up to my lips. The glass was cold, but the warm liquid did its work.

I stopped short of the circle of light cast off by the floods around the house. There were four vehicles parked in front. Two sedans, one with Florida plates. The red Camaro parked next to a white Jeep Cherokee. Lights still blazed in most of the windows. They must've thought they lived too far up the hill to bother with curtains.

I sneaked around back, clinging to the darkness. There was a toolshed. I crouched behind it and surveyed the house from the rear. Construction on a wooden deck, which wrapped around the house, had been brought to a halt. Maybe they were waiting for better weather. The snow wasn't falling any heavier, but it wasn't letting up either.

I light-footed it closer, peeked inside a window.

Two men sat in plush chairs. Looked like a den. One was the short fat one who'd helped knock down the door to my motel room. The other was new. Tennessee Volunteers T-shirt, jeans, house slippers. He had a thick beard and little dark eyes, a dull expression. Basketball game on the television. Beer bottles on the coffee table. I watched a minute. A woman came in, dirty blond, big hips. She talked. The men nodded. She left.

The three original guys plus the new guy and the woman. That was five. So far.

I moved down the length of the house. I watched the kitchen a moment, but it was empty. The dirty blond came in a moment later, started doing something in the fridge. I circled to the side of the house and found a bedroom. It looked pretty neat; the bed was made. I watched a minute, but nobody entered. The living room window. Nobody there.

I started back around the side but heard the front door slam, then a car door. Ignition. Somebody driving away. I looked around the corner of the house and spotted taillights descending the driveway. I looked to see which car was missing from the lineup. The sedan with Florida plates.

I jogged back to the toolshed. I was taking another tug at the Jim Beam when I heard the squealing hinges, looked up to see the back door of the house swinging open. I jumped into the toolshed and pulled the door almost shut, leaving just enough open to watch.

It was the two guys who'd been watching the basketball game. They walked toward the toolshed, buttoning coats. I held my breath, but they stopped halfway, turned to face each other. The bearded guy pulled out a pack of cigarettes, offered one to the other.

"It is—no shit—fucking freezing out here."

They talked low but not at a whisper.

"Tom don't let nobody smoke in the house," said Shorty.

Good for Tom.

"Where did Tina go?" Bearded Guy stomped his feet, hunched his shoulders against the cold. Little flakes of snow dotted their heads and shoulders.

"With Big Dave up to Tina's lake cabin. They took the girl."

"What for?"

"She talked it over with Dave. They thought the girl should be away from here what with that fellow around and all."

"What the hell do they know?"

Shorty shrugged. "She's trained for this stuff, not me."

"This is screwed up." He took quick, nervous puffs on the cigarette. "Nobody said nothing about no kidnapping. We was just supposed to steal some books."

"It was a good plan."

"Well, it's screwed up now."

"It's still a good plan. Or would you rather go back to third shift at the factory?"

"I'm just saying it's all screwed up. Nothing like this ever goes right."

"How the hell would you know?"

"Anyone can see it's screwed up." Puff, puff.

"Stop so much worrying, will you? Let Tina worry about it."

"Tina." He said her name like it was a false idol.

"Come on," said Shorty. "I'm freezing my fucking balls off."

They flicked their butts into the snow. I watched them trudge back, go in the house.

I sighed, took a swig of the Jim Beam. If I'd acted immediately I might have caught them before they moved Amber. I still needed to get into the house to find out where this lake cabin was.

And for Danny. Yeah. For Danny, the bloody hand of justice had arrived. In spite of the cold, I unbuttoned my pea coat, gave myself a clear path for the .32 in the shoulder holster. I'd try the back door. Maybe they'd left it open after having a smoke, but just in case, I thought I'd better look through the shed for something to pry with.

I turned, and the crack of light from the toolshed door fell across a pair of wide human eyes looking back at me.

I flinched back up against the wall of the toolshed, fell down, scattered rakes and shovels, a startled cry smothered in my throat. My heart beat through my ear and my hand. The body hung there from a hook on the wall.

I pushed the door open, let a little more light spill in.

Lou Morgan hung there as dead as it was possible to be.

"Aw, New Guy," I whispered to him. "Aw hell."

I fumbled the cap off the pill bottle. Took one and drank it back with whiskey. My hands shook. I said, "Okay, Lou. You're on the list right behind Bob Tate." And Benny and anyone else who hadn't deserved this.

I went through his pockets, but his wallet was gone along with everything else. In the inside pocket of his leather jacket, I found a cellophane-wrapped cigar about six inches long.

I almost tossed it down but unwrapped it and stuck it in my mouth instead. "Okay, Lou?"

Thanks, dude.

I screwed the silencer onto the end of the .32, grabbed a crowbar from the floor of the shed. I put on a fresh pair of latex gloves. Show time. They'd locked the back door, but not terribly well, no chain or bolt. I pried it open, the wood splintering. A little noisy, not bad. Nobody came to investigate. The door opened into a short hall, washer and dryer on the right. Both machines were running. The noise probably helped cover my entrance. I turned left into the kitchen.

Empty. The sound of the television came from the den beyond.

I entered the den. Shorty's back was to me. He leaned over a CD player, was putting a disc in. He didn't hear me come up behind. I tapped him on the shoulder and he turned.

He saw me, eyes big. His mouth fell open, sucked breath for a shout. I stuck the silencer down his throat, and his lips closed over it reflexively. I pulled the trigger. *Poot.* A miniature volcano of blood, hair, flesh, and bone erupted from the back of his skull. His eyes rolled back, and he slid off the gun barrel with a wet pop as he slumped to the floor.

I looked at what he'd put in the CD player. Johnny Cash. Why not? I pushed it in, hit play. Turned it way up. Picked up the television remote and hit mute. I understood in some disconnected way that the pain medication was mixing badly with the whiskey. I tried to remember how many pills I'd had in the last few hours. At least two.

I heard bizarre, demented laughter. It was me.

I took out the nearly empty Jim Beam flask, held it awkwardly in my bad hand.

The bassline for "I Walk the Line" began, and a woman appeared in the kitchen door. Not the dirty blond, thinner, young and pretty with a heart-shaped face. She saw me, her hand going to the surprised O of her mouth like she'd just let a little girly burp.

Poot.

A little yelp and she pitched forward, kissing carpet.

I took a hit of Jim, fumbled the bottle to the carpet and bent quickly to pick it up before it all spilled out. At the same moment, a shotgun spoke thunder behind me. Somebody had come around through the other hall. The pellets blasted over my head, shredding plaster on the far wall. I spun a small arc, firing quickly to catch my attacker.

Poot. Poot. Poot. Poot.

I'd caught him with the middle two bullets halfway through his attempt to pump another shell into the shotgun chamber. He staggered into the wall, slid down dead into a sitting position. The bearded guy. I heard a scream. People shouting orders back and forth.

I keep a close watch on this heart of mine.

I picked up Shorty's dead body, kicked him ahead of me in

front of the opening to the hall where Bearded Guy had come from. The hall became a hail of gunfire. I wasn't there. I was legging it fast around through the other hall.

In the living room, the ex-military-looking guy was thumbing fresh rounds into his revolver, he saw me—

I keep my eyes wide open all the time.

—butter-fingered the bullets. We both watched them fall in breathtaking, slow motion. They bounced off the carpet. His eyes came back up, met mine.

Poot. Poot.

He fell.

Because you're mine, I walk the line.

Outside, a car started.

I exploded out the front door, dropped the .32 in the snow. The Jeep escaped at a dangerous speed down the steep driveway. I drew the Minelli cannon, fired until it was empty.

Boom. Boom. Boom. Boom. Boom. Boom.

Each shot was accompanied by a spectacular gout of flame. The Jeep's left taillight shattered and went out. The back window disintegrated. I caught the back, right tire just as the Jeep was going into a tight curve. It rolled on its side, sliding down the snowy slope and off the path, snapping saplings, until it smacked into the trunk of a large pine with a sickening metallic crunch.

I watched for a few seconds, but nobody got out of the Jeep.

Going through the rest of the house took only a minute, but they were all dead or gone. On the way back out I grabbed the .32 out of the snow, reloaded the clip.

I skipped down to the truck. The bitter cold, I now found exhilarating.

At the wreck, I went to one knee and looked in the Jeep. Two people hung upside down. The man in the passenger side was new to me, but it hardly mattered. I could tell by the angle of his neck, the way his head was jammed up against the windshield, that he was all done.

The dirty blond dangled from the driver's seat, blood dripping from her nose and one ear.

"Help me," she said weakly.

"Who's that?" I pointed at the dead man in the passenger's seat.

"Tom."

"Good."

"Help." Her voice was a sad, tiny croak.

"I want the girl."

"Tina."

"I know. Where?"

"The lake cabin."

"I know. Where?"

"Up the mountain."

"I thought this was up the mountain."

"More."

"Tell me how."

"Left out of the driveway. Stone Lake. There's a few cabins. People build. It's the only finished cabin. Closest to the dock."

"What road?"

"Stone Lake Trail."

"Okay." I leaned into the cab of the Jeep, reached past her and pushed in the cigarette lighter.

She pawed at me with desperate, feeble hands. "Please."

The lighter popped. I used it to light Lou's cigar, puffed a big blue-gray cloud which twisted away on the dark wind.

"Who are you?" she asked.

"I am the angel of death and mercy. There used to be an angel for each, but now we're the same."

Poot.

❖

A dreadful, slow drowsiness replaced the twisted euphoria of the pills.

I trudged back up to the house, tossed the cigar into the snow.

In the kitchen, I splashed water into my face, drank big gulps from the faucet. I went in their bathroom, took a long leak in the toilet.

I slugged it down the mountain, the snow halfway up my shin. The cold seeped into my bones now, the bottom of my pants wet. I was numb and tired. I looked up, noticed the snow had stopped.

I climbed into the Silverado, cranked it, turned the heat up all the way.

I turned around and drove slowly over the mountain road. Maybe ten minutes into the drive I passed a sign. It was dark, and I went by too fast to read it, but it might have said Stone Lake Trail.

I turned the wheel, and the truck came around sluggishly. There wasn't any traffic, so I crept up on the sign at 5 mph. Stone Lake Trail.

I made the turn. The road was dirt, a steep climb, even steeper than Tom and Tina's driveway, but the truck didn't have any trouble. I flipped it into four-wheel drive just to make certain.

My eyelids were lead. My mouth lolled open. Breath came roughly, heavily. I pulled the truck over, set the emergency brake. I needed the thermos; maybe there was coffee left although it might not be so warm.

It was down behind the passenger seat. I bent down for it. Reached…down.

Down.

TWENTY-FOUR

My eyes popped open. The truck was running, and the inside of the cab was an inferno from having the heat on full blast. I was still sitting on the driver's side but bent over, face against the passenger's seat, arm back behind the seat in mid-reach for the thermos.

I sat up. My back was in knots. The headache behind my eyes meant business. The pain pills had caught up with me, and I'd paid the price. I rolled the window down an inch, welcomed the cool wash of air over my face.

Dawn poked through the trees, bathed the winterscape in shades of orange. The snow on the ground was even and unbroken. An unspoiled wilderness. It looked like a picture postcard.

I flung open the driver's side door, stumbled into the snow, and threw up on it.

I grabbed a handful of snow and held it to my face.

Any one of a hundred things could have gone wrong while I was passed out. Tina might have returned to the house and found the carnival of death I'd left behind. Or the police, same story. Or she might have tried to call, got no answer, became suspicious.

Or maybe they were all still asleep. It was just dawn after all.

I got back in the truck. Up the mountain.

I crept up slowly, the truck bouncing on the rugged trail, until the forest split around a calm, silver lake. The road curved around to the right, roughly following the shoreline. The closest cabin was barely a frame. Through the trees another hundred yards around the lake another cabin was perhaps two-thirds finished. Directly across the lake sat the only cabin in sight which was fully built and clearly inhabited. A thin tendril of smoke oozed from the stone chimney.

A blue sedan in front. It was too far to see the Florida plates, but I knew they were there.

My head throbbed. My mouth was dry, still tasted faintly of vomit. I was in no mood for sneaking around. I followed the trail around the lake, pulled the .32, and set it on the seat next to me.

Dawn stretched across the surface of the lake. A slight but steady breeze pulled at the chimney smoke above the cabin. The cabin was built with brownish-red wood. It had a roof that peaked in the middle like a capital A, and a window above the door—a loft maybe—and a larger window to the side of the door.

I parked twenty yards from the cabin's front door. The lake was close behind, the dock jutting out into deep water, no boats. I stepped out of the truck, stood looking at the front window, but the morning glare kept me from seeing inside. If they were awake, they couldn't help but notice me. I had the .32 in my hand, down at my side like a gunslinger. I was fed up with waiting. Maybe I'd just walk up there, knock on the door. Or kick it open.

The tall, fat one in flannel took away those options when he stumbled from the cabin, firing wildly at me with his revolver. He ran through the snow toward the sedan, keys in one hand, pistol pointed back at me, pulling the trigger blindly. Three shots went overhead. One punched through the truck's windshield.

I threw myself down on the snow, aimed under the truck and fired the .32. I caught him in the ankle, and he went down.

Another shot on the top of the head. He twitched once, and that was it.

I stood. Brushed off the snow. I went to check on him. Dead. I picked up his piece, stashed it in my pocket. It bulged next to the Minelli cannon.

In his attempt to flee, Tall-n-Fat had left the cabin door open. I walked in, stood just in the doorway. The cabin was one big room with a loft overhead, the ladder going up immediately to my right, probably a bed up there. A fire had burnt low in the large, stone fireplace, only glowing embers and gray ash remaining. A large carpet stretched in front of it.

A cot had been hastily erected within warming distance of the fire. Amber lay stretched out on her stomach, eyes closed, hair across her face. She was pale. Her wrists were tied under the cot by a length of cord. Tina sat in a wooden chair next to the cot, her legs crossed, eyes meeting mine calmly. She held her enormous magnum to Amber's head.

I said, "Your pal tried to run. Didn't make it."

"I never really thought Dave had the stomach to go all the way with this," said Tina. "That big ape with the long hair gave us a lot of trouble before we killed him, so when we saw you coming around the lake, I guess Dave decided to cut his losses and go."

"Not you, huh?"

"I've worked too hard," she said. "I requested undercover so I could get close to Jeffers. I don't like FBI work really, and the pay sucks."

"So you found a way to make it profitable," I said.

"Yes. Jeffers was as corrupt as anyone I'd ever seen, but weak, easy to manipulate. My friends and I decided we could just about do anything we wanted. When those ledgers went up for grabs…well, it was just too good of an opportunity to let pass."

"But it blew up in your face, didn't it? A fly in the ointment. Me. So I went in and shot all of your friends dead."

Her eyes grew hard.

I said, "And now I'm here to kill you."

"I don't think so," she said. "You obviously want the girl, or you wouldn't be here. Think you're fast, Mr. Gunman? Not fast enough to—"

Poot.

She took the bullet just above her left eye, her mouth jerked in mid-sentence, and she fell forward in front of the chair, her butt sticking in the air. She still clutched the revolver.

I approached cautiously, pried the gun from her hands and stuck it in the other pocket. It clanked against the other Minelli cannon.

My coat was full of guns.

I went through Tina's pocket and found the locker key, exhaled with relief, and stuck it in my pants pocket.

I slid my bowie knife out and cut Amber's bonds. Once I'd turned her over, I had a good long look. She wore a loose, powder-blue T-shirt and jeans. Bare feet. I checked her over. I'd been through a lot to find her, and I wanted to make sure she was okay.

She had fresh tracks down the inside of her left arm from a needle. They'd been giving her something. That's how they'd kept her quiet. She was passed out now from the junk. I prayed there was no permanent damage.

She looked terrible. Behind the pale, drawn face dwelt a remnant of the beauty my brother saw in her. I brushed the hair from her eyes. So sad and young, but I'd make sure she and Danny had a chance to ride into the sunset.

I touched her cheek. Her eyes flew open.

I sat up, jerked my hand away.

Her eyes grew round with terror, lips pulling up exposing teeth in a horrified grimace. A muted scream tore from the depths of her throat.

"It's okay," I said quickly. "It's me. Charlie."

Her eyes were glassy, unfocused. She didn't recognize me.

Amber thrashed wildly, and I backed away from the cot. She leapt to her feet, darted past me, making little grunting noises of fear as she ran through the front door.

"Wait!" I followed.

She looked back only once, her face a study in pure animal fear, her only instinct to run. Her little, naked feet punched deep holes into the raw snow. I ran to cut her off from the road, moving awkwardly, my hands holding the pea coat pockets to keep the guns from spilling out.

She sensed my intercept course and turned toward the lake. Her feet pounded down the wooden planks of the long dock. I ran after, thinking I had her trapped when she got to the end of the dock, thinking that I'd explain everything. If that didn't work I'd simply grab her, drag her kicking back to the cabin.

It didn't happen that way.

She showed no sign of slowing, hit the end of the dock at full speed, and launched herself, arms spinning, legs still pumping. She hit with a stinging splash, went down, the dark lake closing over her.

"Fuck!"

I hesitated only a moment, then dove after her.

I was swallowed by the watery silence, went down quickly, deep. Every muscle raged against the cold. I forced my eyes open into darkness, the world above a silver blur of daylight. Below me, a white arm beckoning in the murky depths. I was tangled in my pea coat, shrugged out of it. It was gone. I was distantly aware my pain pills were in the inside pocket. No time to worry about it. Already the dreamy wish to succumb to fatigue overwhelmed me.

I pushed the thought aside, stroked toward the arm. Amber came into view, her eyes closed. She floated arms above her, hair a billowing halo. I took her, my hand closing over her thin wrist. I kicked upward, swimming with one arm. The surface seemed a mile away.

They say your life flashes in front of you when you're about to die, but I thought maybe I was seeing ahead, not back. Everything happened in eerie slow motion as I floated upward. The pictures in my head were of Danny and Amber and Ma in Michigan, and of Marcie. Nothing about the monkey cage, my old life, Stan. It was as if I'd shed them into the wet darkness with the pea coat.

My lungs burned, eyes stung, limbs felt lifeless, leaden and slack. I stroked hard.

Please.

I broke the surface, swallowed air with loud, coarse gulps, spit water, coughed. I pulled Amber up next to me. Put an arm around her, swam. She wasn't breathing.

I swam to the dock, reached, my fingertips finding a hold on the rough planks. No way. I didn't have the strength to pull myself up. I paddled for shore. I was about to give it up when I felt the bottom with my feet. I heaved Amber up with both arms, kept putting one foot in front of the other until the lake was behind me.

Amber slipped out of my arms to the snow-covered shore. I knelt next to her, pinched her nose, tilted the head back. Her T-shirt clung to her skin, nipples thrusting against the fabric. I covered her mouth with mine. Blew. Where had I learned this? It didn't matter. I kept at it.

She coughed water. I turned her on her side and let her

finish. She sucked breath, sobbed. We shivered together on the shore, teeth chattering. She let me help her up. We walked with an unsteady sway back to the cabin.

I'd found a stack of cut wood at the side of the cabin under a tarp. I carried in an armload and built up the fire. I turned my back as Amber removed her wet clothes. She sat in front of the fire, wrapped herself in the blanket from the cot. I found a pair of sweatpants a size too small for me, but I put them on and hung my wet clothes next to Amber's on the makeshift clothesline I'd fashioned from a ball of twine.

I rifled the shelf above the little stove and was elated to find a coffee can, but my hopes were dashed when I found it empty. There were tea bags. I boiled water, found cups. I filled the cups, offered one to Amber.

"Tea."

She took it, nodding, staring out the window.

"I'm sorry." Her eyes didn't waver from the window. "I'm okay now. I'm glad to see you." She cleared her throat. "Is Danny...?"

"He's in the hospital, but he's alive. He'll be okay."

That seemed to be enough. She sipped the tea.

I drank mine. A surprisingly soothing warmth started in my belly and spread outward. I felt the wet clothes. It would be a while. I put another log on the fire.

"I'm sorry I ran. I didn't know where I was or who you were."

"It's okay."

She was still rattled, almost catatonic, but she was getting better. She'd been through a lot. Too much. But she was getting better.

She drank tea, her eyes still on the window. "Someone's coming."

I went to the window.

A black luxury car, a Lincoln, parked across the lake. It stayed for a moment, then started the slow circle around the shore. I watched like Tina must've watched, felt maybe like she'd felt. The certainty of approaching dread.

"Who is it?" asked Amber.

"I don't know." Please don't be Mercury.

The car passed the frame of the first cabin, kept coming.

How could it be Mercury? I must've been suffering from the worst kind of paranoia. How could he have tracked me down to Tennessee? My mind whirled.

Jeffers.

Certainly that was it. Mercury could make someone like Jeffers talk easy. He'd say how I'd been there looking for Tina. Mercury could follow the same trail.

The car passed the second cabin.

It didn't matter. Trouble was on the way. How it happened was now irrelevant.

The car stopped well behind my truck, and the driver stepped out.

Lloyd Mercury.

He wore a black suit with a fat, white tie, gleaming wingtips, black overcoat. He held a flashing nickel automatic. It looked like a .357 Magnum Desert Eagle, enough gun to kill me three or four times.

I turned to Amber, put my finger against my lips. She nodded.

My guns were at the bottom of the lake.

I grabbed the bowie knife and the fireplace poker. I scurried up the ladder and found the loft. I kept to one side of the window, watched Mercury carefully. I couldn't open the window without drawing a faceful of bullets, so I watched and waited. Mercury stripped off his topcoat and threw it across the hood of his car, began circling the house to the left.

I already knew the front door was the only way in or out. The two windows in back were small, and he'd have to make a racket of broken glass to get through. He'd see Amber in the blanket by the fire. That didn't matter. He knew somebody was here anyway. He'd seen the chimney smoke, same as I had.

If it came down to speed and strength, I'd lose. But I had experience and patience.

I'd rather have had speed and strength.

Mercury came around the other side of the cabin. He'd finished his survey, and I knew a guy like him wouldn't lay siege. He'd want it done, and he'd come in the cabin right through the front.

I went to the edge of the loft to wait, fireplace poker in my hand, knife sheath stuck in the back of the sweatpants.

He kicked in the front door. Amber didn't even flinch.

"Where is he?" asked Mercury.

I couldn't see him, but Amber turned her head slightly to his voice. I used that to judge his position. Amber didn't say anything, just pulled the blanket tighter around her.

I reached as far to the right as I could with the fireplace poker and tapped the floor of the loft.

The cabin shook with the thunder of Mercury's automatic. Three slugs tore through the wood where I'd tapped the poker. By the third shot I'd already jumped.

I landed in front of him. The pistol was still aimed at the loft, so I swung the poker, caught him on the wrist, and the pistol clattered across the cabin's wooden floor. Mercury took the blow from the backswing on the side of his neck, staggered back. I brought it back for a killer blow, swung down for his head. He blocked it with a forearm, but I knew he would. When his forearm came up for the block, I leapt, kicked him in the ribs. He flew backwards through the window. Glass rained.

A mistake.

He wouldn't just have one gun. I couldn't let him reach inside his jacket or down to his ankle. If he got a pistol out, I was all done.

I leapt through the window after him. Landed on his chest, brought the poker down for a quick blow. He caught my wrist with both hands, twisted, jabbed a thumb into a pressure point just below my palm, and I had to give up the poker.

But I squeezed my injured hand into a painful fist. Punched three times, once across the jaw and twice in the eye.

Mercury twisted, rolled over and bucked me off, kicked out backwards and caught me in the gut. I scrambled to my feet but he was already up.

We faced each other three feet apart. I'd lost the surprise, but I grabbed the knife from behind, drew it, threw the sheath away. I had to stay close, so I could go for him if he went into his jacket for a gun.

But he smiled. A little blood down his mouth, right eye just starting to swell.

I stood cold in the snow, barefoot, wondering what to do next.

"How's it going, Lloyd?"

"Good," he said. "Beggar sends his regards."

"How did you find me? Jeffers?"

"Of course. He said Tina was from Tennessee, and that you were probably headed there too. The phone book had two listings for Tina. This cabin and the house back down the mountain. I went to the house first. You left quite a mess."

"Lloyd, I'm not going back to Orlando. I'm done. I know that. There's no reason to do this. All I want to do is help the girl. She's had it rough. You don't need to bother with me. I'll even tell you where the books are."

He scrunched up his face, thinking about it. "Sorry, Charlie," said Mercury. "Nothing personal, but you've been a whole lot of trouble. Beggar says you have to go. Now, here's what's going to happen. You're going to have to see if you can stick that knife in me before I take three steps back and draw my Berreta. One way or another, we finish it."

Our eyes locked. Then he moved.

He stepped back, his hand flashing into his jacket, and I leapt for him with the knife. It was a trick. His hand came right back without the pistol, and he stepped forward, caught my knife hand and twisted. I kicked him away but had to lose the knife. He swung a fist. I ducked under and punched him in the gut. He caught my arm, pulled me forward, and head-butted me in the nose.

Blood exploded down my face. I staggered back. He came after. I punched. He blocked and kicked my legs out from under me. I sprawled in the snow, tried feebly to scoot away. He pulled his Berreta, pointed it at my chest.

"I just wanted to know," said Lloyd. "I wondered if I was better than you, and now we both know it. I'm going to kill you now. Nothing personal. Beggar wanted me to tell you that this bullet was for Sanchez."

I flinched at the sound of the gunshot. Mercury's face exploded. His blood sprayed across me, dotted the snow with red stars. He fell backwards, landed flat, a grizzly snow-angel.

Amber stood naked, legs spread, Mercury's shiny automatic in her little fists. I wobbled to my feet, went to her, took the gun, wrapped her in my arms. She cried a long time against my chest, both of us barefoot in the snow.

EPILOGUE

I swung in the hammock on the porch of the villa. It had only taken me about two hours to find Marcie after my plane touched down in Acapulco. She was stretched out in a beach chair next to the pool of a luxury hotel, sipping an umbrella drink and reading an art magazine. She burst into tears when she saw me, hugged me hard.

Then punched me square in the face.

We've reached an understanding since then.

Once I'd determined that Amber was going to be okay, I let her have the Impala to drive back to Orlando. I gave her every cent I had on me to make sure her trip went okay and told her it might be six months or so before I could contact her and Danny again. I needed to lay low for a while. She let me know I could contact Danny through Clemson University. She'd see to it.

She really did seem like she was going to be okay as she dropped me off at the Chattanooga Airport. She kissed me on the cheek again, said I'd be in her thoughts.

I put a plane ticket to Mexico on Minelli's credit card.

In the ninety minutes I had before my plane left, I dropped the key to the airport locker in the mail. I used the card Agent Dunn had given me to get the address. I also sent him a note saying one of the conditions for my help was to put Stan in a witness relocation program if they ended up nabbing him. Maybe Dunn would even be grateful enough to do it.

It would be strange for a while without Stan's guiding hand, but I was starting a new life. I was my own boss now.

A slight breeze picked up. I rocked in the hammock. Marcie and I had stayed in the luxury hotel one night before I'd explained we'd have to make her cash stretch for as long as possible. We were waiting to hear if the real estate agent had sold her house. Until then we'd moved into a reasonably safe and clean neighborhood with the locals. Rent on the villa was modest.

I heard someone approach the villa, but I kept my eyes closed. I knew what Marcie's quick steps sounded like on the cobblestones. She climbed the stairs to the porch and put something on my chest. I pretended I was still asleep.

She cleared her throat pointedly, and I opened my eyes.

I was looking straight into the eyes of a big stuffed iguana.

"Please tell me this isn't dinner," I said.

"Do you know what they're charging for these nasty things in the tourist shops?" she asked.

"No."

"Take a guess."

"Twenty bucks," I said.

"Not dollars, dumbass. Pesos."

"I have no idea."

"Two thousand fucking pesos." She put her hands on her hips. "Can you believe that?"

"It's unbelievable."

She grunted her derision at me. "Laugh it up, boytoy. We need to make a living. I could stuff these things in my sleep." She picked up the lizard and shook it at me. "I have a very marketable skill here, you know."

"I can always go in on that deal with Hernandez," I told her. Hernandez was a shady fellow I'd met a few nights ago in one of the local saloons. We got to talking over a few pints of tequila, and he told me about a scheme he had going where he and his pals stole cars in Texas and smuggled them over the border to sell in Mexico.

"No!" Marcie smacked me on the forehead with an open palm. "We don't do things like that anymore. You want me to kick your ass?"

I just laughed.

She tucked the iguana under her arm and went inside the villa. "I'm serious," she called over her shoulder. "We have to earn a living somehow."

I unfolded the telegram that had arrived an hour earlier, read it again.

Stash all counted. Account in your name at Bank of Zurich.
Account number: DH123-45567. Balance: $1,428,076.00.
    —Jimmy the Fix

"We'll get by somehow," I shouted at her.

I closed my eyes. The breeze picked up just a little as I slipped into mariachi dreams.